THE OTHER CHILD

Amy Carver worked for the NHS for fifteen years, spending the first ten as a healthcare assistant in a maternity unit, where she supported women through antenatal care, childbirth and the postnatal period. She later qualified as a nurse and earned a psychology degree, which led her down an alternative path. Now a novelist, Amy draws inspiration from her experiences to create compelling and impactful stories. A mother of three grown-up children and a nanna of four, she enjoys spending time with her expanding family.

Amy Carver also writes psychological thrillers as Sam Carrington. Find out more about *The Other Child* and her other books on Instagram @samcarringtonauthor.

THE OTHER CHILD

Amy Carver

Copyright © 2025 Amy Carver

The right of Amy Carver to be identified as the Author of
the Work has been asserted by her in accordance with the
Copyright, Designs and Patents Act 1988.

First published in 2025 by Headline Publishing Group Limited

This paperback edition published in 2026

1

Apart from any use permitted under UK copyright law, this publication may
only be reproduced, stored, or transmitted, in any form, or by any means, with prior
permission in writing of the publishers or, in the case of reprographic production, in
accordance with the terms of licences issued by the Copyright Licensing Agency.

All characters in this publication are fictitious and any resemblance
to real persons, living or dead, is purely coincidental.

Cataloguing in Publication Data is available from the British Library

Paperback ISBN 978 1 0354 2017 9

Typeset in Sabon by CC Book Production

Printed and bound in Great Britain by Clays Ltd, Elcograf S.p.A.

Headline's policy is to use papers that are natural, renewable and
recyclable products and made from wood grown in well-managed forests
and other controlled sources. The logging and manufacturing processes
are expected to conform to the environmental regulations
of the country of origin.

HEADLINE PUBLISHING GROUP
An Hachette UK Company
Carmelite House
50 Victoria Embankment
London EC4Y 0DZ

The authorised representative in the EEA is Hachette Ireland,
8 Castlecourt Centre, Dublin 15, D15 XTP3, Ireland
(email: info@hbgi.ie)

www.headline.co.uk
www.hachette.co.uk

To every mum finding her way

Prologue

She leans over his sleeping body, inhaling the clean, soapy scent as she places her lips to his soft cheek. He stirs, ever so slightly, eyelashes fluttering. She hums his favourite nursery rhyme until he settles into a deep slumber once more. Tracing the tip of one finger over his forehead, down the side of his face, she lets out a contented sigh.

At last.

This is how it should be.

Loving your child unconditionally is the one thing you expect. It's your purpose as a mother. It should come naturally. Having to fight to find it, that special bond, isn't normal.

But it's all okay now; that's over with. Everything has worked out in the end.

'We're always going to be together, sweetheart,' she whispers.

She checks the straps of his car seat, then closes the door as quietly as she can. It wouldn't be good to wake him now – not with what lies ahead.

Sitting behind the wheel, she glances in the rear-view mirror. Smiles at the reflection of her perfect child.

'You're such a good boy. Mummy loves you.' And she presses her foot hard to the accelerator.

PART ONE

PART ONE

Chapter 1

MUMSTOGETHER – *Sleep Forum*

Baby never sleeps, HELP

ExhaustedNewMum0593 – 24/06 03:21

Anyone else awake? I'd been walking up and down with my 1 month-old son for 2 hours. Put him in his basket. A minute later he's awake! I'm crying now, haven't stopped crying for past week. I am struggling so much and exhausted every day. All the other mums in my mother and baby group put their kids down and they go to sleep at least for a few hours! Why can't I do it? I'm really fucking motherhood up.

Vikkineedssleep – 24/06 03:34

I'm so sorry. Not getting sleep/having a baby who won't settle is so stressful. I remember it well. It will get better. It's not you. You tried co-sleeping?

Mummabear – 24/06 05:15

Shouldn't co sleep it raises risks of SIDS. Just get into a routine & get other half to help more!

Vikkineedssleep – 24/06 05:34

Mummabear – Obvs the safest place is the cot or moses basket but if you follow the advice on Lullaby Trust, it's an option for OP, that's all I'm saying. Not being funny, but judgemental much? We don't know her circs, might not have other half?

ExhaustedNewMum0593 – 24/06 06:21

Thanks. I appreciate you offering advice. I wasn't expecting a walk in the park but this is another level. My OH does his best. Lack of sleep is making me forget things, hallucinate even. Sometimes I look at the baby and think he's doing it because he hates me.

Chapter 2

Louise squirms on the rigid plastic chair, her cheeks ablaze. She quickly looks away. If she pretends she didn't see it, it never happened. Perhaps none of the other mums witnessed it either.

The high-pitched wail followed by a pounding of tiny feet on the brightly coloured flexi-tiles of the playgroup floor gains momentum as the child comes closer. This, Louise acknowledges, is harder to ignore. Has to be confronted.

'Oh, darling,' she says, extending her arms out to him. 'What's the matter?'

The heat in her face continues to increase as she senses – no, she *sees* – all eyes are now on her. On her son. Sweat from running around creating havoc for the past hour flattens his mass of curly blond hair at the temples. He stands, tears abruptly ceased, at arm's length, rejecting her offer of a comforting hug. Of course Alfie's crying has stopped – he wasn't the one on the receiving end of the wallop. Louise side-eyes the little boy in the centre of the jungle-themed playmat, apparently oblivious to the altercation in which he's been involved. His attention is on a wooden beaded maze toy. She hopes Alfie hasn't left a mark on the poor boy's head – it's not as though his fine, fair hair would hide it.

When she's brought up Alfie's tendency to lash out while playing with others, Mark has casually dismissed his behaviour as normal.

'He's a *toddler*, Louise,' he said two nights ago when she tried to talk about it again. 'They don't understand sharing until, what, four?'

'No. The online sources state that most children should understand turn-taking and sharing by three.'

'There you go, then. Most children. *Most*. Plus, he's a few months off three ... You worry too much, love.' He hugged her, kissed the top of her head. Told her she was over-reacting.

So, why is it always Alfie? Louise doesn't recall seeing the other kids bashing each other because they want the toy another one has. They pull and tug, yes – but they aren't violent. She watches Alfie as he returns to the boy on the playmat, her heartbeat erratic. If he does it again now, the other mums will immediately look at her. Judge. Condemn. She and Alfie will become social outcasts. It's taken her so long to pluck up the courage to attend the group regularly, but this amount of stress isn't doing her any favours.

During a therapy session in her first year post-partum, Louise's counsellor had mentioned that Alfie's emotional state could be affected by her own. He could detect Louise's tension. So, she'd set herself a mission to reduce it: signing up to online yoga, meditation, journalling. All the time, in the background, Alfie cried and wailed, never settling, never content. Once he hit thirteen months, he began throwing tantrums.

What was she doing wrong? She gave him security, her time, her love. What else was there?

'Don't think you're alone.' The voice cuts into Louise's thoughts. Halts her incessant overthinking. She sucks in her breath, turns to face the mum who's plonked herself in the chair next to her. Louise's lips twitch as she attempts a smile, but it's tears that are easier to form, and her eyes prickle with them. The woman hands her a tissue.

'Thanks.' Louise takes it and swipes at her dripping nose. When she stops her snivelling, she looks up. 'Sorry, I don't remember your name,' she says. Adding, 'I don't remember much at all these days.'

'Harriet. And no worries, I've only been a couple of times and we haven't properly met.'

'Thanks, you're very kind. I'm Louise.'

'Good to meet you, Louise.' Harriet seems altogether more *together* than her. She's taken time to put on make-up: a subtle, light foundation with a sun-kissed glow highlighter over her chiselled cheekbones. Her perfectly arched eyebrows are neat, not a stray hair in sight, and her minimal soft-taupe eyeshadow brings out the blue of her eyes. She looks Instagram-filtered, yet completely natural. Effortless. The opposite to Louise. 'Me and Jacob used to go to the parent and toddler group next to the library in town,' she says. Harriet signals towards her son. Louise's eyes widen in realisation. It's the boy Alfie hit.

'Oh, right,' Louise says, gulping down the lump in her throat before biting the inside of her cheek. Her stomach clenches at the panic starting to rise there. Should she own up, apologise for Alfie's behaviour?

'But ...' She leans in close, Louise catching a whiff of expensive perfume as Harriet's mouth brushes against her ear. 'Here is *a lot* cleaner,' she whispers, before sitting up straight again. Louise smiles tightly. She's about to blurt out that Alfie is a handful and she's not sure how to manage him, that every day is a struggle, but the moment passes; her urge to offload on to a woman she's only just met is premature and she'll come across as an inadequate mother. 'Not only that,' Harriet says, as some preschoolers rush past them, shrieking happily, 'I thought this one was ... *livelier*.' She gives Louise a gentle nudge. 'In every sense,' she says with a wink, then laughs softly.

Louise's taut shoulders loosen, the tears that had begun to brew again dissipate and she feels herself shrugging off the judgements she'd assumed were being directed at her. Mark is right a lot of the time. She is a bit of an over-reactor. It's obvious to her now that Harriet is aware of what happened moments ago and isn't particularly concerned. In fact, Louise realises, she's gone out of her way to make her feel more relaxed about it.

'You're very understanding,' Louise says.

Harriet narrows her eyes, a thoughtful look on her face. 'You know what might help?'

Louise's forehead crinkles. Help what? Has Harriet clocked the thing she's been trying to keep buried? Is she picking up on her desperation? Louise gives a small yet discernible shake of her head and Harriet continues.

'Playdates,' she says, splaying her hands, palms up as though she's solved a mystery. 'Your little Alfie might be overwhelmed, that's all. Room packed with kids, a cacophony of noise, frantic running around – it certainly gives me anxiety. I'm usually so overcome with the madness of it all I go home for a power nap afterwards, let his dad deal with the childcare.'

Louise doubts Harriet suffers with anxiety, suspects she's simply telling her this to try to make her feel better. She's about to say as much but then concedes – she doesn't know her, and no one should judge a book by its cover, however well designed it is. Instead, she focuses on the other part of Harriet's statement, the one that had provoked a stab of jealousy.

'You're lucky to have him help out. Does he work from home?'

'If he chooses to. Since the pandemic, things have changed a bit for him. He pops into the office sometimes. Probably for some peace.' She throws her head back and laughs, her loose honey-coloured spiral curls tumbling behind her shoulders.

'If I had that opportunity, *I'd* certainly use it,' Louise says, a little too enthusiastically. She clears her throat to cover her embarrassment. Before the conversation can resume, Alfie toddles over to them, going straight to Harriet and dumping a toy on to her lap.

'Oh, well, thank you.' Harriet smiles at him. 'Is this for me?' Alfie grins, then walks away, ignoring Louise.

'You are the chosen one,' Louise says, trying to hide the hurt in her voice.

'Look, can I be honest with you?' Harriet turns to her. Louise's heartbeat smashes against her ribs. Her instinct is to say no, to get up, grab Alfie and escape this place. Avoid, avoid, avoid – her response since the day she'd taken Alfie home in his car seat, his scrunched-up body tiny in the contraption, her own body suddenly alien to her, her heart empty of emotion. There'd been no rush of love, the one she'd expected – was *supposed* – to experience. The birth had been too painful, too rapid, his slippery form ejecting from her in an explosion of fluid – his entry into the world violent. He was born angry. Angry with her.

'Yeah, why not?' she says, her gaze averted. She doesn't want to be looking at Harriet when whatever she's planning on saying is directed at her. She pushes her hands beneath her thighs where their tremor won't be noticed.

'You're being . . .' Harriet's opening words snap Louise back into a rigid stance. Being pathetic? Useless? Selfish? They're all the words she'd use. 'Too *hard* on yourself,' Harriet finishes. Louise sits back, temporarily stunned by this assessment. 'Motherhood is the most precious gift, but it can also be the hardest transition of your entire life. There might be a gazillion online resources, expert guidance, support, blah, blah, blah.' Harriet flicks her hand dismissively. 'But you know what? Sometimes you're better off without any of that. Each of us has our own journey to make and none of us should sit in judgement of another's satnav.'

As Louise is struck mute at Harriet's analogy, there's a flurry of activity all around them and she's jolted back to reality. The session is ending.

'Thank you.' Louise smiles, and for the first time in ages, it's an accurate reflection of how she's feeling. 'My hour's up. How much do I owe you?'

Harriet laughs. 'You owe me coffee and cake. We'll organise that playdate, yes?'

Everything's lost in the noise of the mums and kids reuniting, the bustle of tiny bodies, tired cries as toddlers are wrestled into pushchairs, the scrambling to the door – and among it, Louise misses Harriet leave with Jacob. She looks for her once outside, but there's no sign. It's like she vanished in a cloud of smoke and sparkles: *puff*, like the fairy godmother in 'Cinderella'.

With a lurch of disappointment, Louise realises they didn't swap mobile numbers. She'll have to wait until the next toddler group before arranging their playdate.

Chapter 3

'Time for teeth,' Louise says, her tone upbeat. 'Let's play the Duggee song!' It had worked once around a month ago, playing the cartoon dog and the toothbrush song on her phone, her last resort in the ongoing battle of wits she so often lost.

'No, no, no,' Alfie says, his bottom lip protruding and his eyes firmly closing.

'We need to brush away the little bits of food to make sure your teeth stay strong, don't we? Like Duggee does... see?' She holds the phone in front of his face, encouraging him to open his eyes and look.

'No!' he shouts, his eyes opening wide. He smacks the phone from Louise's hand, then folds his chubby arms in the usual act of defiance. She tenses, fatigue and desperation pulling her muscles and tendons tight to breaking point. Alfie continues to chant 'No', his feet stamping as Louise picks the mobile up and leaves him to his outburst. She stands outside his bedroom door, her back against it, her will and her patience shot to pieces. He doesn't care she's left. She can hear him swiping the cuddly toys off his bed, then moving across to the toy box to make a start on yanking everything from it.

After ten minutes of allowing him to experience his emotions – a concept she'd discovered was the 'in thing' from some influencer's Instagram reel – and using the time to search the internet for a different song that might take his fancy, Louise goes back inside and manages to get the brush into his mouth for a grand total of five seconds before he wriggles away again. Bedtime with Alfie takes around an hour. At least fifty of those minutes are spent cajoling, wrangling and crying. Mostly the tears are hers, though she tries to make sure he doesn't see them. Tonight, they've already been at it for over an hour, and he's only just got into bed.

Another fifteen minutes pass impossibly slowly while she tries to get him to sleep. With all the running around he'd done today, she'd dared to think he'd be out like a light. God knows she could sleep right here, right now. Four stories later, and with not a hint from Alfie that he's ready to surrender, Louise collapses back against his bedroom wall and lets out a long, agonised howl.

'What the . . .' Mark bursts into the room, his face ashen. 'What's wrong?' He casts his gaze about, his hand on his chest. Alfie begins to cry, and he steps over Louise to get to his son. 'I thought something had happened to him.' He wraps his arms around the sobbing toddler.

'Didn't you hear him?' Louise says weakly. 'I've been having a nightmare up here.' She gets to her feet, stares at the sight of her husband and son. Tears roll down her cheeks.

Mark sighs, offers soft, reassuring words to Alfie, then steers Louise out of the room. 'Your mum rang. Why don't you give her a call back while I try.'

Louise inhales sharply before expelling a strangled laugh. 'What a good idea that is,' she says, as she allows herself to be manhandled away from Alfie. She's being pushed away by both of them.

'Yes, I think so,' Mark says, closing the door in her tear-streaked face. Did he not catch her sarcasm? Sure, a chat with her mother will definitely make her feel like a good mum. The usual guilt trip is bound to give her a boost. She could repeat verbatim her mother's story of how Louise had been a miracle – the twin who survived. *I spent weeks in bed when I was carrying you, afraid the bleeding would start again, that I'd lose you, too. The scan showed that one remaining tiny blob still in the sac, and I was overcome with love there and then. You were a battler. I just can't understand how mums don't bond with their babies ...*

Louise shakes her head at the irony. Her mother's lack of support after Alfie's birth, and her habit of sending only sporadic emails while on her regular extended cruises, left Louise feeling stranded. The fiercely stated unconditional love her mother had once professed seemingly had an expiry date.

Louise doesn't return the call.

Instead, she raids the fridge for chocolate and then falls on to the sofa. She's about to reach for the TV remote, thinking she can watch a bit of her favourite reality show, *Selling Sunset*, without being mocked for watching trash, when the lounge door pushes open.

'That was a quick call,' Mark says, drifting in and placing the monitor on the coffee table. The black and white display shows Alfie's contour under the duvet – it's still, peaceful, and his rhythmic breathing is as gentle as a soothing lullaby.

'Not as quick as you getting him to sleep,' Louise says, unable to keep the frustration from her voice. 'I can't believe it took you all of two minutes to settle him.'

'He's overtired, that's all. Sounds like you both had a long day.'

Like every bloody day, she thinks. 'It wasn't without its challenges,' she says, turning on the TV and flicking through the channels.

'I'll pour you a wine, then you can tell me about it,' Mark says. Louise's head snaps to look at him, her mouth agape.

'Oh, okay. Thanks.' Lately when she tries to talk to Mark about her daily troubles with Alfie, he changes the subject or makes an excuse to leave the conversation altogether. He doesn't usually instigate one. She presses her hand to her tummy, to the nervous knot that's formed there.

'Here you go,' he says, coming back in and handing her a large glass of white wine. She notes he doesn't have one. 'So . . .' He perches on the arm of the sofa, looking down on her. 'What happened today to make you lose it this badly?'

Louise gives a short, sharp laugh. Swigs a mouthful of wine.

What's the point?

Chapter 4

'Wakey, wakey.'

Louise opens her eyes, immediately rubbing them to relieve the gritty, stinging sensation. 'What's this?' she says, blinking hard. Mark stands at the side of their double bed, his hands gripping a tray at chest height.

'Nothing fancy. Toast with lashings of butter, cup of peppermint tea.' He shrugs, smiles. He raises his eyebrows, nodding his head towards the pillows. 'Come on, then.' He waits for Louise to get comfortable, then places the tray on her lap. 'Alfie's dressed and downstairs.'

Still not entirely awake, Louise shoots him a quizzical glance, then looks to the bedside clock. It's always set twenty-two minutes fast. A hangover of her uni days when she was habitually late for her lectures and found, through trial and many errors, that twenty-two was the magic number to ensure she wasn't late. Like a flash of lightning, Louise remembers the most likely reason she's being treated to breakfast in bed.

She bites into the undercooked toast, tearing a mouthful

from the slice of hot bread and over-chewing it before washing it down with the aid of the peppermint tea.

'Thanks.' She forces a smile without making eye contact. While she appreciates the gesture, irritation bubbles in her gut. Had he chosen his words more wisely last night, there'd be no need for this guilt-easing brekkie. Mark hovers for a moment, combing his fingers through his sandy-coloured hair, his eyes not meeting hers. He opens his mouth to speak, but a screech pierces the air, and he swallows his words, screwing his eyes up and wincing.

'Hold that apology,' Louise says, her voice monotone. She doesn't react to the onslaught of noise coming from downstairs. 'Alfie needs your attention more than I do.' She pushes the breakfast tray to the side and slides back down the bed, pulling the duvet over her head. Mark's footsteps pound the stairs and Louise closes her eyes and ears. 'I'm not ready for today,' she mumbles into her cocoon.

Louise stands just inside the front door, Alfie balanced on her hip, his hand waving wildly at Mark. He chants, 'Da-dee, Da-dee,' until Mark disappears from view, then wriggles and pushes against Louise, his arms rigid, his face scrunched up into an angry ball.

'Hey, little one,' she says, her tone gentle. She strains to keep hold of him, but fears she'll drop him if his thrashing continues. 'Okay, okay.' A deep ache pulls at her insides, a yearning for a sense of love in place of the chasm of disconnect. She puts him down and he runs off towards the conservatory. They'd made it into a playroom last year. It was Mark's idea to repurpose what had been their dining space into an area for Alfie. His thought process being it would make life easier for Louise to have everything on one level. No more running up and down stairs, or quickly scooping up all the toys from the lounge if someone popped over.

'No one pops over, Mark,' she'd said when he first introduced the idea. He'd frowned, appearing shocked at her statement; argued she was wrong, that of course people visited their house. 'The odd cold caller, perhaps,' she'd scoffed. 'My mother when she fancies it. Your parents infrequently. That's about it.' She wondered if the intention of a designated area was in fact not about her, or the worry of tidying for the rare visitor – but for Mark's sake. He liked order. Not the chaos of toys strewn everywhere when all he wanted was to relax after a long day at the office. A heavy, dragging feeling consumes her now. God, she'd love to get back to work. If only the confidence and assertiveness she had in her marketing job could be applied to her role as a mum, it would make life much less stressful.

Louise peers round the doorframe into the conservatory, observes Alfie. She inhales deeply, fighting back tears. Every thought filtering through her subconscious that she labels as 'not normal' for a mother to have gets added to her ever-increasing list of failures. She might be on the right side of the post-natal depression according to the tick-box assessments she's taken – her scores having decreased with each session – but her faith in that appraisal is low.

Because you lied.

Louise shakes the voice out of her head, beginning to back away from her vantage point. Alfie's happy enough zooming his toy fire engine from side to side, making a nee-nah noise. No use interfering and ruining the moment. She slinks into the kitchen and leans against the worktop. Getting her mobile out, she scrolls through the Facebook groups she grudgingly belongs to at the encouragement of both Mark and her counsellor. One of them, *MumsUnite*, has a dozen new posts, the latest being:

> Anyone know the best places to go with twins – mine are 4 and love animals but getting bored of the zoo after a million trips there 😊

Louise swipes off the page and huffs. She hasn't even taken Alfie to the zoo. The mere thought brings her out in a cold sweat.

A scraping noise outside draws Louise's attention, and she gazes out of the window. The man from next door is walking up the path, dragging his rubbish bin behind him. Louise watches as he struggles to position it outside on the pavement. He's about ten years older than her – around forty, although Mark insists he's more like mid-fifties – and he's sturdy, not exactly weak; it must be really full. How much rubbish can one person accumulate? Is it even bin day? Louise cranes her neck to see if anyone else has theirs out.

Confirming no one does, she turns back. Her breath catches. Her neighbour's standing at the top of his path, just staring at her. She can't recall his name. Darren? Dave? For a moment, he remains dead still, then, perhaps sensing her unease, puts his hand up. Louise hastily throws her own up in response and then he finally tears his gaze away from her and disappears down the side of his house. He's currently single, she knows that much, and, since his wife left, he's been quiet. Keeps himself to himself. Something that at first she appreciated – she was already dealing with a lot, so the absence of small talk whenever they crossed paths outside was a welcome relief. But, as the months wore on, his silence and, more recently, his creepy, lingering stares, have become awkward. Unsettling. She'd never properly met his partner – had heard more than seen her. During the endless hours she spent awake breastfeeding Alfie in the early days, she'd heard their muffled voices through the walls – low at first, then rising – indistinguishable yet thick with anger.

One time, Louise could've sworn she heard the woman begging for him to stop. She convinced herself he wasn't really hurting his wife, her interpretation the result of sleep deprivation and a craving for excitement. The need to entertain herself during the lonely nights. Mark was no help, snoring away beside her. It seemed quite soon after one of these exchanges that Louise realised the woman wasn't living next door any longer. 'Be wary of him,' Mark had said when they spoke about their neighbour recently. 'His missus left him for a reason.' Louise brushed off his warning, reasoning that it'd happened over two and half years ago; why should she worry now?

Louise's eyes are drawn to the wheelie bin. What is he filling it with?

The scream rips through the house, sending Louise's heart rate wild, her blood running ice cold in her veins. She rushes out of the kitchen, propelling herself towards the conservatory. Her eyes dart around, taking in every detail of Alfie and his surroundings, searching for the cause of his distress as she approaches him.

'What? What is it?' she gushes, crouching down beside him, her hands exploring his body for signs of injury. Alfie stares ahead silently, as though in a trance. 'Alfie? Honey – what's the matter?' His lips clamp together, and Louise swallows hard, noting the bluish tinge to them.

He can't breathe.

His toys are age-appropriate, there shouldn't be anything dangerous among them, no choking hazards. Mark made sure of it, not fully trusting Louise during her darkest months to take the necessary precautions herself, and he's regularly checked them since. Something must've snuck through the net. In her panicked state, all knowledge of what to do in this type of scenario disappears, but there's something in the back of her mind telling her she shouldn't try to fish the item out because she could do more damage, push it further down the oesophagus.

Phone 999.

No. By the time an ambulance arrives, Alfie would be dead. *She* has to do something. Act now. What the hell will Mark say if she lets their son choke to death? With her own breath held, she forces Alfie's mouth open and sticks her index finger inside, sweeping it for any foreign objects.

There is something inside. *Jesus.*

Louise's fingertip touches something solid. She manages to hook her finger behind it and flicks it out. The padded heart keyring plops on to the floor, covered in spit. She glances at it, her brow furrowed, then looks back at Alfie.

'You okay, baby?' Tears burn her eyes.

'I not a baby,' he says. Louise presses her hand to her chest, feels the throbbing of her heart against her palm. He's fine. Thank God. But she'd left him unattended for too long – it was her fault. Guilt surges in her belly as she picks up the keyring. How did Alfie even get hold of it? She keeps her keys in her handbag, out of reach. And her handbag was nowhere near the conservatory – she always puts it on the peg in the hallway as soon as she comes home. It's habit. He must've got it earlier somehow – before Louise came downstairs. She pulls at her hair, panic rising again with the thought that if he hadn't made a noise, she'd still be staring out the window, silently judging her neighbour.

Then it hits her. With something lodged in his throat – how would Alfie have been able to cry out? He must've screamed, *then* put it inside his mouth. Or maybe the scream had caused the object to get sucked further back. So, what had caused him to scream in the first place?

She returns her attention to Alfie, who's already moved on from the drama and is now banging a wooden train against the toy box, and gently places her hand over his to stop him.

'How are you feeling, Alfie?' She looks into his eyes, smarting a little when he turns away without a word. 'Can you tell Mummy why you shouted?' she says, putting her hands on his shoulders. Slowly, Alfie turns to face her, but his eyes don't meet Louise's; his gaze fixes on a point beyond her – over her shoulder – into the garden.

'It scare me,' he whispers.

Louise draws a sharp breath, lets him go and stands. 'What did, sweetheart?' Alfie raises his arm, indicating somewhere outside. 'Was it an animal?'

He shakes his head. 'Daddy hiding.'

'Daddy's at work,' Louise says, her voice cracking. She coughs to clear her throat. 'And Daddy wouldn't scare you, make you scream, would he?' she says, forcing a smile.

Alfie pouts, then pushes against Louise, causing her to lose her balance.

'Alfie, don't do that.' She rights herself and before she can say anything else, he goes back to the train and resumes banging it. Louise, her arms tightly folded over her chest, stands at the far side of the conservatory, staring through the glass panels overlooking the lawn. The back garden of their semi-detached house is long, its boundary marked by six-foot-high fencing. It's what separates them from next door and the cul-de-sac running behind the houses. There's no gate, no way to access the property from that end. And the side gate is padlocked – they rarely use the pathway to get to the back, they simply walk through the house. Alfie couldn't have seen anyone in their garden.

Louise turns back and watches her son playing, a strange

sensation creeping over her skin. It's like he knew what he was doing. Had done it on purpose. But what nearly three-year-old could manipulate in such a way? With a heaviness in her heart, she concludes it isn't possible.

No. It's not Alfie; it's her.

She is the problem.

Chapter 5

Mark's car pulls up outside an hour earlier than usual, but Louise doesn't hear the key in the lock for another five minutes. In that time, she's scurried around, picking up the discarded toys and shoving them in their respective containers back in the conservatory, and is sitting beside Alfie on the sofa in the lounge, reading him a book, when Mark enters.

'Well, aren't you two a sight for sore eyes,' Mark says, coming across and scooping Alfie up, squeezing him tight before swinging him around. Alfie squeals with delight, his eyes wide as he looks lovingly at his daddy. Louise averts her gaze, closes the book and mumbles an excuse to leave the room. 'Good day?' Mark calls after her.

Mustering all her energy, she responds, 'Yeah, thanks. I'll make you a cuppa.' It's as though the stuffing has been knocked out of her – and in place of her heart sits a hard stone. Her head lolls, heavy yet empty, while she waits for the kettle to boil.

'You don't look like you've had a good day.' She starts at

Mark's voice behind her, whirls around to face him. His eyes narrow, his expression curious, mistrustful. She's given him reason to be wary of her assertions over the past few years.

'Well. You know . . .' She offers an unconvincing smile.

'No, Louise, I don't. Tell me.'

She recalls the question he posed last night – the 'What happened today to make you lose it this badly?' and she wilts, like a plant deprived of water. She feels as though her body is shrivelling, trying to hide itself from view. She's so far from the person she used to be that she doesn't recognise this woman. Turning away, Louise continues to make his drink, pulling the round decaf tea bag from the caddy and popping it into the mug. Underneath her arm, his hand appears and lies on top of hers, stopping her from picking up the kettle. She feels Mark's breath on the back of her neck, a gentle sigh tickling the tiny hairs there. She shivers.

'There's no point telling you,' she says, her voice already thick with tears.

'Don't say that. Look, I've been a twat. I know it, you know it. And I'm sorry.'

Louise snivels, a brief laugh escaping as she wipes the back of her hand across her nose. 'Yeah – you have a bit.'

'Come on, babe.' Mark twists her to face him and holds her at arm's length while lowering his head to catch her gaze. Louise's pulse judders – his deep brown eyes, dark as pools, seem to look straight into her soul. 'I've been preoccupied with work. But that's no excuse; I shouldn't take it out on you.' He pulls her into a hug, holds her firmly, not letting go. Louise breathes him in, losing herself in his familiar, comforting and slightly musky, woody scent, the hint of Hugo Boss clinging to his skin.

He *has* been throwing himself into work. He *has* been more absent. Louise's body tenses, her muscles contracting with the memory of how Mark felt obliged to take time off to look after her and Alfie when she'd finally admitted she wasn't coping. How his boss had been amazing for the first month, encouraging him to take time off to support them, then, almost as quickly as he'd offered, did an about turn, piling on the pressure for Mark to return because the business was suffering. Christ. *She'd* been the one suffering. But, of course, work had to take priority. How could they pay the mortgage if neither of them was earning? Louise's pay dropped to the basic maternity allowance after eight months, and she'd been in no fit state to go back to work in her marketing coordinator position at that point. They had limited choices.

Louise gently pulls away from his embrace. However warm and caring he's being now, she can't bring herself to tell him about earlier. Her heart jolts at the thought of the near miss involving the keyring. Had she not been able to fish it out of Alfie's mouth in time, would he have choked to death? Would social services have accused her of negligence and charged her with his murder? Her head swims with the flurry of questions, the worry and guilt layering up, threatening to engulf her.

They've left Alfie alone now, though. They're both in the kitchen and he's in the lounge, watching CBeebies by the sound of it. So why can't she admit that he'd put something in his mouth, almost choked when she left him alone for a minute earlier? She'd been in the kitchen, not in another house. Her logical mind says there's no difference between her leaving him alone then and Mark doing so right now. But her critical mind argues there is and, as a mother, she should've known better.

'One of us needs to be with Alfie,' she says, about to go to him. Then she remembers Harriet's comment to her at playgroup, about how her husband takes over childcare while she takes naps. Louise pauses, her thoughts speeding up, and she turns back to Mark. Alfie is their *joint* responsibility. Not just hers. 'Actually, I'm exhausted,' she says, dragging her palms down her face. 'I could do with an early night.' She takes a deep breath, cocking her head to one side. 'You okay to do the bedtime routine and stuff?'

'Oh.' He flusters, looking around as though the answer is somewhere in the kitchen. 'Um . . .'

'I appreciate it. Thanks.' And she scoots up the stairs before Mark can put up a counterargument or suggest an alternative.

It's too light to sleep, too early to settle, despite being knackered. If only they had blackout blinds. A long sigh escapes her. Going back downstairs now would be admitting defeat. Her attention drifts to the wardrobe. A spark of envy had fired when she'd clocked Harriet's effortless sense of style, but what was stopping her from taking care of her appearance? She stands up and begins swiping clothes hangers from right to left. The outfits she wore to work – the sharp, snappy clothes she felt so confident in – are long gone. Left outside for a charity collection after a particularly low day. 'Ugh,' she says to every item. Coming to the last few outfits, she pulls out the dress she bought prior to getting pregnant with Alfie. Its bright, patterned print is so far removed from anything she's worn since – her choice of colours nowadays are dark and plain, safe. Anything else just gets dirty super quick, or stained and ruined entirely. Having a child has dulled her identity.

Louise recoils at this thought, biting down hard on her lip. It had immediately come to mind, so she must truly believe it. She replaces the dress and sits on the edge of the bed, her nose flaring with forced breaths. Then she catches herself in the wardrobe mirror. Glares at the stranger reflected back.

'You don't deserve to be a mother.' Tears bubble and fall. It's no wonder Alfie doesn't feel comfortable around her, when she feels so uncomfortable in her own skin. She lies down on the bed and shuts her eyes tight.

The digital clock shows 2:22 a.m. Has she even been to sleep? Mark's snoring gently beside her. She only vaguely remembers him coming to bed. A dull thud makes her sit up, alert. She listens for further sounds. She flings the duvet off and is on her feet and out of the room, padding across the landing at the second bang. Louder than the first. With her heart hammering, she rushes into Alfie's room, expecting him to be out of bed, wandering around in a dreamlike trance, knocking into his furniture. Her eyes struggle to adjust – his nightlight only offering a dim, orangey glow.

But he's silent. Still.

She kneels beside his bed, lays her hand on his back. There's no movement.

'Alfie?' she whispers.

Nothing.

Louise gives him a gentle shake. 'Hey, darling. Alfie?'

The room darkens further, the walls closing in, the air sucked from the atmosphere. Louise gasps, her hand clapping over her mouth.

He's not breathing.

She gets up, backing away from her son, each stifled breath hurting her lungs. It's as though someone or something is crushing her chest. Sitting on her, preventing respiration.

The scream begins in her abdomen before travelling at lightning speed through her frozen body, erupting from her mouth in an animal-like, guttural cry.

'Louise. Lou.' A calming voice breaks through. 'Lou, babe. What is it?'

'He's ... he's gone. He's dead, can't you see?'

'You're dreaming, Louise. It's a dream.'

'No. No! I haven't even *been* to sleep.' In this moment, her statement makes sense, but looking around, she's also aware she's in her bed, sitting up, her legs covered over by the duvet. Not in Alfie's room. She couldn't have simply climbed back into her bed after finding him, surely? Confusion floods her mind. 'I swear I went to check on him. He wasn't breathing, Mark.' Terror rises again, shredding her emotions, and she claws at her vest top, trying to release the sudden restriction in her throat.

'Calm down, Louise. Please.' Mark's voice mirrors her distress, his words having the opposite effect; her breaths remain ragged. 'Stay there,' he says. 'I'll go check on him.'

Louise's body is rigid while she awaits Mark's yell. Alfie's dead and her husband will see that any second. Time stands still. What will they do? Call an ambulance, even though it's too late? Footsteps across the landing ... *Oh, God – this is it*. Life is never going to be the same again.

'He's fine,' Mark says, scratching his head as he walks back into the bedroom. He shows Louise the monitor, points to an alive, moving Alfie as he wriggles underneath his duvet. She grabs it from him, puts her face up close to the screen. Sees for herself that Alfie is moving. *Alive*. Mark, his face ashen, takes it and examines it again. Louise can tell, despite his assertions, that for a split second at least he'd questioned whether she was right, needed to see for himself. 'You had a bad dream, that's all.'

A nightmare. She hasn't had one of those in a while.

'Nothing happened today, did it?' Mark's voice sounds distant, tired. He positions the monitor on the cabinet at his side of the bed, then looks at Louise. Her posture slackens a little, but the echo of the dream remains etched into her mind.

'Like what?'

Mark shrugs.

Louise thinks about earlier, replays the choking incident. Remembers Alfie saying something had frightened him. It's no surprise she had a bad dream.

'A day like any other,' she says breathily.

'You'd tell me, wouldn't you – if you needed . . . support?'

Louise gives him a fleeting look of confusion. Wasn't she always asking for his support? Had he forgotten how she'd asked him to stay home from work for longer, a request met with a dozen excuses about why it wasn't possible to extend his leave any further? The concern in his eyes makes her realise it isn't *his* support he's talking about now, though. A ripple of shame cascades through her. He means the professional variety.

'Of course I would.'

'I hope so, Louise. Because I'd hate to think of you going through all of that again.' Mark rubs her back, then leans in closer, resting his chin on her shoulder. 'You know I love you, right?'

Does he love her? Or is he saying it from a place of guilt, hit by the realisation that he was absent during a crucial time of her recovery from depression, knowing Alfie can be challenging?

'Yeah, I know,' Louise says, while her internal voice screams the opposite. 'Night, Mark.'

Louise, her insides churning, turns over and, in trying to push out bad thoughts, she allows her mind to drift to the next playgroup session instead. Despite Harriet's assertion that she isn't alone, that motherhood is a difficult transition, she still feels as though she's the only one not coping. Did Harriet have nightmares about her son dying? Louise can't see it. Although she knows full well outward appearances can be deceiving, Harriet was too confident, too relaxed – she wasn't faking it, Louise is certain.

Spending time with her can only be a good thing. Perhaps, Louise thinks, being around Harriet's composure and positivity will help restore her own confidence. She needs a lifeline; she won't let this friendship slip through her fingers.

Chapter 6

MUMSTOGETHER – *Top Tips for Tired Mums Forum*

Working mums help

mummymootoo – 28/07 01:21
> Only just collapsed into bed but as overtired as my kid so doubt I'll sleep for ages! Work tomorrow. God knows how I'll cope. How do others manage work and kids – any tips please?

ExhaustedNewMum0593 – 28/07 02:01
> You're so lucky. I'd do about anything to be in your position right now. 2 months in, and no light at the end of my tunnel of sleepless nights & can only wish I could go back to work. Need a break. Probably get more sleep at work!

Mummabear – 28/07 04:15
> *ExhaustedNewMum0593* Your the lucky one. Get to stay home with your baby not everyone has that option you know. Bit selfish if u ask me! Moan in a different thread.

mummymootoo – 28/07 04:34
> *Mummabear* – hey no bad vibes please. After tips not tiffs 😊

ExhaustedNewMum0593 – 28/07 05:21

Mummabear – Sorry. Thought this was a safe space to be honest. Clearly wrong.

Mummabear – 28/07 05:40

Nope 😊 Just wrong post to comment on if your not a working mom.

AngelFace – 28/07 05:57

OP needs to see helpful comments and tips – not arguing between others? And *ExhaustedNewMum0593* is obvs knackered not selfish. Not helpful for anyone to say such things – *Mummabear* None of us is perfect. Just need to feel supported & know someone has our back.

Chapter 7

The long, floaty dress hangs awkwardly, its cinched waist sitting too high, accentuating her larger hips. Louise sighs heavily. Almost three years, and she still hasn't returned to her pre-pregnancy weight. Her meals mostly consist of salads and smaller portions of what she cooks the family, plus she's been walking almost everywhere, rarely using her car, so it makes no sense. She pinches the polyester material that's snug on her hips, pulls at it until her reflection concedes it's not happening and is about to peel off the dress and revert to her usual jeans and shirt when Mark shouts up the stairs.

'I'm off now. Alfie is eating still. Can you come here?'

Louise's hands bunch at her sides. 'Hang on!' Grabbing the long woollen cardigan flung over the chair, Louise pushes her arms through and wraps it around her body, covering the dress.

Mark, already at the front door, barely glances at her as she descends the stairs, his focus on gathering his briefcase and jacket while simultaneously attempting to swig from his travel mug.

'He's a snail this morning,' he says. Louise stands on the bottom step, frowning.

'Sorry?'

'A snail. That's what he said. It's why he's eating breakfast *incredibly* slowly.' Mark laughs, reaches up and plants a swift kiss on her cheek, then turns to leave. 'I'll try to be back early.' And he's gone.

'Sure,' she mutters to the closed front door. 'Thanks, Mark.' Typical Alfie is choosing to be slow this morning. Butterflies fill Louise's stomach – she can't be late for the playgroup session. What if she misses the opportunity to sit with Harriet? If she's surrounded by other mums, Louise will bottle it and not have the courage to infiltrate the group. She needs to be the first one there, approach Harriet immediately and ensure she gets her mobile number this time.

'Come on, then, my little tiger.' Louise encourages Alfie along, talking of wild animals and how strong they are, how quick . . . anything to speed up the process. It has the desired effect, and, buoyed by her success, she gets him away from the table, out of his pyjamas and into his favourite dinosaur top and jeans without a fight.

'Good boy, Alfie.' She beams. For a blissful moment, a sense of pride washes over her and, looking down at him, her chest fills with a warmth she hasn't experienced for a long time. Fearful this positivity won't last, Louise hurries everything along, and they're out the door ahead of time.

Louise completes the walk to the hall far more quickly than she has done it before, fully focused on her destination, with her mind repeating the planned opening line to Harriet over and over. Reaching the entrance, her breaths rapid, she takes a beat to recover. It's now she realises her armpits are prickling, and she feels sure there will be dark patches of sweat visible once she takes off her jacket. She'll head straight to the bathroom, check her appearance before going into the main hall. Hopefully, Harriet won't be here yet. Louise is a bit early.

With Alfie straining against his straps in the buggy and beginning to vocalise his displeasure at being confined to his canvas prison, Louise's pulse picks up, her anxiety ratcheting up a notch. 'Mummy just needs the toilet, Alfie. You can run around any minute now, darling.'

Louise loses balance while reversing herself and the buggy into the toilets, banging awkwardly against the doorframe. She winces, cursing under her breath as her dress snags on something. Without thinking, she gives it a sharp tug, the perceivable ripping noise causing her cheeks to grow hot as frustration flows through her. Her heart sinks, noting the tear in the fabric. 'Dammit.' She takes a slow breath in, closing her eyes to stop herself from crying. It's not the end of the world. Probably not even noticeable.

Shaking her jacket off, she inspects the now uncomfortably damp armpit areas. If Mark hadn't hollered up the stairs, she'd have changed out of it, into her jeans. As it is, she's encased in a too small, torn and sweaty mess of a dress. Grabbing a few of the green paper towels stacked at the edge of the row of sinks, Louise dabs at the wet patches under her arms, the moisture sucking up into the fibres like it's blotting paper. But before her anxiety can melt away, her eyes widen with horror. 'No, no, no!' Louise leans in closer to her reflection. Sees a splodge of green on her dress where the colour from the paper towels has bled out. Under both arms. *Shit*. She rubs at the stains violently with her fingertips, but only makes it worse. Alfie kicks his feet against one of the stall doors, his patience running out. Maybe she should leave before anyone sees her. She's fooling herself if she thinks she can pull off the 'effortless' look, and this realisation hits home hard when the bathroom door flings open and a group of mums burst in, their toddlers trailing behind them. Louise musters a smile and tries to avoid direct eye contact with any of them. They carry on their loud conversation as if Louise is invisible anyway, clearly too preoccupied with their gossip to even acknowledge her. One of them rolls her eyes at another's 'so superficial' comment, and Alfie, likely sensing Louise's distress, chooses this moment to unleash an ear-splitting scream that draws overly dramatic winces from them.

'It's okay, Alfie, darling,' Louise trills, flustering and pulling his buggy around to beat a hasty retreat. She directs a mumbled apology to the women without glancing at them, her face burning with embarrassment. Why does she allow them to make her feel like this? With her plan of being first in the hall now dashed, her hopes lie with Harriet and Jacob being here already so she can go straight to them, save herself from the continued humiliation of being Billy No-Mates. At least Harriet had bothered to make her feel normal, like any other mum here. Though now she thinks about it, why *had* she? Because she felt sorry for her? Surely she wouldn't have invited her and Alfie on a playdate out of pity.

A wall of noise greets Louise when the door opens. Her eyes flit around the room, desperately seeking Harriet. Alfie rocks in the buggy, keen to escape and join in the chaos starting up around them. Louise ducks down, unclips the straps and Alfie ejects like a rocket, plunging headlong across the floor, knocking children out of his way as he makes a beeline for the toys. No doubt his desperation is because of being confined to the buggy for too long, and that's down to her, but, despite this, she can't help her rising irritation. *Here we go again.*

She looks in the opposite direction, scoping out the seating, then positions herself where she sat last time. Away from the other parents, praying any moment for Harriet to glide in like a breath of fresh air and come and join her. Each time the door swings open, she sits up tall, her breath hitching. And each time, she releases it in a disappointed sigh when it's not Harriet. She keeps her mobile phone in her hand, checks it for the time every few seconds. Her leg bobs, the rhythmic tapping of her shoe against the chair sounding like a metronome. Harriet is running late, that's all. She'll be here. But, after another twenty minutes, with the session in full swing, the likelihood of Harriet and Jacob turning up diminishes.

There. Says everything, she thinks. It was an empty offer of a playdate. Louise was too quick to believe it was genuine. Too hopeful. She should've known better. Could it be that once Harriet returned home with Jacob after their first meeting, Jacob's head came up with a huge bump and she realised she didn't want to subject her precious little one to more of the same from Louise's unruly son? Can't blame her. Hadn't she said this was already the second playgroup she'd tried? Maybe she'd moved on to yet another today, trying each out to find the best one. The first hadn't been clean enough, the second ... too violent.

The one mum who had been nice to her, and she'd ballsed it up.

Or, rather, *Alfie* had.

An ear-splitting scream penetrates her thoughts, and Louise automatically knows it's Alfie that's caused it. She shoots up, rushing to the centre of the room where Alfie has a chunk of a child's hair in his grip and he's pulling with all his might. Louise grabs his hand, unfurling his fingers to release the auburn-coloured strands from it, then yanks Alfie away. She picks him up, gripping him so hard his shouting sounds strangulated, and plonks him into the buggy. Her face flaming, she wrestles his arms into the straps, all the while talking to him as calmly as her hammering heart allows, and with his temper escalating, full-on sobs and snot running into his mouth, she flees the playgroup.

This is one of the times she wishes she had her car. With money tight, she and Mark had decided it was best to have only one car running – and she'd barely left the house the first eighteen months of Alfie's life, so it made sense. Later, of course, they deemed her 'unsafe' behind the wheel, as her low mood was too concerning to put the life of a child at risk. She can't remember now who suggested it – Mark, or Natalie, her counsellor. Was the car still taxed and MOT'd? Christ, she hopes so because it's parked in the cul-de-sac behind their house. She didn't need some busybody reporting it, resulting in a fine. She must check with Mark later.

Once she's out of sight of the hall, Louise stops pushing the buggy and cleans Alfie's face with a wet wipe. She rummages in the bag for a snack – anything to placate him. While sitting on a low wall by the town's clock tower, she watches Alfie tuck into a mini sausage roll, all memory of being dragged away from his peers and the toys forgotten. Her heart rate settles, too – her embarrassment waning a little now there's distance between her and them.

Where else might Harriet have taken Jacob? Louise takes her mobile and searches Google Maps for local playgroups. There are several nurseries in Crowbury, but these are for working parents to drop their kids off at, not for staying to meet new mums like Louise wants. Despite being able to get funding for some hours in the term after his third birthday, she's yet to even put Alfie's name down for a nursery or preschool.

The thought of going home with Alfie now, spending hours cooped up indoors, fills her with dread; a pang of loneliness twists in her stomach and intensifies with each second she contemplates it. She may as well walk around town for a while – at least it's fresh air for Alfie, and she's lost count of how many times her counsellor had recommended exercise to help with the symptoms of post-natal depression. Louise expands the map on her phone with her fingertips and checks out the red pins showing the stay-and-play group locations. Quite close. She could work her way up the high street, through the park to the other side of town, and the route would take her past the two locations where Harriet might be. No need to check out the third. Harriet had already said she wouldn't go back to the group next to the library.

Should she go home first, though? Get out of the stupid ruined dress? What would Harriet think if she saw her looking like a hot mess? Probably nothing, actually. She's not judgemental. Hadn't snubbed her or treated her as though she were invisible. Harriet's a kind soul. That's obvious, because Harriet had approached her. And it's why Louise is drawn to her. Because they're kindred spirits.

With her mind made up, Louise stands, brushes the crumbs from Alfie's lap, tells him they're going for a walk and sets off up the street, pushing the buggy as if her life depends on it.

Chapter 8

Louise struggled to sneak a look into the first playgroup without Alfie thinking they were joining in, but she managed to walk around the perimeter and find a window offering a glimpse. After scanning the parents, she found no sign of Harriet. With her hopes now pinned on the second playgroup, Louise strides along, the buggy at arm's length, her head lowered, her breathing becoming more laboured with each step up the hill. After a minute of this, Louise gives a forced puff of air, and an unwelcome memory of Alfie's birth resurfaces . . .

'Breathe more slowly, Lou,' Mark says, giving Louise's hand a pat, followed by a gentle squeeze.

Louise glares at him, her eyes wide, sweat seeping from every pore on her body.

'I'm trying . . . to push . . . a human . . . out of my *vagina*!' She crushes Mark's hand, moves her face closer to his, and in a low, wheezing growl closely resembling the demon's voice in *The Exorcist*, says: '*You* breathe the fucker out!'

Mark recoils, taking his hand with him, Louise's words spat in such a way he clearly fears for his safety. The midwife can barely hide her smirk, and gives him a knowing look, then returns her attention to Louise, whose feral cries are echoing throughout the labour room.

Louise comes to a sharp stop in the middle of the pavement to catch her breath. Someone bumps into her, mutters their annoyance, and then tuts loudly for good measure.

'Sorry.' Louise says it automatically, even though it isn't her fault; they shouldn't have been so close behind her. According to her counsellor, Louise says sorry too frequently, which – apparently – decreases the value of the word and its intent, lessening the impact of future apologies. During one of Louise's last sessions, Natalie mentioned how it might be because she wants to avoid conflict. She also said it could undermine Louise's credibility, make her appear weak. Insecure. Or had she read that somewhere else – in an article?

'Drink, pleeease.'

Louise snaps out of her thoughts, leaping into action. 'Sorry, sweetheart.' She shakes her head. 'Mummy was far away.' She rummages in the bag for Alfie's drink bottle. It's a stainless steel one – not plastic like most of the other mums at playgroup had for their toddlers. Because it's more durable, resistant to rough use. Alfie has gone through four of the plastic variety during his temper tantrums. Louise finds it and hands it to him. Watches intently as he sucks at the straw, his cheeks hollowing in, and hears each loud gulp.

He had always had a strong suck, right from birth. At first, the mere thought of breastfeeding had been uncomfortable. She'd listened to the instructions given in her prenatal NCT class, squidged the crocheted boobs that had been handed around, watched numerous YouTube videos and Instagram reels – and, although it had seemed so easy, she hadn't been prepared for the initial weeks of discomfort, learning and patience it ultimately required. She'd been determined to keep at it, though, believing it wasn't only best for Alfie, it was best for her too. Good for both of them. A means to aid bonding. Perhaps she should've continued. Not weaned him off the breast at a year old. Would it have made a difference now?

'All done.' Alfie flings the bottle, and it hits the pavement with a clank.

'Alfie!' Louise darts forward, but she's too late. Her shoulders dip, the bottle building momentum as it descends the hill she's just climbed. People stare at it rolling past them, no one attempting to stop it. 'Well, thanks, then!' Making a split-second decision, Louise starts to jog after it. If she's lucky, someone will realise what's going on and at least put a foot on the thing, stop it from travelling any further. Alfie's giggles become more distant, and she wants nothing more than to stop chasing his bottle. There needs to be consequences for his actions; he has to learn that. But she too is gathering momentum now and so she's committed to the cause.

Bloody bottle. Bloody toddler.

With her heart pumping, her adrenaline spiking, she

finally grabs the bottle and stands with it raised in the air, like she's lifting a trophy, triumphant in her win. The moment doesn't last. Her eyes dart about, scanning the place where she left Alfie in his buggy.

But the buggy and Alfie are gone.

A surge of panic whooshes through Louise's body. Her heartbeat – erratic following the jogging – now seems to halt entirely. She whacks a hand to her chest, tries to take a breath in. Where is he? Fragmented thoughts buzz around in her head: *he's been run over. Crushed by a lorry. Didn't put the brake on. Rolled down the hill.*

Louise's legs shake violently, but she starts to run up the hill, still looking in every direction. She hadn't really taken notice of exactly where they'd been when Alfie dropped the bottle. He's probably in a different spot. But they *had* been on the left side of the road, and the bottle hadn't travelled far enough away that she wouldn't be able to see the buggy.

'Alfie?' Her voice sounds strangled. She coughs to clear her throat. 'Alfie.' She can't see him. If only this were a nightmare, like the one she had last night when she was convinced Alfie had died in his sleep. Louise picks up speed, reaches the place she'd left her son only seconds ago. Her breaths rapid, she swirls around on the spot, frantic eyes checking every available angle.

This doesn't make sense.

Louise grabs the arm of a passer-by. 'Have you seen a little boy? He's in a grey buggy and I left him right here.' They shake their head, push on past.

Directly opposite, the door of the butcher's shop is open.

Louise darts across and goes inside. 'Did you see my little boy a moment ago?' Her words rise in pitch as fear nudges ever further into her thoughts, her heart.

Alfie's been kidnapped.

'He's in a grey buggy. We stopped so he could have a drink and he dropped the bottle – I left him for a few seconds to chase it down the road no one stopped no one helped.' Louise's words spill out of her like lava.

This can't be happening.

Her head feels light, woozy, and her surroundings spin as though she's having a vertigo attack.

Someone's arms are on her, around her, as she falls in slow motion to the ground.

Chapter 9

MUMSTOGETHER

Private Message

FROM AngelFace
TO ExhaustedNewMum0593
SUBJECT Hello from the other side
MESSAGE

Hey, hope you don't mind me sliding into your DMs! (Isn't that what the cool kids say – lol) Just wanted you to know I'm here if you need me. Well, at the end of the ether, anyway! If you can't face the forum mob, we can chat privately.

I know what it's like when you're trying to reach out, ask questions, etc in view of gaining SUPPORT – then get knocked back by well-meaning (or the opposite in some cases, sadly) mums who get all preachy or judgey. Remember, they're on the forum for a reason, too. Everyone needs help occasionally, don't they.

Sadly on here, as in life, there are always those who wish you harm.

I've got your back.

Chapter 10

Louise's eyelids flutter open, but her mind can't connect the dots.

Blood. The iron-rich scent hangs in the air, assaulting her nostrils. Her blood? What's she done? There's no pain. It's someone else's blood.

A strobe light flickers above her. Is she in the hospital?

No. Not a strobe light. She squints. It's a fly zapper. And she's not lying down, she's sitting on a chair. Then she remembers; she's in the butcher's shop.

Oh, God – where's Alfie?

'It's okay. You were only out for a short while.' The butcher is eyeing her, his expression one of relief. Alfie is in the buggy beside him. 'Though you did give us a bit of a fright, there. How are you feelin' now?' He smiles, his cheeks bulging like a hamster.

Louise holds her head in her hands, mumbles, 'I'm fine.' Her go-to phrase these days. Just two empty words. Said without meaning. It's easier, quicker, shuts down further questions. Usually. 'But I don't understand.' Louise looks back up, stares at Alfie. He's there. Everyone can see him. He's not a figment of her imagination. Something else that wasn't merely her imagination was the buggy not being where she left it when she'd began her chase after his water bottle. She's sure about it. 'My son ... I didn't come in with him, I couldn't see him, his buggy, on the pavement. He was gone.' Louise's forehead crinkles as she goes over it in her mind's eye.

The butcher ducks down to Louise's level and tells her that a woman wheeled the buggy in just after she fainted. According to them, Alfie was directly outside the shop. He hadn't been missing. He asks if Louise has any medical issues. Did she need medication? Had she been ill recently? After shaking her head to all of his questions and becoming dizzy, she shares how she's had a rushed morning. Did she eat breakfast? Alfie was being a snail, she remembers that. Yes, and then he'd been good, and Louise had been carried along on the wave of success, not daring to stop to grab food for herself. And pushing the buggy up the hill, sprinting after the bottle – she hasn't even had a drink.

No food. No water. Exertion.

A perfect mix to create a meltdown. What an idiot. Not surprising she passed out in the butcher's shop.

'No. But he wasn't outside. Why would I be looking for him if he was right there?'

Had she become disorientated? Ridiculous notion. But the alternative, someone kidnapping him, was more absurd, because if that was their intention, why bring him back straight away?

Alfie is licking a massive lollipop, his little tongue navigating it, sticking to it, completely oblivious to Louise's distress. Sitting contently with one of the customers fussing over him. How long has it been? It's the quietest he's ever been while strapped into the buggy or the car seat. He's not keen on being confined.

'Who—'

'Hope you don't mind, love,' the butcher says, wiping his large square hands down his blood-stained apron, 'but poor little chap, seeing his mum collapse like that—'

'Thanks. I appreciate it.' She doesn't add how the E numbers will likely keep him up all night, doesn't express her concern over the butcher's bloody hands. She's grateful to him. To the person who wheeled Alfie inside.

With a lurching feeling of sadness, Louise questions whether her gratitude is real. She *was* distraught, though, when she thought Alfie was gone – why else would she have panicked? Have ran around looking for him? No matter how challenging Alfie is, she loves him. She just wishes he loved her back.

'Was gonna ring an ambulance, but you didn't hit your head ... should I make a call for someone to pick you up from here?'

The thought of Mark coming to get her and Alfie and having to tell him what had happened brings a lump to her throat. She clears it, shakes her head. 'No, no. I'll be all right, thank you. Just need a chocolate bar or something.' She gazes around for her bag. It's still hanging on the back of the buggy. The butcher – whose name she hasn't asked, but she presumes it's Bernie as that's the name above the door – waves at a younger man behind the counter, indicates for him to bring it to them.

After taking a few minutes to eat a Twix and drink some water, Louise thanks Bernie again, and manoeuvres Alfie's buggy back outside. She can feel eyes boring into her as she walks away. Back down the hill. Her eagerness to visit the other playgroup has diminished after that fiasco. And, given the time, she has to admit defeat – it's unlikely Harriet and Jacob will still be there even if they had been earlier. Not wishing to dwell on 'losing' Alfie, or her fainting fit, Louise focuses her mind on where her new friend might live. She assumes it's relatively local, but Harriet hadn't said if she'd walked or driven to the playgroup venue. Hadn't mentioned her surname, either. Louise hadn't a lot to go on. The disappointment weighs heavily on her shoulders.

Her disillusionment immediately transforms into anxiety once she turns the corner and spots Mark's car parked in the road outside their house. Louise checks her mobile for the time. It's okay. She can say she's been at playgroup, it's not too much longer before it would've ended. Besides, Mark doesn't have a clue how long a session lasts. She lets out a sharp breath and opens the front door.

'Can Mummy have that for a moment, please, Alfie?' Louise reaches a hand towards the lolly, but Alfie screws up his face and turns away, the lolly sticking to his cheek. 'You'd like to get out of this buggy now, wouldn't you?' she asks, her voice almost as sickly sweet as the sugar-filled confectionary her son is gripping in his chubby hand.

'No. Mine. She gave it me.'

It's not a battle she cares to enter into. However, she suspects Mark won't be impressed. 'Let's get you out, then you can have it back,' she says, her voice measured. Alfie glares at her, his familiar look of defiance making her shudder. And, in another familiar move, Louise backs down. She's heard of other parents that do things for 'a quiet life' or because they don't have time to reason with their children. Mostly she's come across those stories online, or on TV. They rarely have happy endings. And they rarely talk about three-year-olds acting this way. They're usually horror stories about the teenage years, when hormones kick in and outside influences are an issue. Social media, getting in with the wrong crowd. Christ. If this is Louise's experience with Alfie now, what the hell will it be like later on?

While bent over the buggy, attempting to unclick the straps, Louise calls to Mark. She senses him behind her, turns and stands up. 'How come you're home at a lunchtime?' she asks, brushing the hair from her face.

'Oh, God,' he says, his eyes wide. 'Are you okay? What happened to you?' His tone is filled with concern, but Louise's stomach flip-flops. Does she look that bad?

'Nothing. Just rushing around after Alfie at playgroup, that's all.' Usually, she'd experience a pang of guilt at lying to Mark – today, she doesn't. Louise turns to smile at Alfie, and she hears Mark's sigh.

'And *that* is?' He points towards Alfie, who has managed to unstick the lolly from his face and is now licking at it contently. Louise raises her eyebrows, quietly thrilled their son actually appears happy for a change.

'He was such a good boy. I thought he deserved a treat.'

'He's not a puppy, Lou.' Mark turns to look at Louise, his eyes penetrating hers. 'Is there something you're not telling me?'

'Like what?' Louise challenges him, staring right back. But before he can offer an answer, she adds saltily: 'I would've thought you'd be pleased we've had a good morning.'

His face softens, and he immediately apologises, giving Louise a hug. The tender moment, the snippet of affection, is brief. He pulls away abruptly. 'You really have been rushing around,' he says, wrinkling his nose. 'Tell you what. I've got half an hour of lunch break left, so I'll keep Alfie occupied while you take a shower.'

'Oh. Right.' Louise glances down at herself, despite knowing what she'll see, and sniffs the air. She grimaces. 'Thanks. I could do with it, eh?'

'I'll make you a ham sandwich and cuppa,' he says, ruffling her hair as if she were the toddler. Then he busies himself with Alfie and, as soon as his back is turned, Louise scurries up the stairs like a mouse whose tail has been trodden on.

In the shower, she allows the hot jets of water to massage her tired skin, listening to the hypnotic sound of the water gurgling, wishing she could stay this way for eternity. Mark said he only had half an hour left before he had to be back at work, though. Reaching lazily for the sponge, she attempts to create a lather with the supermarket own-brand gel and wash some of the embarrassment off her body, down the plughole. But, however hard she towel-dries herself after the shower, an after-effect of it remains, clinging to her skin like a limpet. Once she's dressed in fresh clothes, her more comfortable joggers and a T-shirt, Louise sprays on a hefty dose of perfume and makes her way back downstairs, her tummy grumbling with anticipation of the ham sandwich. It's when she's halfway down that she hears the voices. And they aren't just Mark's and Alfie's.

Her body seems to shrivel in reaction to the unexpected, yet recognisable, tone.

'Oh, fab. *Mummy's* here,' she hisses.

Louise presses her back against the hallway wall, tries to hear what they're saying before announcing herself to them. Forewarned is forearmed. Sue is cooing over Alfie like he's a newborn; her hoarse voice – from years of smoking before having an ah-ha moment after Louise's dad died of lung cancer – spreads through the walls, much like a severe case of damp. Then Mark speaks, his words low and conspiratorial, as though he's telling Sue a secret. The nerve endings in Louise's fingers tingle, her nostrils flaring in annoyance. When her mum made a rare visit, it was these kinds of private chit-chats, snatched pieces of conversation held behind cupped hands, that stuck with her. But she's given them no reason to be worried about her lately. Everything has been progressing the way it should. Hasn't it?

'Why are you here now?' Louise whispers.

Nothing has given them concern.

Nothing they know about, anyway.

Unless Mark has told her mother that he doesn't think Louise is coping again. Is that why she's here now? Ready to 'help' when it suits? Louise's fingernails dig into her palms while her thoughts clash inside her skull. Is she being unreasonable? Too harsh on her mum? She *is* here, after all. That counts for something. Their relationship is strained, has been for quite some time, but, if she were being honest with herself, the fault lay with both of them. When Louise rebelled as a teenager, and locking horns with Sue was an almost daily occurrence, her dad had said it was because they were too alike. Louise refuted it then, and still doesn't want to accept it.

Louise has two choices now. Waltz in and pretend to be delighted to see her mother. Or ... she squeezes her eyelids closed, shakes her head – her still-damp hair flipping from side to side. No. There isn't an alternative. Not really. She sucks in a lungful of air, lets it out slowly through puckered lips, then takes confident steps towards the lion's den.

'Hello, stranger,' Louise says, walking into the kitchen, her chin tilting up. 'Thanks, Mark.' She takes the plate – a round of sandwiches, with some chunks of cucumber and a handful of cherry tomatoes neatly arranged on the side – and goes to Alfie, bending to give him a kiss on his head. 'Nice to see Granny?'

'Nanna,' her mother grumbles.

Louise smiles. 'Course. Sorry. I'd forgotten.' She plonks down on the chair beside Sue and bites into her lunch. Mark chews at the corner of his lower lip, then moves to Sue, putting an arm on her shoulder.

'Got to dash, Sue. Lovely to see you.' He then transfers his attention to Louise, giving her a kiss. 'Be nice to have some company for a bit, won't it, love?'

'Sure,' Louise says, through a mouthful of food. She's well aware the atmosphere in the room is heavy, with menacing clouds banking up; a storm gathering. Months' worth of rain threatens to be unleashed. Mark appears reluctant to leave, hovering in the doorway, but, equally, it's obvious he can't wait to escape the tension. Doesn't want to be swallowed up by the flood. He taps his hand twice against the wood of the doorframe and is gone.

Chapter 11

The days until the next playgroup session passed incredibly slowly, but the second her eyelids opened this morning, her stomach had flipped. *Today will be stress-free.*

Louise silently repeats the positive affirmation over and over in her mind before even getting out of bed. That's the key, apparently – a beautiful day begins with a beautiful mindset. She has a load of other similar phrases written in the wellness journal that Mark had given her – a pretty, spiral-bound book meant as a way to order her thoughts, be mindful. Like therapy, he'd suggested.

Alfie quickly tests her positivity, kicking out at Louise's shins as she tries to get him through each task on the morning routine chart – which is basically a 'good old-fashioned star chart' that her mother had brought with her and insisted she try because 'it worked like a dream with you; you loved being praised', to which Louise had only raised a brow, stopping short of asking why Sue never praised her now – and she purposely ignores his behaviour despite a bubbling of anger threatening to erupt. 'Today will be stress-free,' she repeats through gritted teeth.

Louise pushes the buggy at a steady pace. No rushing means no sweaty mess to contend with when she reaches the playgroup hall. Outwardly, all is calm. But Louise's insides knot and twist.

Please be there today. She looks skyward, the morning sun offering a whisper's breath of warmth on her face. *It's not much to ask, God.* She's not sure why she's brought God into it – it was a faith she'd lost long ago. But . . . it pays to be cautious – just in case she's wrong about Him. *You have to cover all the bases.*

She's on time, not early. That's good – doesn't appear too eager; desperate. Pausing at the entrance, Louise brushes her hair with her fingertips and gazes down at her white blouse, surreptitiously checking under the armpits – no damp patches – and then smooths her hands down her trousers. She's chosen her navy cotton pair because they are roomy-but-smart and don't crease by merely looking at them. With a quick wriggle of her shoulders to release the tension, she opens the door.

It's as though Louise senses her before she sees her. Maybe it's the perfume – or it's simply the positive charge the room seems to hold.

Harriet is here.

Nestled between two of the 'fun mums'. Or should she refer to them as the popular mums – cliquey, even. Louise has never been part of an in-crowd. Even if she were, she's sure she'd be welcoming of others. Not close ranks like some mums at the playgroup seem to do. Louise's heart thuds against her ribs. She inhales slowly, trying to get a handle on her emotions – she should play it cool. Instead of approaching Harriet straight away, and trying to insert herself into the group and come off looking weird, she'll be aloof.

Louise unleashes Alfie, parks the buggy at the far wall and, after nodding, uttering a few 'good mornings' to other parents, goes to help Alfie on the climbing frame.

'I do it,' he snaps, shrugging off her attempt to help him. Her lips press together in a thin line. Out of the corner of her eye, she sees Jacob bound up and so goes to him, interjecting so she can have contact with him instead. Jacob beams at her, laughs, his apple-rosy cheeks plump; she has to stop herself from taking his face in her hands. The world seems to pause as she is captivated by this moment of uncomplicated joy; the tug of emotion pulls at her. Having this little boy look at her with such admiration fills the void in her stomach in a way she hasn't experienced for a long time. If at all.

'Wrong child.'

Louise whips her head around. 'Oh!' She gives an awkward laugh, looking away quickly in the hope Harriet doesn't see the guilt in her eyes – her embarrassment at being caught out.

'Missed you last time,' Louise says, without acknowledging Harriet's comment, but edging towards her own son.

'Ah, yes – was at the hospital.'

Louise's mouth gapes. 'Hope everything's—'

'All fine,' Harriet cuts in. 'It's a once-a-month thing, a sort of "check-up".' Harriet air-quotes with her fingers. 'Nothing exciting but has to be done. How was it here? Alfie have a good session?'

Louise is curious about what would require a regular hospital visit, but doesn't like to ask. 'A bit stressful, to be honest. Compounded by a post-playgroup visit from my mother . . .' Louise rolls her eyes to ensure Harriet gets the gist it was unwelcomed.

'Oh, don't be like that – you'll miss her when she's gone.'

'She's *gone* most of the time. You'd never believe she only lives across town.' Louise is about to go into detail about how the physical distance between them doesn't compare to the emotional one, but senses Harriet's thoughts are elsewhere – a flicker of sadness crosses her face. Maybe she has experienced the loss of her own mother. Louise decides not to harp on about Sue and her lack of support. 'Anyway, I'm glad you're here today, we forgot to swap mobile numbers.' Louise catches a brief look of confusion from Harriet and for an awful moment wonders if she'd dreamt the whole exchange when they last met. She feels heat rise to her cheeks.

Harriet puts a hand to her chin, her forefinger touching her bottom lip in a thinking pose. 'Ohh, so we can arrange a playdate?'

Thank God. '*Yes*. I mean, if that's still okay?'

'Of course. Why wouldn't it be?'

There's something a little off about Harriet today, Louise

thinks. She glances across to the fun mums – had they said something to make Harriet reconsider her invite for Alfie to play with Jacob? They're chatting, and the one with the perfect hair throws her head back and laughs at something the other has said – but they're not taking any notice of Louise. Despite her usual paranoia, she's confident the joke isn't aimed at her or Alfie. And what could they have said, anyway? Harriet is already aware of Alfie's tendency to hit out.

'Right, let me have yours.' Harriet is standing with her phone in her hand, waiting for Louise to say her number. She rattles it off, watching as Harriet taps the digits into her contacts. Then she calls it. 'Now you have mine.' She smiles.

Louise feels the vibration in her trouser pocket. 'Perfect, thanks. When's a good time for you?' Strike while the iron's hot, her mum always said, and Louise didn't want to risk waiting. 'I'm ... *we're* ... free tomorrow.' Louise flinches, blinks hard, realising she has come on strong. Harriet purses her lips, flicks her hair behind one shoulder, then turns to face Louise. The pause seems unbearably long, and Louise's heartbeat whooshes in her ears.

'Yeah.' Harriet nods thoughtfully. 'We can do that. Say ten?'

A warm sensation travels through Louise's body. She's not being fobbed off. She has a firm date. 'Sounds good to me.'

Harriet nudges Louise with her elbow. 'Look,' she says, nodding towards the children.

Louise's attention has been fully on Harriet, not Alfie.

'Oh, wow,' Louise says, breaking out in a smile. 'Look at them getting on like a house on fire.'

'Told you,' Harriet says, with a dramatic air of smugness. 'We're at twelve Vicary Road, by the way. Can't miss us.' She doesn't elaborate, and Louise commits the address to memory. She feels a surge of relief when the session ends and there have been no incidents involving Alfie – no acts of violence towards a single other child. Today has been a productive day.

And tomorrow she and Alfie will spend time with new friends.

Chapter 12

According to Google Maps, Harriet's house is only a twenty-minute walk away. Louise taps on the satellite view on her mobile and drops the little yellow man into the road so she can get a better look. She raises her eyebrows, lets a whistle through her lips. It's a pretty exclusive development – five large detached houses – each with a garage and with bigger than average front gardens. She clicks back to aerial view, a small gasp escaping her as she notes that several houses appear to have swimming pools, including Harriet's. 'Wow. Nice.' Louise sits back, takes a sip of tea and gazes out of the conservatory window into her back garden.

She's lucky to have what she has. She and Mark have worked hard for their modest semi and they both love the area. Louise puts her cup down and rolls her neck, massaging a knot in her shoulder. New house, new baby, she'd remembered thinking on the day she and Mark moved in. It was raining and blowing a hoolie as they rushed to and from the hire van with their boxes in fits of giggles, declaring 'it can't get any worse', moments before thunder began to growl above them. They'd eventually collapsed in an exhausted heap on the sofa, looking as though they'd been swimming with all their clothes on.

Is it the swimming pool Harriet was referring to when she'd said 'Can't miss us'? Can't be – the pool isn't visible from the front, let alone on the approach. Must be something else. Something not noticeable on the map. Doesn't matter now she's checked the location – she knows where to go and doesn't require a landmark. Louise hasn't mentioned the playdate to Mark yet. She hasn't really spoken to him, her mind too full, playing out various scenarios in her mind about how the first date would go. Mostly, Louise conjures only good outcomes, but last night, during a fitful sleep, she was powerless to keep the visions of mayhem from tumbling through her dreams. Why did this feel so huge? Like any hope of a social life depended on it going well?

'Muuummmeeee!' Alfie, his hair a tangled mess of curls, bounds up to Louise, smacking his head down in her lap. 'I'm hungry.' The words are muffled in her skirt. Today's outfit choice took half an hour of pondering and deliberating. Alfie's was, at least, somewhat easier. She'd laid his clothes out ready last night – a pair of long shorts and his blue T-shirt, as it brings out the colour of his eyes. He is a handsome boy; she often stares at him, wondering who he takes after. Whenever her mother has seen photos of Alfie, she's said the same thing: 'He's such a pretty boy. I can't see you in him, Louise.' To which she's never asked if that means her own mother doesn't think *she's* pretty. Best not to ask questions you don't want to hear the honest answer to.

'Aw, you've only just had breakfast. I've got a better idea.' There's no response from Alfie, his face still buried. 'Come on, Alfie – we're going to play at Jacob's house today!' He snaps his head up, narrows his eyes.

'No playgroup?'

'Not today. It'll be just you and Jacob. That'll be nice, won't it?'

Alfie pushes his pursed lips to the side, squinting one eye as he contemplates it. Louise holds her breath, waiting for the feared 'don't want to', followed by a battle until one of them gives in. But it doesn't come.

'Okay,' he says simply.

'Great. Let's get going.' Louise jumps up, not daring to wait in case he changes his mind. It's nine twenty – a bit early, probably, but best to get her and Alfie out the door while he's amenable; she can take a more leisurely walk.

It's the large, four-tiered water fountain in the elevated front garden that gives it away – it has to be at least eight feet tall.

'Blimey,' Louise says, stopping in her tracks outside Harriet's house. 'Look at that, Alfie.' She watches the cascading waterfall, mesmerised by the calming combination of the visual and auditory stimuli. Alfie, though, isn't bothered, and begins to kick against the buggy frame.

'Get out now. Out. Out.'

'Yes, yes. Hang on.' Louise pushes Alfie up the driveway, noting the black BMW parked close to the double garage door. Is that Harriet's husband's car? She did mention he works from home sometimes.

Louise rings the bell – one of those fancy ones with a camera – and stands back from it, waiting for Harriet to answer the door. Moments pass and nerves gather in Louise's belly. She has the right day. She checks the time on her mobile – it is five minutes before ten, but surely that's not too early. Alfie thrashes against the buggy's straps and Louise feels anxiety bubbling. It won't be long before she loses control of Alfie, becomes stressed and flustered and just turns tail and walks away, disappointed with herself – but more with Alfie – for ruining their only offer of a playdate. Sweat breaks out on Louise's forehead, and she swipes at it with the back of her hand.

'For goodness' sake, will you *wait*, Alfie!' Louise bends to placate him, her back to the front door.

'Get out now,' Alfie says again, straining, his face turning a deep red.

'Stop doing that and I will let you out.' Alfie does as he's told and Louise lets him loose. He ejects himself from the buggy and runs straight to the water feature. 'Oh, God. Alfie, no!' With a lightning-quick reaction, Louise grabs a handful of Alfie's top and yanks him backwards, pulling the material taut around his neck. He falls on to his backside and begins crying at an alarming volume. 'Shush, shush, now.' Louise soothes him, then tries to explain how dangerous it is to run off, especially where there's water.

'I told Richard that thing was a death trap. Awful, isn't it?'

Louise swings round to see Harriet standing in the doorway, watching them. 'Oh, sorry. Alfie made a beeline for it. I had to pull him back.'

'I wanted to move house, but my darling husband did not, and decided to surprise me with *that* – some weird kind of bribe, eh?' She shakes her head, then laughs. 'Sometimes I'm not sure he knows me at all. Anyway, come on in. Jacob has been asking "when is Alfie coming?" for the past two hours.'

'Thanks, Harriet.' They go inside, but while they're still in the hallway, Louise says: 'It must be stressful having water in the front *and* back gardens.' Harriet looks at her oddly, motioning for her and Alfie to go on past the sweeping staircase and through a doorway.

'Do you mean the pool?' she asks.

Louise swallows hard. Damn. She doesn't want Harriet to know she's searched her house on Google Maps. 'Yes, don't all the houses in this street have them?'

'You're absolutely right – most do. And yes, it had been a worry, which is why we now have the cover over it permanently. Like I said, I wanted to move house after we had Jacob – to somewhere more child-friendly, possibly closer to my parents, too, but with one thing and another, I agreed we'd stay for a bit longer.'

'I'm glad you did,' Louise says.

Harriet smiles and reaches down to ruffle Alfie's hair. 'Such a gorgeous mop of hair.'

'Can I have a lollipop?' he asks, looking up at her.

Louise immediately steps in, apologising. 'Alfie, we don't ask like that. And I've brought a snack for you.'

Harriet laughs. 'I'm sorry to disappoint you, Alfie. Right, let's find Jacob, shall we? He'll be in the playroom.'

The playroom is double the size of Louise and Mark's conservatory and has wall-to-wall units housing a multitude of toys. So much for one child. Louise's gaze shifts around the room, a mix of awe and worry pulling at her insides. At least at home she knows every toy is age-appropriate; she has no idea if Harriet and Richard have the same level of caution. Given the water hazards, and Harriet's laid-back attitude, she doubts it. Although, as Louise found out, it doesn't matter how careful you are, things will slip through. She'll have to hope Alfie doesn't stick anything in his mouth today.

Alfie goes straight to the train set, ignoring Jacob.

'I'll make us a drink,' Harriet says. 'What's your poison?'

Louise, trying not to fuss over Alfie, replies distractedly with, 'Oh, a coffee, thank you,' and when Harriet disappears from the room, she goes straight to Jacob. 'Hello, Jacob. What are you playing?'

'Just cars,' he says, smiling up at Louise. He zooms a red plastic car between two pillars of bricks, giggling as one topples.

'Oh no, it's crashed,' Louise says, kneeling down beside him and dramatically beginning to rebuild the pillar. 'Quick, Jacob – we must stop the other cars coming through until it's mended!'

Jacob squeals with laughter as Louise madly stacks the bricks and he shouts 'stop' to the other cars. When she's finished it, Louise sits back on her heels, perusing the room. Alfie has his back to them, his attention on a train. It strikes her that she hasn't played like this with him – not from want of trying; he's just always preferred his dad's company. He lets her read books to him, but even then, if he had the choice, he'd pick Mark over her. But Jacob seems genuinely happy to have her in his space. Maybe it's just easier interacting with someone else's child. It's novel for them. And it's possible Jacob is different with Harriet. At playgroup the first time they met, Alfie was keen to show off his toy to Harriet, now Jacob is doing the same with Louise. She shouldn't read anything into it.

'You love your cars?' Louise asks, noting the assortment of them, recognising a few from the film *Cars*.

'Yup,' he says, nodding furiously. 'This my favourite.' He holds up the red one. 'Lightning McQueen. Is he yours?' His eyes bore into hers – inquisitive, bright – and his face lights up with his gap-toothed smile. A tingling sensation stirs in Louise's stomach and, as she smiles back at Jacob, a single tear rolls down her cheek. She brushes it away.

'Good choice. I think my favourite is . . .' Louise reaches over Jacob to grab the yellow car and as she does she touches his hand. A shot of electricity pulses through her fingers. She snatches it away.

'Static shock?' Harriet's voice is behind her. Louise turns, opens her mouth to object because she doesn't think it was static, but has no other explanation to give, so nods. 'It's the laminate flooring,' Harriet says, rolling her eyes. 'Ugh. Seriously, I'm like a walking electricity pylon in this room. Coffee is ready. Follow me.'

'Aren't we having it here?'

'Thought it would be good to have some child-free time.

They'll be okay playing here for a bit. Need to give them some independence.'

A niggling doubt prevents Louise from agreeing. 'I'm not sure that's the best idea ... Alfie, you know ... might—'

'Louise. Stop fretting. It's fine. I have a nanny cam.'

'*Oh*.' Louise wishes she'd known that a moment ago. Had Harriet been watching her from the kitchen? Seen her interaction with Jacob? She gets up and pads after Harriet through a corridor. The rear of the house has been extended, and the ceiling features skylights, allowing light to flood in. Louise tilts her chin up, her face warmed by the sunshine seeping through. 'This is lovely, Harriet.'

But the pièce de résistance is the kitchen.

Louise inhales sharply as they enter. It's a bold choice, Louise thinks as her eyes are drawn to the dramatically dark charcoal units. The backdrop of the white walls lifts the look and, together with the brass elements and accessories, the space has a moody yet glamorous feel.

She pictures Harriet in here with Richard and Jacob – they're all together cooking, laughing and sharing stories from their day as veg is chopped and deposited into Le Creuset pans on the hob. Richard is interested in Harriet's review of her day and listens intently and non-judgementally, and then it's his turn. Their exchanges are meaningful, and they include Jacob, both asking what his favourite part of the day has been. Then, sitting around the large rectangular table, they eat their healthy, home-cooked meal before moving into the lounge for more relaxing family time. Then they both take Jacob up to be bathed and settled to sleep, each reading him a story. The drama, Louise decides, is in the décor, not their lives.

'I can't believe you'd ever want to leave this house. It's stunning, Harriet.'

'Yeah, it is,' Harriet says, casting her gaze around, too. 'But bricks and mortar, material possessions – they aren't what makes a true home, are they?' She looks back to Louise, shrugs. 'It's the people in them.' A strange shiver passes up Louise's spine, tickling the base of her neck. She rubs at it with her hand before changing the subject.

'Richard working from home today?' Louise asks, taking the mug Harriet offers her. She notes the milk froth and smiles at the sprinkle of chocolate powder formed into a heart shape, the way baristas prepare them. She looks around for the posh coffee machine, but doesn't see it.

'No. Office. Talking of work ...' Harriet sits at the kitchen island and indicates for Louise to do the same. 'I'm returning to mine part-time at the end of the month. Have organised for Jacob to go to the other nursery sessions twice weekly, so no more stay-and-play for me then!'

Louise's heart drops. 'Oh, really?' She hears the disappointment in her own voice, attempts to recover. 'That's great. What is it that you do?'

'Well, I used to be a freelance interior designer. Ran my own pretty successful business, actually. But once we decided we'd like a family I slowed down.' Harriet gives a wistful smile, her fingers idly twisting the key on her necklace, 'and given the time and commitment required, realised I didn't want it *all*, you know? Richard's job enables us to live the life we've grown accustomed to anyway, so I just took the less stressful option of a salaried job designing kitchens.'

'Ahh, makes sense,' Louise says, splaying her hands and looking around at the kitchen again.

'I might've had a hand in this creation.' She laughs. 'But with the demands of being a mother, and wanting to spend as much time with Jacob as possible, I took extended maternity leave. Now seems like the right time to ease back into it. Two days a week will allow me to keep my hand in, but still have loads of time for Jacob. I think it's important to have a balance. What about you?' Harriet breaks from talking, picks up her mug and eyes Louise as she sips from it.

Louise gives a jagged sigh. 'I haven't given it much thought.' She averts her gaze from Harriet. She *has* thought about it. That work might give her something to focus on aside from her inability to bond with Alfie. This would be the perfect moment to share her struggles since giving birth. How she's recovering from a really low point, has had therapy for post-natal depression. She sucks in a breath, smiles. 'It's not like my job organising events and campaigns was particularly exciting.' Her eyes close, the right moment slipping by. And she thinks it's too soon in the friendship to be spilling her guts. 'And, like you, I wanted to be with Alfie, so . . .'

'Have you booked him in for the same nursery? I mean, now we've checked it out for the stay-and-play group, I feel confident Jacob will be happy there.'

'I haven't, no. I've been playing the wait-and-see game, I suppose. I'm not *quite* as confident as you are!'

Harriet gives a flick of her hand when Louise says the last bit, a discernible shake of her head. But she doesn't disagree. 'You should consider it – I think you'd be surprised at how much less you'll worry. Not sweat the small stuff. And, honestly, I think we need to maintain our own sense of identity. We're more than just Jacob's or Alfie's mums.'

With the mention of the boys' names, Louise's eyes widen. 'God, they're quiet, we haven't even checked—'

'They're absolutely fine.' Harriet points behind Louise, and Louise swings round. The nanny cam is positioned on the worktop and the large display shows the boys playing cars . . . together. Happily.

'Wow!' Louise's hand goes to her chest. 'It's a miracle.'

'Not really,' Harriet says. 'It's because you aren't there.' Louise inhales sharply, feeling as though she's taken a punch to the stomach. She tries to conceal the hurt by covering her face with her mug as she lifts it to her mouth. 'As I said,' Harriet continues, 'they need to be given some independence. They feel safe, they know we're here – but we don't need to be hovering over them every minute of the day.'

Louise relaxes her shoulders. Harriet wasn't being mean. She was including herself in that, too. And she *almost* tells Harriet about Alfie's choking incident, but stops herself, not wishing to come across even more like the neurotic first-time mother she believes everyone thinks she is.

'You're right,' Louise says, a warm glow swelling inside her. 'Thank you. For today, for inviting us on a playdate.'

'You're very welcome. I'm enjoying the company – but, more importantly, they are.' She nods towards the monitor.

'I knew they'd get on.' Harriet's attention is drawn to her vibrating mobile phone. She glances down, swipes at the screen, then stands up. 'Must get a quick snap of them like this,' she says, hurrying out of the kitchen. Louise sees Harriet on the nanny cam, her back to the lens, presumably as she takes a photo.

'I'll send it to you,' Harriet says when she comes back and shows Louise the image.

'Jacob is such a lovely boy, Harriet. He takes after you.'

'Ahh, well.' Harriet blushes, and it's the first time Louise has seen any hint of vulnerability. 'You must come over again.'

And Louise knows that she will.

Chapter 13

MUMSTOGETHER

Private Message

FROM AngelFace
TO ExhaustedNewMum0593
SUBJECT Better together
MESSAGE

Hey. Just checking in with you. You've been on my mind after our last chat and I see you've been super quiet on the forum. Everything OK?

Don't go through stuff on your own. Take it from me, it doesn't do you any good! And even if you have someone at home that'll help, sometimes it's another mum you need – because they KNOW what you're going through, can empathise with you. It's those 2am feeds, the endless bouts of colic, the engorged breasts, the constant worrying thoughts, the noise in your head – or worse, the totally blank space in your head!

I'm here. Reach out. X

Chapter 14

'I'm going to be a bit late home,' Mark's voice on her voicemail says. 'Don't worry about cooking – I'll grab a takeaway. Message me what you fancy. I left the menu in the kitchen.' Had he popped home for lunch while she'd been at Harriet's with Alfie? Louise finds it on the fridge, held there with the souvenir magnet from their last holiday together. Specifically, *Mark* had bought it. Louise had struggled with allowing it into the house due to barely suppressed memories of those her mother gave with a flourish following each cruise location. Louise slips the menu from beneath the gaudy, plastic Eiffel Tower magnet and scans it.

She can't remember the last time they ate takeout food; is this menu even in date? She's about to search online when a commotion from outside catches her attention. She leans over the sink so she can get a better look through the window. There's a white transit van, its engine still running in front of next door's gate, and a burly man – built like a brick shithouse, her dad would've said – is chest to chest with Louise's neighbour, his raised voice carrying a hefty dose of venom, although she can't make out the exact words. The neighbour takes a step back, puts his palms up, but the brick shithouse isn't having any of it. Louise's heart flutters wildly, adrenaline pulsing through her veins as the aggressor slams the heel of his hand into her neighbour's chest, and he stumbles backwards, arms flailing. Maybe Louise should call 999, as one of them, her neighbour by the look of it, is going to get hurt. But her eyes stay glued to the scene, afraid she'll miss something.

The registration plate. She could at least get that, just in case. The low wall is obstructing it, though. She daren't chance going outside, getting involved in a dangerous situation. Not with Alfie in the house. And then Louise plainly hears words that set her nerves on edge.

'If *ever* find out you're behind it, I'll tear ya limb from limb. Fuckin' rip yer head off. You hear?'

The man backs off, gets into the driver's side of the van and drives away, tyres screeching, smoke billowing. Louise pushes the window open, calls out.

'You okay? I'm sorry, I was going to call the police, but . . .' But what? She didn't want to interfere? She doesn't get to finish the sentence though, as the smell of burning petrol clogs her throat and she coughs, waving a hand across her mouth and nose.

'Oh, no worries, Louise. I'm all right.'

She stares at him. He just used her name, so surely she must know his, but, again, she draws a blank.

'I reckon that'll be the last we see of *him*.' And with those parting words he disappears back into his house.

'I was thinking of putting Alfie's name down for the nursery,' Louise says, testing the waters with Mark. They're sitting on the sofa, their Chinese food balanced on trays while they watch TV. Despite Mark being late, he took over the challenge of putting Alfie to bed. Though *not* a challenge for Mark, as it turns out – he was back downstairs before she'd even decanted their dinner from the foil containers to plates. She tells herself it's because Alfie was shattered after his playdate with Jacob, therefore it must have been an easier task. 'You know, for a couple of sessions where he stays without me.' She's been thinking about it non-stop since being at Harriet's. He narrows his eyes, contemplates her for a moment while chewing. He swallows.

'Okaaay,' he says, his jaw tensing as if he's waiting for a negative punchline.

'That's all you have to say?' Louise repositions her tray and twists fully to face him, searching his brown eyes for clues as to what's running through his mind right now. He takes a noisy breath in through his nose. Purses his lips. Louise waits while he arranges the words he wants to say in his mind before speaking them. He didn't always used to be so considered. When they'd first met, his mouth opened and words tumbled out without much thought. He spoke what was on his mind, openly and honestly, not caring how anyone else felt about it. She'd loved that about him at first. It was refreshing, funny. All that changed once she became pregnant, then had Alfie. He told Louise one morning, after she'd lost it with him due to lack of sleep, that he was scared to say anything. Felt he had to always walk on eggshells.

'Well,' he says, placing his fork down and turning to face her. 'He is almost three. And I think he's ready.' He lays a hand on her shoulder. 'But that's not what's in question, really, is it.'

Louise closes her eyes in an extended blink and inhales slowly, mustering the courage to speak up for herself. She knows what Mark is getting at; they've had numerous half conversations about it during the past year.

'I'm ready, too, Mark,' she says, making her voice strong, determined, so that her belief is in no doubt. 'It's time for me to get back to work. Resume normal life.' The words seem to suspend in the air, frozen in time and space.

'Have you spoken to anyone else about it?' Mark's frown, together with his monotone delivery of this question, indicate he's not entirely happy; he's not on the same page as Louise.

'No,' she lies. 'It's not like this has come out of the blue, Mark. I thought you'd be pleased that I've reached this stage of recovery.' Louise pulls away from him, plonks her food tray on the floor and gets up from the sofa, her muscles twitching. She paces.

'I *am*. Christ, love – of course I'm pleased. You've done brilliantly. I'm just . . .' He sighs heavily, gives a brusque scratch of his head. 'Concerned, I suppose. It's not been that long since—'

'It's been almost a year.' Louise glares at him, trying with all her might to keep her words steady, measured.

'Yeah,' Mark says. 'I guess. Look, put his name down. He might not even get a place straight away. We'll see where you're at once he's accepted.' He gets up, too, goes to Louise and wraps his arms around her. 'It's great your confidence is returning, Lou. Really. I'm proud of you.'

And, while he seems genuine, Louise can't help but feel a tug of apprehension, and she shivers as a snake of unease slithers over her skin.

Like Mark doesn't quite believe his own words.

Chapter 15

'Cheers!' They clink their glasses together, ice cubes tinkling against each other. They're posh gin glasses – huge, with long, fancy stems.

'Here's to cheeky afternoon gins,' Louise says, grinning. It's been quite some time since she's partaken in daytime drinking, and this feels a little like a naughty secret known only to her and Harriet. A frisson of excitement ripples through her – maybe she's now considered to be one of the 'fun mums' too.

'Here's to regaining some of our own independence!' Harriet says. They fall into a comfortable silence. Louise is picturing how that might look, and she assumes Harriet's doing the same. 'You seen anything of your mother?' she asks, pulling Louise back from her daydreaming with a jolt.

'Oh, no. I've had some texts. I've kind of ignored them. That makes me a terrible person, doesn't it?'

Harriet swallows a large gulp of gin, shakes her head. 'No. Family relationships can be . . .' She pauses, squints as though she's grappling with finding an appropriate word. 'Complex,' she states, slapping her hand down on the granite worktop. She widens her eyes, then blinks, trying to refocus them. Louise wonders if she'd had a gin before Louise arrived. She looks back, over her shoulder, checking the boys on the nanny cam monitor. Alfie is a different boy when he's here. More sociable, calmer. Happier. Her mind flits back to Natalie telling her that Alfie picks up on her emotions and thinks that maybe, because she's been in a better place these past weeks, it's rubbed off on Alfie. She smiles.

'It's not funny,' Harriet snaps.

Louise scrunches her face in confusion, then realises. 'God, no. Of course not, sorry. I was just smiling looking at our boys.'

'Oh, yes, I see. Bless them. Though, looks can be deceiving.' Harriet, gin in hand, slides off the stool and leaves the kitchen. Louise, frowning, watches after her, then glances at the nanny cam and sees Harriet enter the playroom and approach Alfie. 'Hey, buddy. Having fun?' Harriet's voice is quiet through the speaker. Louise shifts in her stool, half stands, poised to follow, but she waits. Watches and listens. Harriet puts her glass on the windowsill and crouches down beside Alfie. He lifts his head, and she ruffles his hair, the same as she did the first time they came here. Harriet continues to engage with Alfie, but Louise can't make out what she's saying. Then she abruptly gets up, retrieves her drink and leaves without appearing to even acknowledge Jacob. Louise looks away from the monitor just as Harriet returns and resumes her position at the kitchen island, a faraway expression on her face.

Louise twists her glass, the liquid swirling like a mini whirlpool. She watches it thoughtfully. 'What did you mean?' she says, not looking up. 'When you said looks can be deceiving?' Now she raises her eyes to meet Harriet's, is caught up in her hypnotic blue irises as she waits for Harriet to offer an answer.

'Well, you know ... Not everything in life is what it seems, is it?' Her words smudge together a little. Louise raises an eyebrow. She can't disagree with this sentiment, but the context in which Harriet uttered the words doesn't seem to fit. She tries to grasp the feeling that's swimming around inside her brain, just like the ice in her glass, and almost plucks it out before it swims away.

'Far from it,' Louise says, instead, then takes a sip of her gin. Footsteps approach from behind her and she turns, expecting to see Alfie.

'Oh, hello.' A man, who Louise presumes is Richard, strides into the kitchen. He's tall, dressed in navy suit trousers and a white open-necked, long-sleeved shirt that's been neatly rolled up, revealing tanned, muscular forearms. 'Richard,' he says, his voice strong, confident as he thrusts a hand towards her. 'You are?'

'Louise. A friend of Harriet's.' She puts her glass down, wipes her right hand over her jeans quickly before shaking his. 'Our children go to the same playgroup.' Louise smiles broadly, keeping eye contact. His grip is firm, his handshake consisting of one forceful pump. As their hands unlock and he pulls his arm away, she notices what looks to be a tattoo visible beneath his sleeve.

'Great,' Richard says, giving a closed-mouth smile. He moves to Harriet, kisses her fully on the lips. 'Did I miss the party invite?' He lifts an eyebrow, taking in the gin glasses. Harriet's is almost empty.

'Thought you were working at the office today?' Harriet forms her words carefully, deliberately, as if attempting to mask the slurring. To Louise, it makes her appear even more drunk. A bolt of guilt shoots through her. Is she to blame? Does it look to Richard that she is? Not the first impression she would've chosen to make in front of her new friend's husband. They're in charge of two toddlers. What must he think? She eyes Richard warily.

'Popped back for some files.' He casts his gaze around, before it settles on the nanny cam. He squints, appears happy that all is in order, then goes to a cupboard and ducks down. Louise's heart stutters as she realises it's the cupboard that Harriet put the gin bottle back into. 'I could stay, though, if you need me to,' Richard says, standing up again. His face is neutral, but Louise catches what she thinks is concern in his tone. Harriet waves it off.

'We're good, thanks. Aren't we, Louise?'

Louise swallows, shifting in her seat, uncomfortable at being put on the spot. She nods.

'Okay. Maybe let up on happy hour, though, eh?' Richard says. 'Responsible adults, and all that.' He turns to Louise. 'I didn't see a car ...'

'Oh, no. I walked,' she says to quash Richard's obvious worry. 'And I've only had the one.' She holds up her glass as if that's proof. She thinks she notices a flash of something in his eyes. Disbelief? She needs to pull this back. 'You've an amazing home, Richard. It's no wonder you don't want to leave—'

He sucks in a breath, looks a little flustered before finally muttering, 'Thank you.' Then he makes his excuses and walks out the way he came. Soft voices are heard over the nanny cam as Richard enters the playroom and spends a few moments in there. Then the sound of the front door closing brings the conversation back into the room.

'Take no notice, Louise. He's just jealous he's not joining us,' Harriet says flippantly. 'He's not normally so rigid. Working too much, you know how it can be.' She goes to the cupboard housing the alcohol, and as she refills her glass, she looks pensively at Louise. 'You and your husband should come over sometime. I could cook for us all.' Harriet hovers the bottle over Louise's glass, but she hastily puts her hand over it, shaking her head.

'No, thanks.' She thinks of how she 'lost' Alfie the other day when she was stone-cold sober; she really didn't need any kind of repeat performance enhanced by being under the influence. Harriet pauses, the gin bottle in mid-air, and Louise thinks for a horrifying moment that she's offended her; that she thinks she's turning down the offer of dinner, not a drink. 'I won't be able to walk home again if I have another,' she adds, to clear up any confusion. Harriet screws the lid back on and sits down.

Louise doesn't immediately jump at the meal idea, mulls it over for a moment. Does she want to share Harriet with Mark? 'And, yeah, a meal would be nice. Thanks,' she says.

Then, in the hope it will be forgotten, she changes the subject, and they discuss work plans and nursery placements, school and beyond. Before she knows it, they've been chatting for half an hour without once having checked on the boys. Louise's pulse skips, the sudden realisation she hasn't heard a peep from them all this time smashing into her consciousness.

'Right, I must get off. Mark will be home soon, if he isn't already.' She slips off the stool and hurries into the playroom. Her mind races when she spots Jacob, but not Alfie. 'Where's Alfie?'

'Hiding,' Jacob says, beaming up at Louise.

'Ah, I see. I love hide-and-seek, too,' she says, her voice catching. She doesn't like the game at all, and never plays it with Alfie. She's sure he wouldn't know how to play – let alone stay still and quiet enough. If he were in the room, she'd know it by now. 'Which way did he go?'

Jacob points to the door. A chill slips down Louise's spine. He obviously hadn't come in the direction of the kitchen, as they'd have seen him. If she and Harriet hadn't been so busy drinking and chatting, Alfie wouldn't have been able to sneak out undetected. Louise turns, bumping into Harriet coming the other way. Apologising, she explains the boys are playing a game and Alfie has left the playroom.

'Oh. Jacob, I told you both to stay in here, didn't I.' Her reprimanding tone seems over the top to Louise, especially as it's not up to Jacob to keep her son in tow. 'You stay here, Louise, I'll find him.'

God, Louise hopes he hasn't got up to any mischief.

How embarrassing if he's broken something. She bets pretty much everything in this house is something of high value – probably from John Lewis, or bloody Harrods or something. Not like breaking something at Louise's house which is most likely from IKEA or Poundland. Luckily, Louise doesn't need to worry for long, as Harriet returns with Alfie moments later, hand in hand and giggling.

'Alfie, sweetheart,' Louise says, going up to him and bending down to his level. 'You need to stay with Jacob. Don't go wandering off, okay?' He looks up at Harriet and smiles, then slowly turns to Louise.

'Yes, Mummy,' he says. 'We go home now.'

Louise begins to usher him towards the hallway. 'Thanks for having us over again, Harriet.' Then she whispers, 'Hope Alfie didn't get into anything he shouldn't have when he was hiding?' She's keen to avoid giving Harriet a reason to not want them to come again. Not just because she's enjoying having female company – someone who she feels, despite the obvious differences in their lifestyles, she can resonate with – but because it really is having such a positive impact on Alfie's behaviour.

'It's fine, honestly,' Harriet says. 'Alfie knows now that he shouldn't wander around the house, and that room is out of bounds ...' Harriet glances down a short corridor leading to the other side of the house. Louise follows her gaze and notes a light-wood door at the end. 'It's the study. Richard uses it when he's working from home,' Harriet says, then mouths to Louise, 'He doesn't like people going in there.'

Outside, Louise gulps in the fresh air, allowing the

coolness of the late afternoon to balance out the effects of her alcohol consumption. She hadn't had a lot, she tells herself – not as much as Harriet, at any rate – but, as someone who, over the last three years, hasn't had more than the occasional glass of wine, it has likely hit her harder. She gets the impression Harriet is a regular social drinker. She envisages her at lunchtime get-togethers with neighbours and friends, the kids making their own fun while the adults chat about the latest news and sip Pimm's. As though her mother is walking right beside her, Louise hears her saying, *You never did have a wide friendship group, weren't invited to lots of parties, and it didn't change when you reached adulthood.* Louise doesn't want that for Alfie. She needs to keep in with Harriet – she's her only link to a normal mum's group.

Checking the road both ways before crossing with Alfie, Louise catches sight of a man as he darts round the corner that leads to Harriet's house. For a split second she thinks it's Richard, and wonders if he's going back to see if Harriet's still drinking; he'd seemed a bit off when he saw the gin glasses. But he was driving, not walking, and this man is stockier than Richard, and not as tall. More like her creepy neighbour. Louise does a double-take, but he's out of sight. She glances over her shoulder several times during her walk home, but doesn't see him again. Maybe she'd imagined it.

Later, with Alfie in bed and asleep without too much fuss, Louise sits on the sofa with her legs sprawled over Mark as they silently watch TV. She glances at the photo on the wall of the lounge, a canvas print they'd had done for Alfie's first birthday. In it, the three of them are smiling, though behind Louise's eyes there's a hidden sense of disquiet. Something she's never quite rid herself of, maybe because she's not sure of its reason for manifesting in the first place. Hard to eliminate a feeling if you can't put your finger on the cause. It was a few months before the official diagnosis of post-natal depression, so Louise had always put it down to that. The feeling still lingers, though. She turns away from the portrait, back to blankly staring at the telly, and consciously exchanges those thoughts with better ones of her time at Harriet's. It was good to chat in a more private space, with a mum who has interest in her. Wants to share her wisdom, and help Louise with the daily challenges of motherhood by offering advice and support. And she seems to genuinely like and get on with Alfie.

Then it hits her. Everything at Harriet's seemed like perfection, the epitome of a happy and contented household – bar one notable exception. Louise hadn't spotted a single family photograph adorning the walls or displayed on units. Not even one of Jacob.

Chapter 16

Jacob hasn't let go of Louise's hand for the entire walk back to Harriet's. Alfie wanted nothing more than to jump into his buggy and be pushed following the playgroup session – a task Harriet gladly offered to take because she needed the buggy as a 'crutch'. Concern nudges at Louise's thoughts – Harriet's been pale and unusually quiet this morning. Not her usual self. But when asked, she claimed to be 'fine, just tired', so Louise let it go. Now, with Jacob's warm hand in hers, they lead the way, chatting about animals and wildlife along the path, with Louise giving the odd glance behind to check her own son and Harriet's progression – a residual unease still clings to her from the other day, when she believed she'd lost Alfie, lingering like the smell of garlic on her skin after a curry.

A warm glow builds inside her as Jacob lifts his honey-brown eyes to hers and smiles. He's such a cheerful little boy; the way his lopsided grin gives him a cheeky look reminds Louise of Mark. A split second later, Louise's spark of happiness is replaced with a sense of guilt and she takes a deep breath in through her nose, blinks to prevent the tears of frustration. Why can't she feel this way about Alfie? Although he's behaved much better of late and the tantrums have lessened, the gulf between them hasn't. It's on her – she knows that. She's the one who needs to make more effort. Louise promises herself she will. Later, when she's home. Right now, she's enjoying this moment too much to spoil it. And, besides, Alfie's happy with Harriet.

After a subdued cup of coffee sitting at the kitchen island, a far cry from their last gin-fuelled meeting, Louise breaks.

'I know you said you were just tired, Harriet . . .' She pauses, leaning forward to look into her friend's eyes to check if it's wise to question her. There's no flash of irritation, so she carries on. 'You would say if there was something bothering you, wouldn't you? I mean, fine if you don't want to talk about it, of course. I only want to be here for you, like you have for me . . .' Louise trails off, unsure where else to go from here, and sits back. The silence stretches. Louise begins to play with a rough edge of her fingernail, waiting for Harriet to say something.

'Oh, for God's sake!' Harriet springs up from her stool. Louise's pulse thuds in her neck, her eyes widening in alarm. Shit, she hadn't meant to upset her. Harriet storms past her, heading down the corridor towards the playroom, mumbling something about 'that boy'. Louise's relief Harriet's reaction wasn't the result of what she'd said is short-lived when she hears the calls of, 'Alfie! Alfie, where are you?' Louise closes her eyes, sighs. He's obviously gone off on a wander again. By the time Louise catches up with Harriet, it's too late. Alfie has been in the previously declared 'out of bounds' area of Harriet's house – the study, where Richard works.

'Oh, again. I'm sorry, Harriet. Alfie, baby, we don't go in this room, remember?'

'Of *course* he remembers,' Harriet says sharply. Her jaw is tense, her features stony. Her reaction seems excessive compared to her usual laid-back attitude. Uptight, frazzled. More than just tired, in Louise's opinion.

'Do you want us to go?'

'Don't be silly.' Harriet snaps back into her usual self – the flash of anger extinguishing as though a bucket of water has been poured over it. Louise hesitates, hovering in the corridor with Alfie's hand grasped in hers. The door to the study is still open, and Louise's gaze flits inside. She barely sees a thing before Harriet reaches for the handle and pulls it closed.

'Maybe he should lock it,' Louise says.

'Why, when most people understand simple instructions?'

Louise feels herself blushing. 'Point taken. Alfie is an inquisitive one!'

She has the urge to leave regardless, then spots Jacob's face peeping round the corner, his fair hair falling over one eye.

'You want to play cars now?' The squeak audible in his voice tugs at her heart. She hopes he doesn't think they're fighting. Alfie's fingers wriggle until his hand escapes hers and he quietly walks back towards Jacob, leaving Louise and Harriet standing within a foot of each other.

'Sorry,' Harriet says, swishing a hand over her forehead and back over the top of her hair. 'Sleep deprivation is a killer, eh?'

'Is it Jacob?'

Harriet shakes her head. 'Not really. I need the bathroom. See you in the kitchen.' She turns away, and even though the temptation to enter Richard's study is overwhelming, Louise knows it would spell disaster if she were to be caught. It might even be a test, she thinks. She scurries back to the kitchen and resumes her position on the stool, angling it this time so she can see the boys on the nanny cam. Harriet's mobile is on the worktop, the screen unlocked. The background photo is the one Harriet took of the boys in the playroom the first time they were here. She said she'd send it but never did. Curiosity compels Louise to pick it up – and she taps on the camera icon to access the photo gallery. Aside from the one of Jacob with Alfie displayed on the home screen, there are two other images. Louise's brow furrows. These have been cropped. In each one, Jacob's been removed, leaving close-ups of Alfie. Maybe Harriet planned to send them to her, but forgot.

A door opens, and Louise quickly exits the gallery and scoots the phone back across the worktop, readying herself for Harriet to enter. She can't very well ask about the photos right now, as she'll know Louise has used the opportunity to snoop on her phone. Louise plasters on a smile, swivels in her stool to begin the discussion, but it's not Harriet.

'Oh.'

'Not even a "Hello, Richard"?'

'Sorry. Hi, Richard.' Louise unconsciously twists her wedding ring. Christ, that had been a close call, then. If he'd come home a minute or two earlier, he'd have caught Alfie in his study. She wonders what his reaction would've been. Anger? Harriet certainly appeared concerned enough.

'Why the frown?' he asks, his eyes narrowing.

'This?' She points to herself. 'Oh, it's my resting bitch face.'

Richard gives a short snort of laughter, then asks where Harriet is. Louise tells him she's in the bathroom, and he starts to make himself a coffee. His demeanour is casual, relaxed. He doesn't seem bothered about her being at their house again. Probably just glad there are empty mugs instead of gin glasses this time.

'Want one?' he asks, nodding towards Louise's mug. She thinks about it; the time is getting on and she doesn't really want to fill up with any more liquid or the walk home might be uncomfortable. Her bladder hasn't been the best since giving birth. Another thing that hasn't returned to normal. 'Difficult question?' Richard stares at her.

'Go on, then.' She pushes her mug towards him.

'Is it something that happens to all of you?'

'Sorry?'

'The thousand-yard stares, the inability to make decisions,' he says. 'Harriet's the same since Jacob.' He's smiling, but there's a hint of contempt in his voice. Louise bristles, but forces a laugh.

'Yep. Apparently our brains are pushed out along with the placenta.'

'Hah! Well. Don't get me wrong – I'm not being a misogynist. And given what you women go through, I'm not surprised things are hazy for a while.' He stirs milk into the two mugs – she notes he isn't making a drink for Harriet. *Where is she?* Louise looks over her shoulder, but there's no sign. What does Richard expect her to say in this situation?

'Just need a bit of support through it, I guess. I'm sure we'll bounce back, like we're expected to,' she says pointedly. Richard gives a furtive glance before lowering his voice.

'You know, Harriet was hellbent on leaving the area after Jacob was born? This place was packed up, all ready to put on the market. But literally overnight she had an about-turn. Told me she didn't want to leave. And Harriet gets what Harriet wants . . . So, we didn't.'

'Really?' Louise leans her chin on her hand, confusion tripping through her mind. She's sure Harriet said it was the other way around. 'Moving house is a big decision, though. And after giving birth – wow, that would be a stressful time to do it!'

'Yes, true. At the time I put it down to her having pregnancy difficulties and taking a while to recover from them, then the traumatic birth. Better to have the familiarity, I suppose. But my point remains – decisions are no longer straightforward with her.'

Louise is taken aback by Richard's openness, but leans forward, intrigued to know what he means about Harriet's traumatic birth. 'I totally understand that – I went through something similar . . .' She catches herself, stopping mid-sentence, her heartbeat crashing. She hasn't even told Harriet about her post-natal depression yet. She shouldn't be confiding in Richard first. She skips over that detail, but mentions that Alfie was apart from her the first day after giving birth due to requiring emergency care and, because of this, it affected her negatively – made it difficult to bond. Richard nods, takes a sip of his coffee, then looks straight into Louise's eyes.

'Same, actually. I think that impacted Harriet, too – she wasn't herself for those first days of Jacob's life – probably a common feeling for mums who've had babies in a special-care unit.' Louise wants to ask more about it; Harriet's never talked about the birth. Although, to be fair, neither has she. It's almost as if they've both been avoiding it, yet it sounds as though they shared similar experiences. Reading between the lines, Louise concludes that it's very possible Harriet also suffered post-natal depression. They might have more in common than she realised. Maybe that's why they've been drawn to each other.

'You two having a deep and meaningful?'

Louise spins round to see Harriet standing in the kitchen doorway, Alfie holding on to her thigh.

'Hey, my little one,' Louise says, getting up and moving towards him. He ducks behind Harriet to avoid her outstretched hand. Louise pulls it back, stands up straight and looks to see if Richard and Harriet have noticed her pain at this rejection. But Richard isn't looking; he grabs his coffee and gives Louise a nod as he goes to leave.

'I've a few things to finish off. I'll be in the study,' he

says, passing Harriet and Alfie. He ruffles Alfie's hair, the same way Harriet has done a few times, and, for a moment, the scene in front of her freezes as if it's been paused, and Louise looks on as if *she's* the stranger – not Alfie's mum. The thought that the three of them look more of a family unit than she, Mark and Alfie do lights up like a neon sign in her mind.

Chapter 17

MUMSTOGETHER

Private Message

FROM AngelFace
TO ExhaustedNewMum0593
SUBJECT Location, Location!
MESSAGE

So glad we connected. And how serendipitous that we live quite close to each other!

I understand your reasons for not wanting to meet up in person yet – there's a reason we're both on this website ... It's kind of scary, isn't it? Making the leap, I mean. There's a safety in being an anonymous nickname on a forum. Jeez, it's worse than dating 😄

Just know that I'm still here. Reach out whenever you need to. I need this connection too. I feel so alone. X

Chapter 18

'Alfie, get down from there,' Louise says, dropping the pile of clean clothes on to his bed. 'That's for your toys, not for you to stand on.' He's dragged the toy box from its usual position to underneath the window in less than the minute she's taken to collect the laundry from downstairs. Thankfully, there are locks on the windows – another safety measure Mark put in place.

He doesn't move. 'Bin lorry,' he says, pointing out the window. Louise looks out, sees it's the waste lorry. Sometimes the recycling one comes first, but rarely when she needs it to be that way around.

'Oh ... *typical*.' She grabs Alfie, scooping him up in one arm. 'We've got to catch them!' Alfie jiggles against her hip as she rushes downstairs and plops him down in the conservatory. 'Stay there – I'll be two minutes.' She curses under her breath and runs out the front door, waving her arms frantically in the hope of stopping the vehicle's progression. If it were just the recycling lorry, she wouldn't be bothered – they're not filled to the brim like the wheelie bin. The slow hiss of brakes, followed by a shout of 'You're lucky', allows her stress levels to drop again.

'We take bets on whether you'll remember,' the man says, smiling widely as she drags the bin to him.

'Oh! Well, I'm glad to offer some entertainment value. Not to mention financial reward.' Louise gives a stiff smile in return, watching as her bin is emptied and the lorry pulls away.

A barely contained burst of laughter from behind her causes her to turn sharply. It's her neighbour. He's standing, his arms folded across his chest, observing with apparent glee.

'Really? Is it that funny to you?'

'Sorry, Louise. I'm sure you're not the only one who forgets their bin.'

'I do have rather a lot of other things to think about,' she snaps.

'Good that you've been busy. Friends are time-consuming, though; it's why I don't bother.'

Why is he bringing up friends and sharing his lack of them with her?

'Yes. And, anyway, you forgot yours, too?' Louise indicates to the lack of wheelie bin outside his house.

'Didn't fill it this week, so no point putting it out.' He *has* stacked his recycling boxes, though, and Louise can't help but stare at the number of empty bottles and cans, plus takeaway containers and Amazon packaging. She gives a sad smile. She's about to go back inside, without further conversation – as she'd usually do – but her feet remain stubbornly planted to the spot; a strong sense of inquisitiveness – or nosiness, if she were to be honest – keeps her there.

'You don't seem to go out much.' Louise's mouth is dry, the saliva evaporating on her tongue. She fidgets, transferring weight from one leg to the other like an awkward teenager who has never spoken to a person 'IRL'. *What is wrong with you?*

'No point in that, either,' he says matter-of-factly.

Louise wants to ask why, although from what Mark has said, and from what she's gleaned from the town gossips about 'that weird bloke living next to you', she can guess the answer. But it's been ages since his partner left – surely he's had new relationships in that time. The narratives of him being a loner, a bit odd, and the fact 'he keeps himself to himself', all things he *must* have heard, might well have something to do with him not putting himself back out into the dating scene.

Then she remembers she thought she saw him near Harriet's house. Has he been following her? She's caught him watching her numerous times – has he progressed to stalking?

Louise gives a shake of her head, tries to dispel the thought. He's just said he doesn't go out much; it probably wasn't even him.

'I'm sorry,' she says, realising he's waiting for a response. She squirms at her inability to come up with some words of wisdom or, at the very least, something more positive about his situation.

'Can't get hurt if you don't put yourself out there,' he

says. And as though he senses Louise's awkwardness, or perhaps because of his own, he gives his usual nod and turns to walk down his path. This, she realises, is the most conversation she's ever had with him. She stands still for a moment, the man's sadness crashing over her like a wave. Then, in a split second of impulsiveness, she shoots across to his recycling box and ducks down so he can't see if he looks around. She rifles through the neatly folded and stacked cardboard and gives a whispered, triumphant 'Yes!' when she finds what she's searching for. An address label.

Andrew Pullen.

Finally, she has his name.

With a bounce in her step, Louise steers Alfie into the hall and lets him join the group of toddlers already playing in the ball pit. The swirling whirlwind of anxiety usually in her belly is absent today and in its place sits a sense of contentment. She spots the playgroup manager and strides up to her.

'Morning. Can I speak with you a moment, please? I want to enrol Alfie into the nursery.'

Five minutes later, Alfie's on the waitlist for two full days a week and Louise is back in the main hall, slightly shaky, but proud of taking this step. She seeks out Harriet, keen to tell her the news. At first she doesn't see her, but then she spots her among the fun mums. Louise swallows hard and pushes her shoulders back in an attempt to control the mental wobble this scene causes.

You've got this. You're one of them now.

Before she reaches them, though, a mum Louise doesn't recognise marches up to Harriet, and she has Alfie in tow. Louise's pulse flutters. Oh, God, what's happened while she's been out of the room? *Don't let this moment be ruined.*

'Your son's been looking for you,' the woman says to Harriet. 'Got upset when he couldn't spot his mummy.' She offers Alfie to Harriet like some kind of prize, and Louise hurries across ready to claim her child. She stops short when Harriet's voice, sharp and loud, rings out.

'He's not mine!' she snaps. 'You should really check before assuming.'

'Oh, I'm so sorry. He looks just like you . . . You're right, I shouldn't have assumed . . .'

'Hi, Alfie,' Louise says, swooping in and taking his hand.

'There you are,' Harriet says, her usual charm returning in an instant. 'Bit of a mix-up.'

Louise looks to the other woman, smiles. 'I'm his mum. Thanks.'

After the woman leaves, Jacob comes up to Alfie and Louise offers them both a snack. Harriet stands, watching, her eyes glazing over. Her reaction seemed a bit extreme to Louise, and she can't help wondering if there's something going on for her right now. She's preoccupied, not her usual bright and breezy self.

Louise asks Harriet to keep an eye on the boys while she goes to the toilet. As soon as Louise closes the cubicle door, she hears some of the fun mums enter the bathroom.

'I have no idea why. I mean, seriously . . .'

Louise freezes. Are they talking about what just happened?

About why Harriet is even friends with Louise? She blows air from her cheeks. You never overhear anything good about yourself – it was one of her mother's favourite sayings. But Louise stays silent inside the cubicle, waits, head tilted to hear better. She needs to know.

'Zac said he thinks we brought the wrong baby home from the hospital because neither of us are creative, but Tabatha's like a child Picasso!' This is followed by laughter, and Louise's concerns dissolve. They're just chatting about general stuff; random things that come up in conversation. Things friends usually talk about. She flushes the loo, goes out to the sink and, without overthinking any more, inserts herself into their conversation. Finally, she's broken through the invisible barrier, joining the group as if she belongs there.

Chapter 19

Later that evening, Louise is watching Alfie when the freeze-frame scene of Harriet, Richard and him in their kitchen shoots into her mind and she relives the gut-wrenching feeling that they looked more like a real family than her own did. Alfie's curly hair and blue eyes a match to Harriet, to the point she was even mistaken for Alfie's mum; his ease around her. And it's in this moment that the fun mums' conversation about not bringing the right baby home comes back to her.

What if *she* brought the wrong baby home from hospital?

No sooner has she had this thought, Louise dismisses it. It's absurd to even consider it. That sort of thing doesn't happen in this country. Getting up and going into the kitchen, she pours herself a glass of water, her hand trembling. With her back against the worktop, her eyes screwed tight, Louise forces herself to think about something else. Immediately, her mother's face pops into her mind. She groans. Why her?

'You okay, love?' Mark joins her, laying his hand on her shoulder. 'You're very quiet this evening.'

Louise gulps down the rest of the water and smiles. 'Yeah, fine, actually. Been busy, but, all in all, it's been a pretty good day.'

'Oh, Lou. You have no idea how good it is to hear you say that,' Mark says, his eyes brimming with tears. Louise puts her hand on her chest, tries to speak, but emotion clogs her throat. Seeing his vulnerabilities, too, makes her feel closer to him. All too often in the past, it's been Louise's fully on show, not his. He embraces her firmly, pressing her against his chest. 'You and Alfie are everything to me. Your happiness is my happiness.'

Louise is tied down in a room filled with spiders, trapped, her movements restricted so she can't brush them off, much less escape them. Hundreds of hairy legs scurry over her writhing body, run over her face ... and as she opens her mouth to scream they pour in, and she chokes.

She sits bolt upright, coughing, her hand to her throat, the duvet a tangled mass between her legs. Grabbing her phone off the nightstand, she illuminates the area around the bed. Mark's beside her. His breathing steady. She couldn't have screamed out; there's no way he'd have slept through that. She allows her pulse to settle, telling herself she's safe – there are no spiders crawling over her – but she knows that, really. Knows the actual reason for her nightmare was nothing to do with arachnids, and everything to do with the thought she'd tried to suppress earlier.

The digital clock reads 00:22. Smack on midnight, then. She starts to neaten out the duvet, kicking it with her feet to make it reach the bottom of the bed, and her foot hits something that doesn't belong. She withdraws her leg sharpish, the remnants of fear not having quite left her body. Tentatively lifting the corner of the duvet, and with her mobile as a light source, Louise peers beneath it.

'Oh, you stupid woman,' she whispers, some of the tension seeping out of her taut muscles when she sees the metal coil binding. It's only her journal. It must've been on top of the duvet earlier, and it became buried when they climbed into bed. She reaches a hand under and retrieves it. The pen is still wedged between the pages, only, she doesn't recall getting it from the drawer and writing in it.

Despite the fuzziness in her head, her heavy eyes, and the sinking, sickly feeling of tiredness sitting like a stone inside her, the prospect of getting back to sleep now is zero. Her mind simply won't allow it. Careful not to disturb Mark, Louise checks Alfie's monitor and, seeing him settled, takes the journal and slips it back into her bedside cabinet, then heads downstairs.

The small lamp in the lounge casts a soft glow, enough to see by and kinder on her eyes than the main light – and sitting with her mobile dimmed, her legs tucked up, Louise opens Google. Her finger remains poised over the keys, the cursor flashing inside the search bar. Is she really entertaining this ludicrous notion? She doesn't *want* to find evidence backing her theory, but the niggly, prodding sense of something being 'off' that's needled her mind for almost three years drives her to tap in the phrase 'swapped at birth', and she hits the search button. Closes her eyes.

Her fingers are rigid round the case of her mobile, her other hand taps at her mouth. She's not sure what she's even expecting to see, what information the search engine will display. It's not as if it's going to return a result that she needs.

It's an extreme way of making herself feel better about her shortcomings, to explain away her lack of bonding with Alfie, she realises. After a few more seconds, she lifts her eyelids and focuses on the screen. A deep thudding rocks her upper body, her heart racing as she begins scrolling the list of hits her search has found.

After clicking on a few scary headlines with shock-value buzzwords – most of which inevitably turn out to be clickbait – and some others about historical baby swaps in other countries, Louise is relieved to find while there've been near misses, and cases where babies have been temporarily swapped by accident within the UK, they were all swiftly rectified – within minutes or hours – and all during the maternity stay.

She has to accept the reason she hasn't truly bonded with Alfie, the reason he doesn't seem to like her, is not due to some bizarre baby swap theory – it's simply because she hasn't tried hard enough. The post-natal depression has impacted far more than she's realised, and she's likely not alone in having some disturbing thoughts. Having learned from Richard that Harriet also struggled initially is like a smack in the face. Why hadn't she noticed before? Too caught up in her own stuff. Maybe Harriet was drawn to Louise because she recognised in her the same things she was feeling towards Jacob. Whatever it is, Louise can't shake the uneasy sensation deep in her gut that Harriet's hiding something from her.

Chapter 20

The flowers cost more than Louise anticipated, but she can't very well turn up with a pathetic bunch of five wilted nondescript stems grabbed without thought from the petrol station. Mark gives her a questioning glance as she returns with a reasonably sized, richly coloured bouquet for fifteen quid, having gone AWOL for the past ten minutes when they were meant to be conducting their weekly supermarket shop. He mutters something about why there's need to buy any at all.

'She's been good to me,' Louise says, ignoring the perplexed shake of his head. 'And, besides, it makes you feel good when someone gives you flowers.' She raises her eyebrows, pushes her mouth to one side to ensure he gets the hint. The last time he'd bought her any was Valentine's day. A bunch of wilted flowers from the petrol station.

'Just don't get why you're stressing over a posh bouquet when they're just wrapped in supermarket cellophane anyway – they look the same as the cheaper variety to me.'

'I'm going to ask for them to be wrapped in pretty tissue

paper, or get some myself—' But her words fall on deaf ears, Mark already walking away because Alfie's fidgeting in the trolley seat. Louise starts off after them, then halts. Sue, dressed entirely in black as though she's in mourning, has blocked the queue and is fussing over Alfie. What timing. Louise is about to sidle off up the nearest aisle to avoid her when Mark waves her over. There's no escaping now. Louise plasters on a smile.

'Hey, Mum. Didn't know you shopped here.'

'Only popped in for some supplies.' She jiggles the items in her basket towards Louise, offering the proof. 'Poor Janet – remember her, love?' She doesn't wait for a response, carrying on with the story of how her long-time friend recently lost her dog in a hit-and-run accident, and they were about to carry out a ceremonial scattering of his ashes in the garden.

'Oh,' Louise says, surprised at Sue's compassion. 'That's sad.'

'The way people drive, speeding around like it's Brands Hatch. Honestly, it makes me worry. What if it'd been little Alfie, eh?' She squeezes his cheeks with one hand. 'Doesn't bear thinking about.'

'Did anyone take responsibility?' Mark asks. Louise gives him an exasperated look – trying to communicate that he shouldn't encourage further conversation. People around them are pushing past, deciding to go the self-service route rather than staying to listen.

'No. Cowards. But one of Janet's neighbours has one of those recording bells, you know the ones? Well, they caught it – could see it was a white van, but wrong angle to get details.'

'Ah, white-van drivers . . .'

'Mark,' Louise says, tutting. 'They aren't all the same, you know.' And then a flash of memory comes to her – her neighbour's altercation was with a bloke in a white van. She'd forgotten to tell Mark about it. 'Anyway, Mum, we must get on. Our frozen stuff will be defrosting and Mark's dropping me to a friend's before going home.'

An astonished expression alights on Sue's face, and for a moment Louise braces herself for the questions. But instead Sue flaps around them. 'Yes, yes. Okay,' she says, going to Alfie, kissing his head. 'Bye, my sweetheart,' she coos. 'Perhaps Mummy will let Nana come over and visit this week.' She looks to Louise and, rather than allow the awkwardness to stretch, Louise nods.

'Sure.' The likelihood of her mother actually popping over is slim, may as well look like the better person here.

'Those curls,' Sue says to Alfie. 'They are cute. Don't know who you got those off. Your mummy's hair was wispy and straight as a die.' She gazes from Louise to Mark. 'Must have skipped a generation.' And then, finally, a gap opens up and she shimmies through the line to reach the checkout and is gone.

Louise rubs a hand over her forehead. Why is every interaction with Sue so stressful?

'Don't take it to heart,' Mark says. 'She doesn't mean anything by it.'

'By what?'

'She's just winding you up, that's all. I'm sure Alfie gets his beautiful locks from you. She's probably just forgotten what you were like as a toddler.'

Louise's thoughts turn to the mad baby-swap theory again. Her mother had mentioned how Alfie didn't really look like either her or Mark when she'd seen photos, or on the rare occasions she'd spent actual time with them. Was there anything in it? Could her mother have picked up on things she'd been too tired, or depressed, to even consider?

'Ah, so that's the reason for overthinking the flowers,' Mark says, pulling the car up at the end of the driveway and gazing up at Harriet and Richard's house. 'Keeping up with the Joneses.'

'It's no such thing.' Louise gets out and opens the back door to retrieve Alfie from his car seat. 'She's invited us both here for a meal, actually.' Louise screws her eyes up; she hadn't meant to let this slip – she'd wanted to keep Harriet to herself.

'Oh, really?' He makes a face. 'Not sure they're our type . . .'

'I wasn't aware we had a type.'

'What's the husband like?'

'If you listened to your wife, you'd know,' Louise says. 'He seems nice enough.'

'Nice, eh? Not convincing me, Lou.'

'Alfie and Jacob get on so well. He's had such a positive impact – you can see that. It would be good to encourage it, and so if that means the parents need to be friends, too – I'll do what it takes.'

'Doesn't sound like a disaster waiting to happen *at all*.'

After a few disgruntled remarks in retaliation, Louise slams the car door and she and Alfie begin the walk up the drive towards Harriet's. Richard's car isn't there.

'Flowers!'

Louise turns to see Mark's hand sticking out the car window, proffering the bouquet. She jogs back towards him, thanks him for remembering.

'After all the effort you went to for them.' He says it with a smile, but Louise senses his mocking tone. She swipes them from his hand, flashing him a tight smile in return.

'Christ, Lou – watch him!'

In the brief space of time it's taken Louise to retrieve the flowers, Alfie has made another beeline for the water feature in Harriet's garden. Flustered by Mark's tone – when it was him who called her back, creating Alfie's opportunity in the first place – and the burst of adrenaline at seeing him teetering on the edge of the fountain, Louise yells 'No!' at the same time as beginning to run. In a blur of movement, Harriet is there, plucking Alfie from harm's way, scooping him up and pulling him towards her. They fall back, landing on the grass lawn. The whole thing appeared to happen in slow motion.

'Bloody hell! Thanks, Harriet.'

'Good job I saw what was happening on the doorbell video. Couldn't believe he was on his own.'

The blood drains from Louise's face, power leaving her

body as she stands with the bouquet hanging from her limp arm. She turns back to where the car is, its engine idling as Mark watches on, and points without speaking. Mark puts an arm up – then, obviously satisfied all is fine, drives away. 'I was halfway up when he called me back,' Louise says. 'I'd left these in the car.' Louise holds the bouquet up now. 'Wanted to show my appreciation for all you've done.'

Harriet manoeuvres herself and Alfie so she can stand. She keeps hold of him, his legs wrapping round her middle. Louise bites down on her lip – the desire to apportion blame to Harriet for having such a dangerous item in her garden is overwhelming. As is the wish to shove the bouquet she'd thought so hard about into the wretched fountain. Instead, Louise stands there, transfixed by Alfie in Harriet's arms. It looks so natural. He's not struggling to get free – he's comfortable. Trusting. As though they share a connection.

'Come on then,' Harriet says to Alfie. 'Would you like some juice?' Alfie nods, his little fingers twiddling with the key pendant on Harriet's necklace. She eases it from his hand, tucking it beneath her top, then walks inside, leaving the door open for Louise to follow. Watching Harriet with *her* son, it strikes Louise just how similar they look. It makes sense the mum at playgroup thought Alfie belonged to Harriet.

Even more so than the other day, Louise feels like an outsider looking in.

Still determined to be the one Harriet confides in about the struggles Richard let on about when they spoke last time, Louise sucks up her paranoia and, when they're positioned in their usual spot at the kitchen island, Louise opens with a comment about Alfie's birth – how she'd found the experience to be a far cry from her expectations. The birth plan she and Mark had worked on for weeks going out the window when the labour progressed so quickly that Alfie was born less than three hours after her first contraction.

'Wow.' Harriet's eyes are wide. 'That's unusual for a first, isn't it?'

'Yep. And, trust me, not as amazing as you'd imagine. So many people afterwards remarked how lucky I was, how they wished theirs had been so simple. But it was awful, like my body didn't really get a chance to figure out what was happening. Poor baby flew out of me in a mass of meconium and was whisked away, while I basically collapsed with shock.'

Harriet's forehead creases and she looks thoughtful. 'I'm sorry. I know what you mean, as well. Those people who demand to tell you their birth story, whether you want to hear it or not, and then whatever it is, it's *always* more dramatic, worse, alarming, than yours. Damn annoying, isn't it?'

'Oh, sorry. I'm doing just that, aren't I . . .'

'No, no. I wasn't meaning you, silly.'

Pleased to be finally having this chat, Louise goes all in, giving more detail as her confidence grows. She is nearing the point of telling Harriet about her post-natal depression and her challenges bonding with Alfie when Harriet's face crumbles and she buries it in her arms.

'Oh, Harriet. What is it?' She thinks she knows, of course – this is what she's suspected since Richard let on, and this is her moment to shine, show Harriet she can be a good friend and supportive of her needs, like Harriet's been with her. Harriet will be feeling vulnerable. Louise is well aware of this, has to be careful not to put words in her mouth. Give her time to articulate her struggles. Harriet says something.

'Sorry, what was that?' Louise narrows her eyes, unable to make out what Harriet's saying, her words too muffled through her tears and folded arms. She gets up and walks around the island, lays her hand on her shoulder, giving it a gentle squeeze. Harriet lifts her head and sucks in a deep breath.

'Nothing. It's nothing. Sorry.' She rubs at her eyes and gets up. 'Ignore me.'

'No, I can't. Honestly, you've been amazingly supportive of me. The least I can do as your friend is repay that.'

'Really, Louise, I'm fine. All the talk of birth has just set me off. Not like me to succumb to emotion. Sorry.' She leaves, and a moment later Louise hears her voice on the nanny cam – soft, honey-warm, it's like listening to a lullaby. But Harriet's not speaking to Jacob, it's Alfie. Louise inches towards the playroom, stands and watches from the doorway. And it's only when Harriet glances around and sees her that she silently moves towards Jacob.

It could be Louise's imagination, but she senses a shift. And if Louise has noticed how they each have a better bond with the other one's child, has Harriet, too?

Chapter 21

MUMSTOGETHER

Private Message

FROM AngelFace
TO ExhaustedNewMum0593
SUBJECT Are you there?
MESSAGE

Hey, another DM from me! Hope you're good – and the little one? Is he sleeping better?

Do you mind me offloading on you? It's been a rough day if I'm honest. I hope my last message didn't put you off. I'm not needy, honest! (Well, ok, I *am* a *little bit* needy). I'm not having the best time with my partner, you know how it is . . . they don't always offer the support you crave, do they? I know we have that in common at least, from what you've said before. There's stuff I haven't felt comfortable sharing on the forum, but as we have bonded, I didn't think you'd mind if I shared some of it with you? Get it off my chest, so to speak.

Maybe we could speak properly, if you're up for it? I wouldn't ask, but there's something about you – I feel like we've connected for a reason. I think we can help each other.

X

Chapter 22

Harriet thrusts the invitation into Louise's hand the minute she enters the playgroup hall, and at first she assumes it's for the previously mentioned meal for the four of them. But then she watches as Harriet works the playgroup room, swiftly moving from one parent to the next, handing out at least another five. Her stomach lurches. Not an exclusive invite for just her and Mark then. What is this? Trying to hide her disappointment, she shields herself from view before tearing the thick cream envelope open.

Jacob is 3! Join us for a pool party to celebrate.

Oh, thank God. She inhales sharply, turns around, and grins as she heads back to the fun mums.

'Aren't they a little young for a pool party?'

Louise is amazed to hear someone else voice this opinion, even though she'd had the same thought. And hadn't Harriet herself expressed she thought it was a risk and covered the pool? She listens, her head tilting as her own thoughts swell like a balloon filling with anxiety in her mind. Alfie's near miss with the huge water feature in the front garden is still fresh in her mind. She doesn't relish the opportunity for him to get into even more trouble. Clearly, and thankfully, she's not alone in her thinking.

It's the fleeting look of distress on Harriet's face that propels her into action, though. A sudden need to be by her side, defending her friend, offering backup.

'Don't you ever take yours swimming?' Louise says, stepping forward. 'Come on. This will be great fun – and in a much calmer, and may I say it, stunning location.' Louise grins at Harriet. 'I, for one, will be there with Alfie. Thanks so much, Harriet.' Louise holds the invite up like a trophy, before popping it into her bag. And her reaction sparks the desired outcome from the others, who then all follow suit, gushing their thank yous and exclaiming how amazing it will be.

'Yes, I thought it was the perfect opportunity to celebrate on his actual birthday this year. It's so nice when it lands on a Saturday, isn't it?'

'Oh.' Louise pulls the invite back out of her bag and stares at it. How had she missed it? 'The date didn't register. I'm not sure . . .' Everyone's staring at her. She was the one to make a fuss, and now she was about to say she couldn't make it. 'Never mind. I'll sort it.' Louise gives a wave of her hand, like whatever it was, it doesn't really matter, and the conversation starts up again. Louise can't distinguish the words; she can only hear the voices as if they are a long distance away.

Harriet has organised a third birthday party for her son. Louise hadn't even considered a party for Alfie.

But that's not the reason her heartbeat is thrashing against her ribs, or the whooshing of blood dulls the surrounding sounds. Jacob's birthday is the same day as Alfie's.

Louise doesn't hang around once the session ends. Someone asks if they've missed the starter gun as, head down, she thrusts the buggy through the doorway and out of the building. She pushes Alfie at speed along the pavement and around the corner, out of view of the playgroup mums within seconds. She doesn't slow down, and by the time she's approaching the house, her breath's ragged and the nape of her neck is slick with sweat.

A white van, its engine idling, two wheels bumped up on to the kerb, is between hers and her neighbour's house. Louise slows to a stop, catches her breath. Alfie, who has been quiet up until now, begins to whine. She pretends they're playing a game of spot-the-bug to placate him for a moment, while really her focus is trained on her next-door neighbour's house – on the van belonging to the man who'd threatened Andrew. Then, her neighbour had said something along the lines of hoping it would be the last they'd see of him. Obviously his hopes were now dashed. What did this guy want from him? Louise gulps, her throat dry as she reaches into the bag hanging from the buggy and gets her mobile. She could capture the number plate this time. If something has happened, at least she'll have evidence of the vehicle involved. Maybe it's even the same white van responsible for Janet's dead dog.

She opens the camera app, but there's movement from Andrew's path, followed by pounding footsteps on concrete, and she fumbles the mobile, almost dropping it. *Dammit*. Louise whips the buggy around so they're facing in the opposite direction, and ducks out of sight behind a bush, afraid of alerting the aggressor to their presence in case it fuels the issue. But if he really has hurt Andrew, a photo of him would be helpful to offer the police. If she hesitates now, she'll miss the opportunity.

Is this white-van man the aggressor, though? It's what Louise had assumed, given his behaviour and angrily spoken words, but what had he said again? Something about if he ever found out Andrew was behind it, he'd tear him limb from limb – or words to that effect. Behind what, exactly? Perhaps all this man was doing was trying to find out what had happened – was he a relative of Andrew's ex?

Was her neighbour, not this white-van man, the one Louise should really be worried about?

Louise allows the noise of the engine to die away before moving, then walks with purpose towards their house, chatting away to Alfie as though nothing out of the ordinary has occurred. At the top of her path, she hesitates, tilting her head to try to see inside Andrew's front window. The blinds are down and from this position she's unable to see a thing. She taps her fingers on the buggy handle, contemplates whether to bite the bullet and go and knock on his door. Check all is okay. She'd have to come clean, tell him she'd seen the van speed off, say she was concerned for his wellbeing, because not once since he lived there has she popped in to check on his welfare. He wouldn't believe her if she fabricated some random reason for her being there.

She casts her gaze about to see if anyone else is watching, then backs away from her house, pushing Alfie towards Andrew's instead.

'Want to go home,' he says, wriggling in the buggy.

'Shh. In a minute, Alfie.' Louise continues down the path, listening out for signs of life. She reaches a hand up, knocks on the front door. It's ajar. 'Hello!' Louise calls, her voice shaky. 'Are you in?' She pushes it fully open, alert now for any noises. There's a thud, and Louise turns sharply, a hand flying to her chest. Breath hisses through her lips. 'Jesus,' she whispers, seeing Alfie's feet kick out again. 'Hello.' Her voice is louder this time.

Silence.

She can't go inside and leave Alfie on the doorstep. And she won't take him inside. There's no telling what scene they'll be faced with. Louise takes a step back, looks down the side of the house's exterior. She's seen Andrew disappearing down there a number of times; it leads to the back garden the same as their house's does, only there's no locked gate here. Perhaps he's not responding because he's in the shed or something.

Please let that be it.

'Hey, Alfie, we're just going to look in the garden, okay?' Her tone is meant to be reassuring, although it's for her sake more than Alfie's.

'No. Don't want to.'

'We're going to play I-spy,' she says, hoping it acts as a distraction as she creeps around the back. 'I spy with my little eye, something coloured—' The word 'green' sticks in her throat the second she turns the corner.

'Daddy,' Alfie says.

'That's not Daddy,' Louise says in a whisper. She squints at the figure wedged between a fence panel and a bush near the bottom of the garden. The fencing that separates their properties. He has his back to them, and based on the fact he hasn't moved, Louise assumes he hasn't heard their approach. Is he watching her house?

Adrenaline spikes through her. What the hell is he doing? She shouldn't have ignored her instinct that it was him she saw near Harriet's, that he was following her. If he realises she's caught him red-handed spying on her house, or whatever he's doing, she could be in danger here. Backtracking is her only option, and before Alfie calls out. The white-van guy hadn't hurt him, after all, then. None of it made sense. Louise hurries away from Andrew's house, scuttles back to her own and locks the door as soon as they're inside.

'We'll play upstairs,' she says, lifting Alfie out of the buggy and carrying him to his bedroom. She sits him down among his toys and goes to her bedroom, inching towards the window. It overlooks the back garden.

Andrew isn't there.

She tilts her chin, trying to take in as much of the gardens as she can. No sign of him.

'Alfie,' she says when she returns to his room. 'Did you think you saw Daddy just now?'

He nods. 'Daddy hiding.'

God. That's it. The words he uttered before, after he screamed and choked on the keyring. She'd forgotten about what he'd said, too many other things on her mind, but now she knows that wasn't the first time her neighbour had been spying on them.

Louise shudders, the tiny hairs on her arms all rising. He's gone from being a bit creepy to being a potential threat. A sudden thought rises to the surface of her mind: what if his wife didn't actually leave? Usually, Louise would talk herself out of such wild theories, but his behaviour isn't normal. Maybe one of the couple's arguments got out of hand, and he harmed her. Accidentally, or otherwise. *Shit.* What if he *killed* her?

Chapter 23

'I had an odd encounter earlier,' Louise says, trying to sound nonchalant as she slides the knife through the carrots, the rhythmic chopping vibrating through her hand.

Mark stops pouring the wine, holding the bottle in mid-air. 'Oh?' he says. It's a fleeting pause in activity before he recovers and continues to fill his glass. He stands with one hand on the worktop as he takes a gulp. Louise gets the feeling he's dreading what she's about to say.

'Yeah. Now I'm getting out and about more, you know, it's like I've emerged from a fog, and I'm seeing things more clearly.' Louise gives a small laugh, then faces Mark.

'Are you going to elaborate?' He puts his glass down and Louise mirrors him by resting the knife on the chopping board. Her eyes flit towards the kitchen window. The streetlamp opposite is already on; they're eating late tonight because it took her so long to get Alfie to settle. No doubt because of being frightened by the neighbour again. Despite Louise finally convincing him it wasn't his daddy and reassuring him that the neighbour was simply gardening, not hiding, Alfie remained cautious. He hadn't, however, said a single word about it to Mark when he got home from work. She'd hoped it had been forgotten, but during each of the three stories she read to him, he mentioned 'hiding' and being scared multiple times. It had to be discussed with Mark – they needed a united approach to ensure it didn't become an issue. Cause him to suffer with night terrors, like she did. Her own had begun during childhood, getting significantly worse once she hit puberty. With Alfie's behaviour already a concern, she couldn't bear to imagine adding that into the mix.

'I meant to talk to you about it, but with one thing or another, it's slipped my mind. Until today.'

'Christ, Lou. You're taking storytelling to a whole new level here, love. It's not a Netflix series – you can drop the tension and cliffhangers.'

'I was only trying to explain why I hadn't mentioned anything before.' Louise shrugs, sighs. 'So, a couple of weeks ago I was standing here, and heard a commotion outside.' Louise pauses, takes a step towards the window, peeking outside. She rubs her hands over her bare arms, brushing away the tingly sensation. Then, her voice lowering, she tells Mark about the angry man, how he sounded as though he was threatening Andrew.

'Andrew?'

'Yeah. Our *neighbour*?'

'Oh, right. Drew, yes.'

Louise narrows her eyes. The last time they spoke about their next-door neighbour, she was sure he hadn't recalled his name either, let alone used a nickname. 'I didn't know you two were that friendly.'

'We're not mates. I barely see him, thankfully – just the occasional superficial interaction over the years. I've told you before there's something about him I don't like ...'

'Yeah, I remember you saying to be careful of him. Anyway, I think perhaps you're right.'

Mark's mouth drops open as if this is the first time she's ever uttered those words. 'Can I have that in writing?'

'Ha ha.' She gives him a playful slap. 'No, seriously, I'm getting a strange vibe from him.' Louise decides in this moment not to divulge *how* she caught Drew in the act of spying on them, but she does mention she's seen him watching their house, and tells Mark about the white-van man. The ensuing discussion is lively, both she and Mark animated as they throw out various theories of who the van guy is, what he wants with Drew, and what he might be referring to when he said, 'If I *ever* find out you're behind it.'

They're still talking about it when they climb into bed close to midnight.

And for the next half an hour it fills Louise's thoughts, and she nudges Mark a few times to ask him about Drew's ex. 'You ever talk to her?'

'Honestly, I can't really remember what she even looked like now. You?'

'No,' Louise admits. 'I spotted her leaving the house early some mornings – she wore a uniform of some kind, I think. She seemed young. As in, younger than Drew.'

'I know age doesn't really come into it,' Mark says,

yawning, 'but it was one of the things that struck me about them, too. Huge age gap.'

'You think the white-van man is her dad?'

But there's no response from Mark. Louise crosses her hands over her chest and stares at the dark shadows on the ceiling. Sleep won't come to her so easily; her mind is awash with a thousand thoughts. And now, in the silence of the room, Louise finds herself going over Harriet's invitation. A needle of concern pricks at her; is it a coincidence the boys were born on the same day?

You're doing it again.

Louise tugs at the duvet, bringing it up under her chin. Is the new drama with Drew a convenient cover to allow her to push aside the paranoid feelings about Alfie not being her child? Natalie's voice is loud inside her skull. *Do you find you make things up to stop yourself from confronting the real issues? Creating problems elsewhere might be your way of coping with internal difficulties – a form of masking.*

Her fallback, a mechanism she's used for as long as she can remember, has been to compartmentalise: put the most pressing issue – the painful one – in a box and tuck it away, then open a different box, usually one not directly affecting her. Focusing her attention on a lesser problem allowed her to avoid the distressing one.

It wasn't until speaking regularly with Natalie, when her depression was at its worst, that she gained enough self-awareness to recognise when she was employing this tactic. Now, lying on her back, her eyes wide and nerves all on edge, Louise fights with her inner voice saying there was a mix-up at the maternity unit, that her son was swapped for another. A technique Natalie taught her during an early therapy session exploring the limiting beliefs Louise held about herself – like when she'd say she was a terrible mother – was to gather evidence to dispute it. She was asked to pay attention to things during the day where it was clear she was being a perfectly good mum.

Louise knows her mind won't settle until she's at least made notes of her whirling thoughts about Alfie – written down any evidence she can think of disputing her theory of him being the wrong child. Worse, that it was Jacob he was swapped with. That would be too much of a coincidence, surely – a child in the same playgroup? She pushes the duvet aside and, with the phone light on, eases her journal out from the bedside table. It still has the pen keeping the place of her last entry. Her breath snags in her chest as she opens it, the scrawled words jumping out at her. She must've written this the other night, before she found it under the duvet. She guesses her mind had been unable to let go of a thread of doubt then, too. She can't remember writing it, or what thought had occurred to cause the scribbled demand, but something had.

Check baby diary.

She quickly replaces it and gets out of bed, compelled to follow the lead.

Chapter 24

'Christ, Lou. What are you doing?' Mark stands in the doorway to the conservatory rubbing at his eyes, his Australia-shaped birthmark on his lower abdomen just visible above the band of his boxers. Framed there with the light behind him, he looks like an underwear model from one of the mail order catalogues Sue used to run as an agent back in the day, earning a bit of extra cash through commission – the same catalogues Louise used to eagerly flick through, giggling over instead of searching for Christmas presents to add to her list.

'Looking for something. Obviously.' She kneels back, surveying the stack of children's books she's pulled out from the storage chest, a weary breath escaping her.

'I see that.' He shakes his head and turns to leave again, tired and clearly not wishing to get involved.

'Where did you put the memory box?' The last place she saw it was in the nursery that they've since redecorated to make more toddler-appropriate.

Mark pauses, looking skyward. Louise feels the

annoyance coming off him in waves – the fingers of each hand are clenching and unclenching while the rest of him remains still. She watches as he weighs up the pros and cons of whatever he's thinking of saying next.

'With the photo books, remember?' he says, his words measured. Mark is able to come across as calm and angry at the same time, a juxtaposition Louise hasn't fully understood even after the years she's known him. If she asks him how he manages this feat, he claims to be unaware of possessing such an ability. That it's her interpretation, not his intention, leading her to this conclusion.

'Oh, yeah. Course.' They'd started to transfer some of the digital photos and ones from their phones on to canvases or into books – one of the only good pieces of advice from her mother, who felt it was a shame in this digital age that there were no albums to sit and reminisce over. She complained that images on phones were not the same – a bit like her hatred of Kindles over paperbacks. And so Louise did both. She kept photos on her phone, but also ensured the important ones were compiled into albums. 'Thanks.'

She jumps up from the floor and bounds past Mark to reach the lounge. She finds the cardboard memory box containing the pregnancy diary behind a row of photo albums. Louise drags the books off the shelf and takes the box, shaking it to jiggle the tight-fitting lid loose. Inside is Alfie's remaining ankle tag – she'd lost one, presumably in the leg of a Baby-gro while they were in the maternity unit – his cot card, birth certificate and the pregnancy diary Louise had started writing in the day she'd missed her period right up until she brought her baby home.

Mark pops his head round the door. 'It is two a.m., though. You coming back to bed?'

She slips the small diary in her pyjama pocket. 'Yep. Coming.' She'll read it later when Mark's left for work. She doesn't want to give him reason to worry. Think she's acting strangely. Although they shared some theories about Drew earlier, she isn't about to tell him about her rather more concerning theory about them having brought someone else's child home with them. Her pulse jitters as an image floats across her mind's eye. She and Mark standing over the crib, him looking on adoringly as their baby son grips his finger.

What if that baby really was someone else's?

Of course, many people adopt children – they don't necessarily bring up their biological offspring – but that's a choice, a specific decision they made. She and Mark decided to start their own family. Their own flesh and blood. How would Mark react?

Alfie belonging to other parents would change everything.

With a long breath in, then a slow release of the air, Louise brings her heart rate down to its normal level. It's no good worrying about something that hasn't happened, might never happen, because she's probably getting carried away – jumping to the more theatrical conclusions.

You always were a bit of a drama queen. Sue's voice, of course. But she has to admit her mother has a point. Louise had been chosen to play Juliet in the Year 7 play,

THE OTHER CHILD

and several teachers gave her feedback afterwards, sharing their belief that she had been extremely enthusiastic. Which Sue later translated as meaning she'd basically overacted. Something she continued to do, according to her school report, throughout each drama lesson until she dropped the subject in Year 9. Mr Patton had subsequently told her form teacher that he'd been somewhat relieved by her decision.

'Screw you, Mr Patton.' Louise follows Mark back upstairs, but turns towards Alfie's bedroom and pushes the door ajar. He's slept better since having playdates with Jacob. He's been far more content, too.

And hasn't *she* been?

She stands with her arms folded and listens to his soft, snuffly breathing. He mumbles something in his sleep, turns over so she can just make out his face. He pulls his cuddly dog closer and settles again. Maybe she's creating problems where there are no longer any.

If Alfie has managed to alter his behaviour, then shouldn't she try?

Louise pulls the door to again and pads along the landing to their room. In the dim light the bedside lamp offers, Mark's bare torso is visible above the duvet and his arms are behind his head. For a moment she thinks he's watching her, but he's too still; he's asleep already. She takes the diary from her pyjama pocket and goes to put it with the journal in the drawer, but her fingers clamp round it, unable to let go.

A quick flick through wouldn't hurt. It would more likely put her mind at ease right away, rather than allowing herself to dwell on what 'check baby diary' meant. She'll likely find she'd written those words because she knew, deep down, there was nothing untoward, and actually reading her diary would confirm this. She sits on the edge of the bed and positions it under the lamplight and, with her nerves tingling, opens the A6-sized notebook. After reading a couple of early entries, where her excitement was off the scale, then a later one where she was lamenting the joys of morning sickness and how it was, of course, all-day sickness in her case, Louise skipped towards the back of the notebook and read one of the entries after she'd given birth.

All the alarms went off this afternoon. Lots of rushing around – was told we might have to evacuate the ward. Turned out it wasn't a fire, thank God. Apparently a water leak led to a flood, which caused the short. Second hospital this month to have issues. I blame the government – post-pandemic the NHS seems to have gone to the dogs.

Alarms going off wasn't exactly unusual, and she can barely recall it even happening, so an evacuation obviously hadn't been required. Louise blaming the government for shitting on the NHS also wasn't anything new. Even now there is a new party in power, she doubts change will happen quickly enough to save it. Her eyes start to lose focus in the poor light, the words blending together. She's not gaining anything by doing this now. She places the diary in the drawer along with her journal and slips into bed, laying her arm over Mark's stomach, circling her fingertips round his convex belly button. He stirs, turns over, and pulls her arm so it's draping over his side. She snuggles into his back, and, relishing the closeness, allows her body to relax.

She'll go see Harriet – tell her it's Alfie's birthday, too, own up to the fact she hadn't planned anything. Maybe Harriet will suggest they make the party a joint one. It's the kind of thing she would do. A warm sensation seeps through Louise – how amazing would it be to have his first proper party somewhere cool like Harriet's and to celebrate it with Jacob? With thoughts of swapped babies and suspicious neighbours put to one side, she finally falls asleep.

Chapter 25

MUMSTOGETHER

Private Message

FROM AngelFace
TO ExhaustedNewMum0593
SUBJECT Sorry
MESSAGE

Sorry I didn't make today, something came up.

Having a few *issues* with the other half at the moment. Always wants to take control. Said I shouldn't be even contemplating work – thinks a mother's place is at home and all that patriarchal bull. What century are we in?!

Chapter 26

As predicted, Harriet's reaction when Louise confessed to not organising a party for Alfie was to suggest they make it a joint party. She didn't miss a beat. Gave her trademark flick of the hand, rolling her eyes when Louise put up a counterargument of why she couldn't possibly accept the kind offer, and immediately began talking about how she was sorry she didn't think of it to start with.

'Honestly, Harriet, *you* shouldn't be sorry. God knows how, but it hadn't even come up, had it – the boys sharing the same date of birth, I mean – so how could you have?'

Her eyebrows pull together as she appears to contemplate the question. 'True, and it was a rather hasty decision on my part to throw a pool party –' she leans in close – 'and, between you and me, Richard is really not best pleased about it. All the unwanted extras wandering about the place – the *noise*.'

Louise gives an awkward smile. Is that how he thinks of her and Alfie, too – unwanted extras? 'It isn't everyone's idea of fun, I guess.' It isn't *her* idea of fun, if she were being honest. 'I've never particularly enjoyed large get-togethers. I understand where Richard's coming from.'

'Oh, Louise. Ever the diplomat, eh?'

'Well, I try.' If Harriet could see her in her own environment, in her dealings with Sue, Mark and Alfie, she doubts this would be the label assigned to her.

Louise's head lolls forward, a heaviness overcoming her, and she closes her eyes as she lays her forehead on her folded arms on the kitchen island. Weeks' worth of anxiety, tiredness and stress has decided to take its toll right now, this second – her entire body fights with her brain to shut down.

'Christ, Louise. You okay?'

'Sorry. Think this has been brewing for a bit. I'll get home. Feel the need for a lie-down.'

'You can't go home like this. Have a rest in my room. I'll look after the boys and you have an hour.'

And before she's able to put up a fight, Harriet's hands are under Louise's armpits and she's guiding her up and along the corridor. They pass the forbidden room and take a right. Then Harriet ushers her into a large bright room – another modern, airy space – and makes her sit on the end of the bed while she plumps pillows, then tells her to lie down and relax. Harriet presses a button, and the daylight blots out as though there's an eclipse of the sun.

'Don't move from there. I'll come get you if I need you, otherwise rest for as long as you need.'

'Thank you. Please, though . . . don't let me nap for more than half an hour or I'll never sleep tonight.'

'Sure.'

Louise doesn't hear the door close, but after a few minutes of silence, assumes Harriet has left. Her eyes flutter closed.

Louise's eyes spring open and she sits up, fear surging through her veins. She can't see anything. Blood pumps hard to her vital organs, her fight, flight or freeze response in a frenzy. Where is she?

What was the noise that woke her?

What time is it? Where's her son?

It takes several seconds of panic before her brain finally works and she remembers where she is. She'd asked Harriet to not let her sleep for longer than thirty minutes. The grogginess she feels in her head, the stickiness of her eyes, makes her think it's been far longer than that. Gathering herself, she edges off the bed and feels around for the remote Harriet used earlier to close the blinds. She's slow, purposeful, not wanting to knock something over – an expensive lamp or a glass of water. Her hand closes around an oblong, plastic object and she runs her fingertips over it to find the buttons. Concern makes her hesitate. What if she opens the blinds and it's pitch-black *outside*, too? Could be the middle of the night for all she knows.

Her pulse bangs again, her ears clogging with the sound of rushing blood.

'Stop panicking,' Louise tells herself, her voice a strange echo in her head. She'd always loved the idea of a blackout blind, something to block the glow of the streetlights outside their house, but now that she's experiencing one, she's rapidly changing her mind. Someone could be in here – lying in the bed beside her, even – and she'd be none the wiser.

With this thought, she sweeps one hand across the top of the duvet, while at the same time her other hand presses all the buttons. Her mouth is dry, lips open, ready to scream if her hand touches something or someone. The blind opens in slow motion. Her adrenaline subsides as the light floods in, revealing only her in the bedroom. She lets out a sigh.

After checking herself in Harriet's floor-to-ceiling mirrored wardrobe doors and brushing her fingers through her hair to neaten the sticky-out strands, Louise checks around to find a clock. She gives a small humph. She's had about twenty minutes of sleep.

Harriet probably wouldn't wake her for another ten minutes at least.

She tiptoes towards the door, pressing her ear against it. Harriet and the boys are on the other side of the house, so unless they were being unusually noisy, she wouldn't expect to hear them. Neither would they hear her. An idea percolates. She really shouldn't nose around. But this is an ideal opportunity. Louise can't put her finger on why, exactly, but she's an urge to sneak into the forbidden room.

Richard could well be home now, though. Probably shouldn't risk it. Especially as she doesn't even know why she's compelled to go in there. It's the study where Richard occasionally works, a place he wants to keep sacred, Harriet's already explained. So why does it hold an element of intrigue? All off-limits, out-of-bounds areas tend to have the same pull – an attraction – though, don't they? Particularly true for kids and teenagers. Louise remembers Sue's rule about her not entering the cellar – a case of keeping her safe, she'd said. It had spiders, and was dark, so, to begin with, Louise had no problem adhering to the rule. By the time she was twelve or thereabouts, though, the feeling there was something interesting down there outweighed the fear of a few arachnids. Each time she passed the doorway leading to it, she'd put her hand on the latch, testing her bravery, until, one day, she got back from school and Sue was out and she took the opportunity. What had been down there? Louise can't even recall now. But the point is people don't necessarily grow out of the desire to enter an off-limits area.

Louise creeps along the corridor, stopping outside the study and listening. There're no sounds coming from inside. She knows the room isn't locked, so slowly depresses the handle, opening it a crack just to be sure. He isn't in there. Nipping through the gap, Louise is inside and closing the door behind her within seconds. For a moment, she stays absolutely still, her hearing heightened as she waits for a sound on the other side – a sign she's been rumbled. If Harriet goes to the bedroom and doesn't find her there or in the bathroom, Louise is in serious trouble. Not hearing anything, but aware she needs to be quick, Louise casts her gaze around the room, adrenaline coursing through her.

It doesn't look the way she'd imagined Richard's workspace. But then Harriet had said it was a study, and that Richard only uses it when he's working from home. Given the subtle hints of her personality here, perhaps Harriet was the one who used the room more often. The walls are painted a soft green; two are lined with vertical white-oak wood slats, giving the room a sleek, ultra-modern feel that matches the rest of the house – or what she's been privy to, anyway. Louise pads across the thick cream carpet towards the L-shaped desk. She brushes her fingertips along the high-gloss edge, admiring the neatness and lack of clutter on its white surface. Everything has its place. Louise wonders if the minimalistic style is because Harriet and Richard were about to move house. Hadn't he said they'd packed up, all ready, before Harriet changed her mind? Now she thinks of it, that might also be the reason for the lack of any family photos or other personal trinkets around the house.

She hasn't got time to linger here. And with a quiet huff of dissatisfaction, she turns away from the desk. As she does, her foot snags on something. She winces, looks down. It's a small cardboard storage box. Glancing towards the door to check the coast is still clear, Louise ducks down and opens it. Flicks through the content of mainly documents – insurance forms, utility bills and receipts. Then she spots a photo among the paperwork. She removes it, studying the image. It must be Jacob, when he was just a few days old by the look of it. It's the first baby photo – well, any photo – she's seen. Why does Harriet have it tucked away in a box of admin? Maybe because it was a traumatic time she doesn't want to remember. Louise sucks in a breath; it sticks in her lungs. She can relate to the pain of that. A part of her wonders if Harriet is also questioning her bond with her son, and that's why she can't bear to have photos of Jacob up.

Louise runs her fingertips over the glossy print. Baby Jacob is lying in a plastic crib like those in the neonatal units, no Baby-gro on, just a nappy. Poking above the nappy line, she notes a birthmark. Louise brings the photo closer to her face. Is she imagining it, or does the small coloured splodge looks like an island? She puts her hand to her heart. Feels the thudding. It looks like Australia.

Chapter 27

There's a roaring in Louise's ears. That birthmark is highly unusual; Mark always jokes he's one of a kind. Yet now she's staring at one in miniature, the same distinctive shape and colour. How is it possible? She should take the photo. No one would notice it's missing – it's stuffed in a box with paperwork. But what then? If Louise had the photo, how could she prove she found it at Harriet's? Resisting the urge to pocket it, she places it back in the box. She must be running out of time.

Louise peruses the room one more time, her eyes desperately trying to find something deserving of Harriet's reaction to Alfie having been in here. There's a small unit standing against the far wall – antique-looking, incongruent with the rest of the furnishings. Louise gently pulls on each of the two drawers, but they don't open. There's a single lock above the top drawer. She didn't see a key anywhere on the desk.

As Louise closes the study door, she hears footsteps approaching. Darting back towards Harriet's bedroom, she pretends to be just coming out, rubbing her eyes and yawning as Harriet comes into view.

'Feeling better?' Harriet stops and stares at Louise, her eyes narrow. Her tone is offish and immediately Louise's pulse splutters. Was her act not convincing? She can't let on where she's been, what she's found. Not yet. She needs to pull herself together.

'Yes, thank you. Have the boys been all right?' Louise walks towards Harriet, who backs off.

'Of course. Didn't you think I could manage the two of them?' She gives a flicker of a smile. Then, as if she realises she's being unreasonably antsy, she adds, 'We've been playing all together. It's been lovely, actually.'

'Oh, good. And thanks again. I clearly needed that extra rest.'

Louise follows Harriet back towards the kitchen, turning to go into the playroom. But it's empty. A twinge of alarm plucks at her, and she's about to ask where the boys are when she spots them through the tall glass windows. They're with Richard out in the back garden.

'Don't worry,' Harriet says, as if sensing Louise's discomfort. 'The pool is still covered. Won't take it off until the party.'

Louise swallows down the lump in her throat. How come Harriet hadn't mentioned Richard a second ago, when she'd made the comment about managing the two boys on her own? 'I didn't realise Richard was home.'

'Well, you wouldn't have, would you? You were asleep.'

There's something in the way she utters the sentence

that puts Louise on edge. She glances to the nanny cam on the kitchen unit and her entire body freezes. It no longer shows the playroom. The image currently on the screen is of a hallway and door. The door to Richard's home office.

Fuck.

Is there any likelihood they *didn't* see her sneak in there? She should own up. Give Harriet some sob story, a reason to justify invading their privacy. Her mind blanks. She's no defence, or not one she can easily come up with on the spot. She can't mention her suspicions yet – she'll seem crazy. A large part of her still believes she *is* crazy. Buying time, Louise closes her eyes, blows air from her cheeks.

'Look, Harriet, I'm sorry. There's no excuse, and honestly, it's not like I *planned* to …'

'What on earth are you rambling on about?' Harriet lays a hand on Louise's arm and Louise opens her eyes. Sees only concern on Harriet's face.

'I – I want to explain—'

A loud squeal interrupts Louise's confession, followed by a dramatic roar, and two toddlers run between her and Harriet. Richard is close behind, pretending to be a monster.

'Richard!' Harriet stands back, throwing her arms in the air. 'You'll give them nightmares.' She shakes her head, looks to Louise. 'God, I'm sorry. Men just don't *think*, do they?'

'He's only playing – they look like they're having a good time,' Louise says, watching them disappear back outside, glad of the reprieve.

Harriet turns her back, fusses around with the empty mugs. Louise hopes the previous conversation has been forgotten, then Harriet speaks again.

'Listen, Louise. Are you okay? Honestly I'm worried about you.'

'Oh.' Louise recoils, eyes wide. Here it comes – Harriet knows she's been snooping, will probably kick her and Alfie out. Then what? How can she forget what she saw in Richard's office?

Harriet's eyes glaze over. Like she's shutting off from the world; doesn't want to see anything. Or doesn't want others to see what's behind them. 'You know, going through a trauma can be a reason people project? It's a defence mechanism,' she says.

Louise nods. This isn't what she was expecting. Maybe she's safe. And projection – isn't that what Natalie is always talking to her about? Sounds like Louise isn't the only one in therapy.

'Yes, I've heard this. Did ... did your therapist explain that to you, too?' Louise says tentatively. She needs to get Harriet to open up, see what she can find out.

But Harriet's withdrawal is immediate. She pushes back from the kitchen island, expression stony.

'I don't have a therapist, Louise.' There's a tightness to her voice and Louise's breath catches. She's overstepped.

'If you don't want to share your experience with me, it's fine. I'm not forcing you to talk before you're ready.' Louise keeps her voice soft. Like a soothing lullaby. Like a therapist, she thinks. 'Richard mentioned you'd had a rough time after Jacob's birth and spent time in a special-care unit ...' Harriet's eyes widen. 'He wasn't speaking out of turn, only in response to me telling him my experience.'

'And where was I when this tête-à-tête was occurring?'

'In the bathroom, I think. Anyway, my point is, I've noticed you're sometimes a bit ... aloof with Jacob. I think maybe we have that in common? I mean, you know, we both seem to struggle to bond with our respective boys – and I think being separated from them when they were first born is a major factor, don't you?' Louise shuffles her feet, wishing now she'd sat down on the bar stool because her legs are shaking.

'You mustn't give weight to what Richard says. But I'm sorry to hear *you* didn't have a good experience.'

Louise rolls her shoulders. Evidently, Harriet isn't going to give much away. 'Which unit were you on with Jacob?'

Harriet's face pales, a haunted-looking expression covering it. Louise waits to see if she's going to answer. She senses Harriet's story is more traumatic than her own. After a while of Harriet not responding, or even moving, Louise finally asks outright, 'Were you apart from Jacob for a long time?'

The words seem to shake Harriet from her trance, and she snaps her head round to look at Louise. 'What?' she says, taking a breath and putting both hands on the island as if to steady herself. She frowns and closes her eyes. Louise's stomach knots. She can hear the kids and Richard a stone's throw away and making a racket, their excited shouts permeating the kitchen despite being outside. It's not the right moment.

'Sorry, bad timing. But I'm always here if you want to talk. All these playdates and we haven't even touched upon the important stuff really, have we?' Louise puts a hand over Harriet's. Harriet snatches it away.

'You really should be leaving. Mark'll be thinking you're not coming home.' And, with that, Harriet lurches forward, knocks on the window and beckons for Richard to bring in the boys.

'Oh, erm . . .' Louise hesitates. 'Maybe I can call you later. I don't like to leave the conversation—'

'Date night tonight. I'll catch you another time.'

Louise reels from the clear brush-off. Could this spell the end of their playdates? Christ, Alfie loves being here – and so does Louise. Harriet is the first real friend she's made since having Alfie, and Louise can't deny she loves being around Jacob too. She thinks again of the photo, the birthmark. She *has* to keep seeing them, at least until she figures out if this is all in her head.

Before she can respond, the boys stomp in. Alfie's pouting, his arms crossed.

'Time to go home to Daddy now, sweetheart.'

'Don't want to.'

'We'll see Jacob again soon.' This seems to do the trick, his face softening.

'Okaaay.'

'Bye-bye, Lou-Lou,' Jacob says, rushing up to give her a hug. Louise touches the back of his shoulders, his warmth making her fingers tingle. There's a finality to the moment – like it's the last goodbye, the last time inside this house.

But Louise won't let this be the end. She has to make this right.

Chapter 28

The door slams behind them like an audible full stop and, for a split second, both Louise and Alfie are completely still, standing on the step like abandoned children. Louise's mind is whirring with thoughts of the study, the photo, Harriet's uncharacteristic coldness. Maybe she didn't like Louise prying, but she suspects it's more than that. Harriet must have seen her on camera. Louise has ruined everything. She fights back tears. The feeling of emptiness she'd had before meeting Harriet returns to the pit of her stomach. She gives a small shake of her head to snap out of her reverie, and looks down at Alfie, tries to smile. Her mouth is stiff, her lips dry.

'Hey. You ready to go home to see Daddy?' Alfie nods and they step down. Louise automatically turns to reach for the buggy. A surge of regret moves through her like a wave. It had been her bright idea not to bring it today, deciding the walk would do them both good. Her earlier flood of tiredness returns, but, taking a deep breath, she starts walking. And, with no need to prompt him, Alfie takes her hand.

It's a quiet journey, sluggish, too – Alfie's had a boisterous time with Richard. He's exhausted and, although not complaining yet, Louise fears a meltdown might not be far off. Should she call Mark? He could meet them halfway.

'Shall we have a quick rest here?' Louise points to a wooden bench set back from the pavement. There's a plaque on it and when Alfie's climbed up he runs his fingers over it.

'What it say?'

Louise's eyes struggle to focus, but as she peers at the silver plaque her curiosity piques. There's no name, which is unusual for a memorial bench. It simply says: *Until we're together again*. She reads it to Alfie, then searches for any other identifying information. Nothing apart from the carpenter's stamp, or at least she presumes that's what it is. Her mind wanders, thoughts about whether the words relate to a lost loved one, or whether it could be more cryptic, like two lovers who met around here, but aren't able to be together. Forbidden love. Like Harriet's forbidden study.

Louise leans back, tilts her head skywards. The clouds are high, no rain forecast today, thankfully, but they've a yellow tinge to them. Her lids are heavy, swollen. She really hadn't been making it up about being tired at Harriet's; the overwhelming need to sleep had come on so strongly it had taken her by surprise.

Mark's mobile goes to voicemail. Louise leaves a message telling him the route they're taking in the hope he picks it up before too long.

'Come on, then, Alfie. Let's see if we can spot another

bench along the way.' She doesn't think there are any, but she needs to give him something to focus on.

Alfie scuffs his feet along the pavement, tripping a few times. Louise pauses, checks to make sure his shoes are on properly, and they are. It's tiredness. She might have to carry him a little way. It's downhill for this bit, though. Louise looks around and sees the butcher's shop she ran into a few weeks ago, convinced she'd lost Alfie. She'd put the incident down to her own tiredness then. Her paranoia. Is it even possible to imagine something like that, purely because you're fatigued? The mind is an amazing thing, capable of feats beyond her comprehension, but, standing here now, it seems a stretch. It's hard to understand how she could have missed seeing Alfie's buggy when she looked back from down the road. Even with her stress levels high at that point, *not* seeing something is surely less likely than seeing something that isn't really there. Like a mirage appearing in a desert when you're hot and exhausted. She hadn't considered it before, but what if someone had actually taken Alfie – even if only for a few moments – and then brought him back while she was in the butcher's? But why would anyone do that?

A horn blares and Louise jumps, spinning round to see a car coming down the hill behind them. It slows down and the passenger window lowers. A man whistles. Not a wolf whistle, thank God, just one of those intended to gain someone's attention. At first, Louise doesn't clock who it is, then her muscles all tense up at once. It's her neighbour.

'Hey, Louise. I'm heading home. Need a lift?'

Louise grips Alfie's hand tighter and starts walking again. The dark grey Volvo estate crawls along beside them. 'Thanks, Drew, but I called Mark.' She feels a flush of heat in her face, keeps looking forward.

'Honestly, it's no problem.'

She side-eyes the car. Is it his? She's never seen him use a car before and not once has she seen this Volvo outside his house.

'New car?'

'Borrowed, as it happens.'

Alfie fidgets beside her, his hand wriggling, pulling away from hers. 'Alfie! You must hold Mummy's hand.' Louise shoots Drew a glance. 'Thanks, but Alfie needs a car seat.' Her mind conjures the last image she had of Drew, staring through a gap in the fencing at her house. Spying on them.

Drew stops the car. 'As luck would have it, there's one in the back already.' He smiles, catching Louise off-guard. It seems genuine, but she can't help thinking how odd this all is. A borrowed car that conveniently has a car seat? She halts, looks at the mobile in her hand. No missed calls, no new messages from Mark.

'Um, I . . .' She stumbles over her words, competing thoughts clashing inside her head. 'I don't know that Alfie would—'

'I'm holding up traffic. I'll pull in there,' he says, pointing to a loading bay up ahead. 'And you can hop in.'

The phrase 'what's the worst that could happen?' runs through her mind. She looks down at Alfie, whose eyelids are heavy, his face pale, and considers the consequences of declining Drew's offer. Louise nods. 'Okay.'

Oh, God. What are you doing?

As she guides Alfie to the lay-by, Drew gets out and opens the rear passenger door, beckoning to them. A flicker of nerves dances across her skin as she approaches him. Peering into the back, she notes the car seat is an ISOFIX make similar to the one they have in Mark's car. At least she can relax a little on the safety front. She'd feel terrible if she allowed Alfie to travel in a seat not suitable for his weight.

You'll just allow him to travel in a strange man's car.

'I'll let Mark know you're bringing us home,' Louise says, after she's strapped Alfie into the car seat and ensured it's tight. 'Don't want him scouring the roads trying to find us.' The call goes to voicemail again. A quiver of concern runs through her. Why isn't Mark answering? He's been home early most nights, but the one time she needs him he's not there. She sends a WhatsApp message instead. The conversation she and Mark had about Drew the other evening comes back to her as she climbs into the passenger seat. That, together with Drew's own admission of rarely leaving the house, brings goosebumps to her arms. Did Drew lie to her?

Louise looks over her shoulder to check Alfie is okay, then turns to Drew. His focus is on pulling out into the road, so she has a few seconds to take in his features. This close up, he appears younger, she thinks. But he's shaved since she last saw him, his chin smoother – perhaps it's that. When Mark's had a beard in the past, it's definitely aged him – the smattering of grey adding a few years at least – not that she's ever shared this observation with him. From the side profile, Drew's jawline is long and angular, his chin jutting out, and his nose is narrow. He reminds her of an older Robert Pattinson, an actor who she'd once had a crush on. Along with a million other people. Drew catches her staring, and she quickly starts talking, as if she's only just turned towards him.

'Surprised to see you this way. You said you didn't get out much.'

'Had a few things to sort out,' he says.

'I see. Thought I saw you the other day, actually. Up near Vicary Road?'

The silence stretches and Louise's heart flutters. It was him, then. Must've been. Maybe he knows someone on that road – but then why not say? Christ, maybe he really *is* stalking her. He's clearly not offering up an answer, so she changes tack.

'Whose car is it?' she asks, trying to sound nonchalant.

Drew sucks in a breath, releasing it slowly through his nostrils. His fingers tap on the wheel, fast and uneasy, like a nervous tic. 'My sister's.' He stares dead ahead. It doesn't seem she'll gain any more from him; his body language is closing off, his shoulders stiff, his torso rigid. She waits a beat.

'Is she local?' Louise presses.

'Not far away.' He snaps down the indicator, turning right at the bottom of the hill. Alarm flutters in Louise's chest. This isn't the way home. She shifts in the leather seat, pulls at her seatbelt; it feels as though it's constricting her lungs.

'And she doesn't need it?' Her voice shakes and her mind races to come up with an excuse to get out of the car, continue on foot. Drew swerves around a pothole, sending Louise pitching sideways. He apologises and curses the council for its lack of maintenance.

'Let's just say –' Drew glances at her – 'my little sister's having a spot of trouble with her husband, and I'm ... *helping*.'

'Oh. I'm sorry to hear that.' Louise swallows the rising bile. 'Does that guy in the white van have anything to do with this?'

'He's a problem, for sure.'

Louise's attention drifts. They've been driving for longer than it would've taken her to walk, and in the wrong direction. She's about to query it when she clocks the one-way signs. Of course. Her route is different because she walks it. Hasn't driven for so long the road layout has changed. Her stomach unclenches, and she turns to check on Alfie again. He's asleep. Louise groans.

'I know,' Drew says. 'Seems neither of us is great at choosing partners.' Drew blinks several times, sniffs loudly. He must've assumed she was groaning at what he'd said, not because her son has nodded off, which will cause no end of hassle when she tries to settle him for bed. But as it is, his response gives Louise a chance to do some digging. No longer quite so interested in the white-van guy, she uses Drew's admission of wrongly choosing his partner to steer the conversation to her real area of interest – the missing wife.

'I'm so sorry, by the way. About the breakdown of your marriage. It must've been—'

'We weren't married. Thank heavens for small mercies.'

'Oh, right. Well, I have to admit – and this makes me a shocking neighbour, I know – but I can't really remember her. I was totally absorbed in my own world.' Louise raises her eyebrows, gives an apologetic smile.

'Yeah. I know.' Drew nods. 'You were heavily pregnant. Every time we saw you, *she* commented how bi—' He coughs, his face turning crimson. 'Never mind. Anyway, point being, I don't expect you to remember her. Wish I didn't.'

'That bad, huh? How did you get rid of her in the end?' Louise bites her lip, cringing at her careless use of words. But, as Drew basically called her fat a second ago, she thinks she'll get away with her phrasing. She watches for his reaction. He keeps his eyes forward, but his jaw tightens, the clenched muscles visible. Whatever happened between them, he plainly hasn't let it go.

'Turns out she was a pathological liar.' His voice carries venom with what sounds like years of bitterness. Drew switches on the radio, signalling the end of the conversation, leaving Louise with a list of unasked questions swimming inside her head.

He didn't divulge how his girlfriend had left.

If she'd left at all.

Chapter 29

With her house in sight, and Drew indicating to turn into their road, Louise allows herself to mentally relax. The physical tension, though, is harder to relieve – although that's not all down to Drew. It's been building and building since Harriet's. She rubs the back of her neck, the muscles grinding and crunching beneath her fingertips. She hasn't pushed Drew further about his girlfriend's departure. A part of her doesn't want to provoke him while she and Alfie are trapped in his car – it's not as though she could merely jump out and escape at any sign of danger, leaving her son in the back with a man she suspects is capable of killing. Her curiosity can wait. And, given it has already got her into trouble once today, it's probably unwise to tempt fate.

Louise's pulse picks up when she's unable to spot Mark's car, though. She expected to see it. Was hoping he'd be home by now so he can meet them at the car, get Alfie out and carry him inside. Grateful to Drew for picking up his wife and son when he failed to.

'What time is it?' She cranes her head to see up ahead.

Maybe he had to park further away than usual. Parking on the street has become harder over the past year. One-car families becoming multi-vehicle families adds to the ever-increasing issue of space. Or lack thereof. That's why she's tucked her car away around the back of the cul-de-sac. The battery's probably flat from the car sitting unused for so long.

'Um, coming up for six.' Drew reverses into a space between two parked vehicles. Louise lets out a wince as the tyre squeals against the kerb. 'Out of practice,' he says, his focus flicking between the side and rear-view mirrors, his hands throwing the steering wheel this way and that to manoeuvre as the parking assist beeping grows louder and faster.

'I don't trust those things. Do you want me to get out and check how far you've really got?' Louise doesn't wait for a response. She flings the car door open and gets out. Standing at the rear of the Volvo, she beckons him to come back further, then taps the roof of the car when he's only an inch to spare. 'You're good,' she shouts.

Drew climbs out and joins Louise on the pavement. Standing side by side, Drew's arm gently touching her own as they both look into the car at an angelic, peaceful child, Louise considers that another part of her feels safe with him. Aside from the weirdness surrounding him spying on them from his back garden, and her own imaginings of what he's done with his ex, he hasn't given her cause to *fear* him. It's not like he's ever been aggressive with her, or physically intimidating. And wouldn't she get some kind of warning sign if he meant her any harm?

This is the most time she's ever spent with him – and she feels at least she's gained something from the journey, other than not having to battle with Alfie to walk all the way.

'Ahh. Seems a shame to wake him,' Drew says, his voice hushed.

'Oh, it absolutely doesn't.' She gives a gentle laugh. 'Trust me. He'll be a nightmare to get to bed – or he'll be wide awake at four in the morning.' She sighs. 'Maybe even both. Not fun.'

'Yeah, I've heard.'

'Oh, God. Have you?' Louise lowers her gaze. How embarrassing. It's easy to forget it works both ways. If she can hear noises from next door, it stands to reason he can hear them. 'Well, you'll know I'm not great at coping with sleep deprivation, then.'

'No judgement here, Louise.' He shuffles his feet, then cocks his head to make eye contact. 'I can carry him in for you, if you like. It'd be kinder to wake him gradually.'

Louise hesitates. Mark isn't home. Is it wise to allow him into their house? But . . . oh, what the hell. 'If you don't mind.'

She leans in and clicks the belt open, and gently removes Alfie's arms from the straps. He makes a little snuffling noise, like an animal being disturbed from its hibernation, but doesn't wake up fully.

'Lovely when they're like this. All innocent and angelic. Guess I'll never know this now.' Drew's face crumples, and for a moment, Louise thinks he's going to break down in tears. She lays a hand on his arm, but can't find the right words. He sucks in a breath and reaches in to lift Alfie.

'You've been a knight in shining armour today,' Louise says. 'Saved two maidens in distress.'

'I'm not so sure about that. But, thanks.'

After Drew pops Alfie on the sofa, then leaves, Louise calls Mark. It goes to voicemail again. 'Hi. It's me. Calling for the third time. Hope you're not out looking for us.' She gives a nervous laugh. 'Are you working late? Let me know.' After a slight hesitation, where she contemplates making a snarky comment, she hangs up and checks WhatsApp. The two ticks next to the message she sent remain stubbornly grey.

After nudging Alfie awake, Louise paces the conservatory, tapping her mobile against her thigh, mind whirring. She thinks again of the photo – should she talk to Mark about it when he finally returns? No, it's not enough. She shakes her head, tries to focus on Alfie. He's curled up on the sofa, his eyes wide and staring. Usually, that's a sign he's ready for bed, but having slept for about fifteen minutes in the car and another five once inside, Louise guesses she has about half an hour before he has his 'second wind'. Maybe it's wiser to put him up now, before that happens.

'Story time,' she says, scooping him up off the sofa. And, incredibly, he doesn't fight her, and he's asleep after one story. Louise switches the monitor on and tiptoes out of his room. There's still no sign of Mark when she looks out the kitchen window. Her chest fills with a bubble of anger. He might've at least sent a bloody text. Well, she won't be cooking tea for *him*. She rummages in the freezer, pulls out a frostbitten, ready-made meal likely to have been in there for over a year, and brushes off the iced snow. Chicken curry. That'll do. She bungs it in the microwave and after eight minutes, gives it a stir and plonks it out on a plate. It doesn't particularly resemble the picture on the cardboard packaging, but then they rarely do. She takes it into the lounge on a tray and devours it while watching *Selling Sunset*, trying to forget the day's events.

Afterwards, with still no word from Mark, Louise grabs her laptop for further distraction. She opens YouTube; perhaps some funny animal videos might help. But it's not long before the shock of what she found coupled with the burning shame of Harriet's rejection resurfaces. But, now she thinks about it, Harriet's behaviour was off too. If she saw Louise snooping, why not just say something? Or was it just Louise's questions about Jacob's birth that made her switch like that? Does she suspect something too?

Louise opens a new tab and googles Harriet's name. No personal social media accounts, but she finds her business one – Custom Kitchen Design. Louise scrolls through photo after photo of gorgeous bespoke kitchens on Instagram, fighting a surge of jealousy as she thinks of their small, fit-for-purpose kitchen. She's not sure what she's looking for, but she's not going to find it here.

She thinks of her diary entry about the alarms going off at the hospital, the same day Harriet was there, in the same ward. She searches Sommerby maternity unit and enters a few different terms. Nothing appears about that hospital, but there are news articles mentioning disrepair of hospital buildings due to lack of funding and basic care and attention. No surprises there. Strange how she doesn't recall the specific incident in SCBU happening, though. What else has she forgotten? She closes her eyes, bringing to mind the image of the birthmark in the photo. Might she have written about Alfie having been born with a birthmark in her diary?

She needs to read it again properly. If it reveals nothing, maybe she can let go of this once and for all, stop looking for excuses and focus on bonding with her son. And if it proves her theory then, well ... she doesn't want to think about what happens next.

With a glance at the monitor to make sure Alfie is still asleep, she goes to the kitchen to make a cuppa, then returns with it and the diary, sits in the low, comfy chair in the corner and starts reading from page one. Tears fall on to the paper, each drop spreading in slow, irregular blots. The ink beneath blurs and smudges. Louise dabs at them with the cuff of her sleeve. The things she's documented here seem brand-new to her. She's forgotten so much of those first hours without her baby after they whisked him away. And when she could finally hold him, she detailed her sense of disconnect from Alfie, how it felt different from what she'd imagined.

Then she gets to an entry already stained with tears, and her heart squeezes. She feels so sorry for the Louise in this diary, how she felt alone and afraid of how her body and mind were reacting to the birth of her baby. But it's more than that. It's like watching a horror film and seeing the danger before the character does. Knowing harm will come to them before they do. The unfolding story in Louise's baby diary was heading in a bad direction, and she instinctively knew they were about to enter a dark alleyway.

Louise reaches an entry written two days after she had given birth.

Strange thing – dreamt I was feeding Alfie, but when I looked down it wasn't him. I jolted awake, panic-stricken. But the baby was in my arms – so maybe I hadn't been dreaming. One of the SCBU nurses was sat with me. She said I fell asleep while breastfeeding, assured me it was common with sleep deprivation and that was the reason she'd stayed with me while I fed. She was so reassuring. I hate being here, though. Nothing feels right. Just want to go home.

Louise's heart drops like a rock thrown into a pool. Shit. What if it hadn't been a dream?

Who was the nurse? Louise can't remember her name.

Her lack of bonding with Alfie, her feeling as though something is missing – she's tried to put it all down to her faults, her inability to step into the role of mother – but what if it's *not* her? What if she just doesn't have the mothering instincts for Alfie because he's really *not* her flesh and blood? While she doesn't find any mention of the birthmark – and why would she, if they handed her Alfie from the start – there's enough here to ring alarm bells. There's only one way to be sure. Louise searches 'home DNA tests'.

It looks a simple enough process to do a home test for both maternity and paternity screening, but each would need to be done separately. For now, only maternity will be required. She has to find out if she's Alfie's biological mother first. From her brief research, she finds that the test involves a simple cheek swab from herself and Alfie. Should be relatively easy.

No upfront lab fee, just pay postage and the lab fee when you send the samples back.

Her trembling finger hovers over the proceed button. God. Why does it feel like she's betraying Mark? Going behind his back like this. It's such a mad idea; who even does a DNA test unless on the telly? But she owes it to herself and her family to get proof. If nothing else, to give her the peace of mind she needs to move on. Louise adds it to the basket, then hammers out the details of her address and payment option for the postage. It's a small enough amount to go unnoticed by Mark.

Once we process your order, your DNA testing kit will be sent via 1st Class Royal Mail.

Well, no going back now. It's for the best, Louise tells herself. Because, when the test is done, the truth will be unquestionable.

Chapter 30

MUMSTOGETHER

mummymootoo – 28/07 01:21
   Did you see the drama on here?
   reaches for the popcorn

Mummabear – 28/07 04:15
   Did someone get banned? Inappropriate contact or something.

mummymootoo – 28/07 04:34
   Yeah, they messaged a member privately. Broke community rules. Caused quite a stir

Mummabear – 28/07 05:40
   Can't see it now.

mummymootoo – 28/07 05:44
   Nope. Got deleted 😵

AMY CARVER

EMAIL

FROM AngelFace
SUBJECT URGENT

Thanks for swapping emails. We need to talk. Must be in person.

Chapter 31

Once she'd received the dispatch notification from the BioLab company, Louise hovered by the front door, anxiously awaiting the package to shoot through the letterbox. Then she bolted up the stairs to hide it in her bedside drawer before Mark could query what it was. Now, hearing the slam of the front door as he leaves for work, nausea grips her. If she's to carry out the test, this is the ideal time. But the weight of the guilt keeps her rooted. Her hands wring in her lap, conflicting thoughts surrounding the ethics of what she's going to do battling inside her head.

It's just a swab. It's not invasive, like a blood test. And I'm doing what's best for Alfie. For all of us.

'Mummy is just popping upstairs for two minutes; will you be okay?'

Alfie nods and pulls a truck from the toy box. Swiftly retrieving the DNA test, she runs back down to the conservatory and sits reading the instructions word by word. She can't afford to mess this up. Once she's committed the steps to memory, she performs the test on herself first. It's easy, a simple cheek swab, just as advertised. She can make this a bit of a game for Alfie, a promise of a treat, or say it's playing hospitals. She's not proud of herself; the twinge of guilt as she verbalises her lie grows when she pretends to conduct a test on his cuddly monkey first, intensifies as she then sweeps the swab inside Alfie's little mouth.

But it works. He allows her to do it without a fuss. With her hand still shaky, she places the swab on to the paper to dry and carries on with the next steps. She has to hope and pray Alfie forgets about it and doesn't say anything to Mark that might alert him to her betrayal. At least she'll have him in bed and hopefully asleep before Mark even gets home tonight. *Thanks, Brad.* Has to be the first time she's been grateful to Mark's shit of a boss for making him stay late again.

A rush of relief swoops through her when both samples are safely in their containers and packaged up. She stares at the padded envelope, takes a long, deep breath, then snatches it up and puts it inside her bag. It has to be sent today; she can't risk Mark finding it.

'Hey, Alfie,' she calls. 'Let's go to the park, shall we?'

He looks up from his toys, his little brow furrowed as though she's asked him a difficult question. 'Can I go on the swing?'

'Of course.' And Louise waits until he's in the buggy and they're out the front door before she adds, 'We're going into town to post something first.' There's a small post office round the corner, but with the local gossip as it is she's reluctant to go in there. It could fit directly into the post box, but she wants proof of posting in case there's any issue. She shudders at the thought of having to conduct another test if this one gets lost.

Her gaze skims the streets, nerves on edge, hoping she doesn't see anyone she knows. Getting into a conversation at this moment is the last thing she needs. She just wants the package gone. It's as if it's visible through her bag, that everyone will know what she's done. Maybe she *is* deluded.

Before she can dwell on this possibility, her attention is caught by a woman coming out of a café ahead of her. *Shit*. It's Harriet. She looks distracted as she strides along the pavement. Now's not the right time for a confrontation, so Louise quickly steers Alfie's buggy into the entrance of a charity shop to avoid her. From there, she cautiously peers out to check which way she walked.

Louise's breath catches as Drew steps out of the same café.

She retreats into the doorway again, her mind spinning with possibilities. Had he been *with* Harriet? Or is he following her? Louise watches, heart racing as Drew hesitates on the pavement, then heads up the hill. Is it just coincidence her neighbour was in the same café as Harriet? Part of her wants to run after her, ask if she knows Drew. She hesitates for so long that by the time she moves Harriet's too far ahead to catch up. And, after what happened, maybe it's a good thing.

Besides, she has a job to do. She mustn't allow herself to become sidetracked with conspiracy theories.

Chapter 32

Louise paces the conservatory, her phone gripped in one hand, knuckles blanched white. The notification pinged an hour ago – the email sits in her inbox, unread. She thought she'd open it immediately when it arrived. But, now that moment has come, her mind and body are awash with emotions she didn't expect, and the knot in her stomach intensifies with each step she takes. Aside from the guilt that's been eating away at her since she first ordered the DNA test and swabbed the inside of Alfie's cheek, a sense of dread now consumes her. What if it really is negative? What will that mean in reality?

She taps the phone against her chin as she does another circuit of the conservatory. Despite Alfie playing, all she can hear is her own heartbeat. 'Open the damn thing!' she mutters under her breath. With a churning in her stomach, she clicks on the new email. It feels like several seconds pass, time stretching as she waits to read the result. Her eyes flit over the words and she scrolls down, then back up. Nothing makes sense. The words are all muddled.

She closes her eyes, counts to five, then opens and reads it again.

> **Results inconclusive.**
> It is very rare for a maternity case to be inconclusive. However, occasionally we may detect a natural change in one of the DNA markers which means that it does not match as expected.

'What the hell does *that* mean?' Louise's legs fold beneath her and she collapses on to the beanbag. Inconclusive. Does not match as expected. She looks at Alfie, and her thoughts spiral. In reality, she'd expected a positive result – was ready to accept she'd overreacted. She swipes a hand over her forehead, carries out a frantic internet search, which only heightens her anxiety – *An inconclusive result is received when we are unable to confidently draw a conclusion from the similarities between the samples we have received*. In her mind, all it can possibly mean is that they aren't a match. The email doesn't state the samples were insufficient, or corrupted, and it doesn't say it was a lab error. Her breath comes in ragged gasps.

This was meant to be her turning point – the moment she could let it go. Dispel the voice in her head saying her baby was accidentally swapped at the hospital. But all she's achieved is the opposite. Her fear now backed up with science.

Alfie is not their child.

PART TWO

PART TWO

Chapter 33

Louise opens the wheelie bin lid and tosses the bunch of once soft pink, now crispy yellow-edged carnations inside. Mark's apology flowers had lasted over a week – surprisingly long for a late-evening garage purchase. He'd explained why he'd had to put work first, but his words had bounced off her. At that point, she'd been more concerned about what *she'd* done – ordering and performing a DNA test on herself and Alfie behind his back. And, since the inconclusive result, she'd thought about little else.

Should she tell Mark? Her chest tightens, and she puts a hand to it.

'It's not bin day today.'

Louise swings round. 'Oh, hey, Drew.'

'Looked like you were miles away there. You okay?'

Louise narrows her eyes. She's barely slept since the DNA test came back a few days ago. After the initial shock, she took a step back, told herself it wasn't categoric evidence that Alfie wasn't hers. But it certainly isn't evidence that he *is*. Nothing makes sense right now. There's a niggling feeling she's missing something vital. A key piece of information that would offer proof. But of course she can't share any of this with Drew.

'Fine, thanks,' she says finally. She thinks back to the café, where she saw him and Harriet. Should she ask him about it? But what's he going to say? It's a café in a small town where they both live – it means nothing really. But she feels an urge to scratch that itch, to solve at least one of the mysteries rattling around her head. 'Good to see you getting out more.'

He gives a confused look. 'Is that sarcasm?'

'No! Sorry, I mean, it was last week, during the day. And just a café in town, not like a night out or anything.' She gives a little laugh. 'Tried to catch up to you, but seemed you were on a mission.' She watches as his face crinkles and he shakes his head in denial. 'It was definitely you, Drew.'

'Probably just getting a takeaway coffee then. Like you do.'

She crosses her arms. He's not convincing her, and she's pretty certain he wasn't holding a cup when he left the café. Pressing him on it seems over the top, though.

'I can't remember the last time I had a decent coffee. Always too many other things to do when you have . . .' She trails off. It's a bit insensitive to talk about having kids when Drew shared his belief he'd never have the opportunity now.

'Kids? Yeah.' He gives a sad smile. 'Your Alfie must have a birthday coming up.'

'Yes. In two weeks, actually.'

'You know,' he says, gazing up, 'I remember it so well. You bringing the little fella home.'

'Oh, really?'

'All scrunched up in the car seat. Mark carrying it down the path, you following behind. You looked so ... *tired*.' Drew sucks in a breath, releases it slowly through pursed lips. He shakes his head. 'Everything changed after that day.'

Louise straightens. 'What do you mean?' She braces herself for Drew saying something about his life being disrupted by the crying baby, or her wailing in the early hours when she couldn't get Alfie to feed, or sleep. But he doesn't carry on. He turns and walks away, leaving her with her mouth agape. The vibration of her mobile interrupts the urge to run after him and demand to know exactly what had changed and why, and she retrieves it from her pocket. Her heart plummets.

Harriet's name shows on the caller ID. She rushes back inside, puts the mobile on the table and stares at it. It's been a week since Harriet threw her out of her house. Or that's how it'd felt, anyway. With each trill of the ringtone, each jolt across the table as it vibrates, Louise's pulse thuds harder.

Do I really want to face this? She pushes her fingertips into her temples, then lurches forward and grabs it, hitting accept before it goes to voicemail.

'Hey, Louise. Where has this week gone?' Harriet gushes.

A sense of relief, mixed with a nervous twist of anxiety, writhes through Louise's insides. Hearing Harriet's voice after thinking she'd blown their friendship is a welcome sound, but it also brings into blinding focus the enormity of what Louise suspects. Maybe she needs to distance herself from Harriet while she figures things out.

As she battles with the pros and cons, she realises she's missed much of what Harriet's been saying.

'Sorry, Harriet. Say again. Alfie distracted me.' Louise wrinkles her nose at the lie.

'I said, I've checked with Richard and he's fine about it.'

'Oh. Well . . . that's good of him.' Louise is glad this conversation is happening over the phone. At least she can hide her humiliation at having been caught snooping around his home office, although her voice carries enough shame. 'And you? I mean—'

'Well, of course *I'm* fine about it. It was my idea!'

And then the penny drops. This isn't about her entering the study. It's about the meal. After some backtracking on Louise's part, and the checking of calendars, they set the dinner date for two nights' time.

'I'll look forward to seeing you all,' Harriet says. 'Will be good to get together before the boys' birthday pool party. Given the men still haven't met.' Louise imagines Harriet giving her usual flick of the hand. 'And it's been a long week; I've missed seeing Alfie. As has Jacob, of course.'

A sudden, overwhelming instinct it won't end well presses down on her. What if Harriet suspects the same thing she does? That by some terrible coincidence their boys were mixed up in the special-care baby unit when the flood occurred. Is that why she took photos of Alfie? Because she's looking for similarities, too . . .

THE OTHER CHILD

Part of her brain screams at her to back-pedal and decline the meal invitation, say she's just realised she has an appointment or something. But a stronger instinct tells her that she needs to get back in that house, to see them all together in the same room. She needs to look Harriet in the eye and see if she suspects what Louise thinks she knows.

Chapter 34

Mark stands in front of Louise's wardrobe mirror, fiddling with his tie and muttering under his breath as he undoes it and starts again. He's taken longer to get ready than she did. Louise watches him from the doorway, Alfie by her side, swishing and pulling at her skirt as though it's the parachute canopy they have at playgroup.

'Surprised you haven't hired a tux,' she says jokingly. Mark's fingers stop moving, his arms dropping to his side. He turns to look at her.

'Meaning?'

Louise swerves the question, instead asking Alfie to stop swinging from her clothes. She knows Mark is nervous about meeting Harriet and Richard, and making a joke out of it isn't warranted. *She's* nervous, so isn't in a position to criticise. She too wants to make a good impression, despite already knowing them both, and bought the skirt especially for the occasion. Not a second-hand purchase, either. She doesn't share the reason behind her own keenness to impress. How she wants to appear normal – a good person. Not one who sneaks around in other people's houses; someone who can't be trusted.

After another ten minutes of fussing over their appearances, the three of them clamber into the car.

'Wave to your friend,' Mark says, throwing his hand up and waving madly towards Drew's house. 'He seems to still be keeping an eye on you.'

Mark pulls away, and Louise casts her gaze up as they pass, seeing Drew at his upstairs window. Watching them. Her skin tingles.

'I didn't say he was watching *me*,' she says, though that's exactly what she's been thinking. As if worried he can hear them, she puts her palm up towards Drew. He returns the gesture.

'Oh, so you don't think he's a creep who possibly murdered his girlfriend now?'

'Mark!' Louise turns sharply to look at Alfie, but he's oblivious. 'Please don't say stuff like that in front of him.'

'He doesn't know what we're talking about,' Mark retorts. He gives Louise a sideways glance. 'So . . . *do* you?'

Louise's mouth opens and closes soundlessly. Having got to know Drew better recently, she now finds it hard to believe he'd kill someone. But she still can't shake the feeling that he watches her too closely, that he's hiding something. Something stops her sharing this with Mark, though.

'Oh God, probably not. Just my imagination running wild!' she says with a forced laugh.

As the scene transitions from the dense cluster of cookie-cutter terraced housing estates to more open spaces and greenery, the vast lawns and driveways of the more exclusive detached houses appear. Louise's stomach knots, and she massages it with her hands. She swallows the rising acid, regretting now that she didn't have lunch.

'Any topics off the table?' Mark asks, breaking the silence in the car as he swings into the driveway with ease, as if he's done it many times before.

Louise stiffens. 'No. Why would there be?'

'No need to be defensive, Lou. I was just checking. I don't know what you have or haven't talked about.'

Louise apologises, blaming her abruptness on feeling nervous. Which is true. But the nerves aren't really about the meal. And there *are* off-limits topics, just as there are off-limits areas in Harriet's house. But she wants Mark to feel relaxed. He's good at talking to people, getting them to open up. Maybe he can get Harriet to share more.

Sucking in a deep breath, Louise unbuckles her seatbelt. Once out of the car, anticipation of the evening ahead makes Louise's legs go limp, and she has to put a steadying hand on the roof of the car. How will this go? The last time she saw Harriet, things had been frosty, to say the least. But she wouldn't have them round if she hadn't forgiven Louise, would she?

It's Richard who greets them, opening the door and making a sweeping motion with his arm as if he's inviting guests into Buckingham Palace. Not that Louise has ever been there. He's wearing a long-sleeved, casual-yet-stylish patterned shirt – the top buttons are undone, revealing a patch of fair chest hair – grey wool trousers and brogues.

Louise immediately side-eyes Mark, who looks more like he's turned up for a business meeting. He doesn't seem perturbed. Her mouth twists. She guides Alfie in first, and Richard says, 'All right, mate!' and ruffles his hair. 'You go ahead and find Jacob. He's in the playroom.' That poor child is always in the playroom, Louise thinks. Alfie beams up at Richard before running off. Then Richard turns his attention to Louise, and he grasps her upper arms and looks her up and down, visually appraising her. Louise's muscles tense, her throat constricts. Did Harriet tell him about her being in his office?

'Hi, Richard,' she says, forcing a smile.

Richard bends and leans in, kissing her lightly on each cheek. Something he's never done before. 'You look delightful, Louise. New skirt?' Louise's face reddens as she mutters a rambling response, but Richard's already let her go and is now welcoming Mark, extending his arm out to him, a warm grin spreading on his face. She steps back, watching as they shake hands. Mark's is overly firm, his shoulders stiff, jaw tight. He appears confident, though, not like he had earlier when he was fussing over his appearance. But then, she guesses, he's probably out to impress Richard and Harriet, too.

They move through the house towards the kitchen, Louise noting the look of awe on Mark's face as he sees the grandeur for the first time.

'Welcome, welcome!' Harriet says, arms opening wide to embrace Mark. 'I've heard so much about you.' Then she turns to Louise. 'You look *gorgeous*, Louise. How are you?'

She moves in for a hug, and, with the affection seeming genuine, Louise melts into her arms. The waft of Harriet's perfume transports her back in time to their first meeting at playgroup, and Louise remembers how Harriet approached her and made her feel seen. Normal. *Accepted*. But Louise pulls away, unable to let her guard down. There's so much uncertainty right now, and she senses the undercurrent of mistrust moving silently beneath the surface, aware there's a threat of her being sucked under. For a moment, it seems as though no one knows the next move – everyone has forgotten basic social skills – and an awkward silence sits heavily between them. Then Richard steps in, taking the reins.

'Right! Shall we sit?' He guides Louise and Mark through the kitchen, the aromas filling Louise's nostrils, towards the dining area. Louise has only glimpsed this area before, as they've spent most of their time in the main part of the kitchen or in the playroom. The table is beautifully set with flickering candles, sparkling glassware, and linen napkins elegantly folded into roses. Louise checks for signs that Harriet's had help to set this up but finds no evidence. How does she do it all? No one can be this perfect. Harriet must have flaws, though she hides them well. And, if she's this skilled at masking them, Louise wonders what else she could be hiding.

Louise and Mark sit at the table first and, while Harriet flits about in the kitchen, the sound of clanging plates echoing through the space, Richard fills two glasses with non-alcoholic drinks, 'for the driver and the chef', then wine for himself and Louise. The boys are called to the table, and Richard tells them to choose where they want to sit. Louise watches on curiously as Jacob immediately sits next to Mark. Alfie makes a fuss, also wanting to sit next to his daddy.

Louise pats the chair next to her. 'You can be next to me,' she says. She might've guessed his response, which is a resounding *no*. 'Okay, love,' she says, her voice clipped. 'You've probably seen enough of me today.' Louise gives an awkward laugh and glances around at the men.

'Kids are so funny sometimes, aren't they?' Richard says, taking his spot at the head of the table. 'It's all or nothing, I find.'

'What's all or nothing?' Harriet says, swooping in with a plate in each hand.

'Attention,' Richard says, without adding context.

'Oh. Yes. I agree.' She puts the plates in front of the boys.

Louise shifts in her chair. 'I feel awful sitting here doing nothing, Harriet. Can I help?'

'No, no. You're our guests! Stay put.'

After Harriet has brought in all the plates, she sits next to Louise and makes a toast, holding her glass of water up high.

'To new adventures, and new friends,' she says, and they repeat it with added vigour. 'Now, tuck in! I didn't sweat over the oven all day for you to just look at it.'

'Women don't sweat, dear—'

'They glow,' Harriet finishes. 'Yes, yes – so you say. Well, that'll be your little secret, my love.'

'Oh, really? I thought secrets were your domain, darling.' He laughs, as though to prove he's joking, but Harriet's terse 'Ha ha, you're funny' comeback is incongruous.

'This is delicious,' Mark pipes up, barely understandable with his mouth full. He's done it to stop the awkwardness, Louise guesses. She wishes he hadn't, because it was getting interesting. An insight into Harriet and Richard's relationship – a peep into their real life behind the glamorous façade. Aside from a few fleeting moments, she's not really seen them together before. There's a definite edge to the atmosphere.

The food is good, but Louise struggles with each mouthful. She is hungry, the growling noises attest to that, but her tummy squirms and she's afraid she'll regurgitate what she eats right here at the table. She senses something odd between Harriet and Richard. He's certainly not as relaxed as she's seen him on previous occasions. Mark is doing the thing he does when he's nervous – the twitchy smile, the jerky hand movement when he's talking. And what's with that *laugh*? Every time Harriet says anything, even if it's not remotely humorous, he roars; his chin tilting up, his mouth wide as if he's been told the funniest joke ever. He's *flirting*. He won't admit it. If Louise were to bring it up later, he'll deny it, saying he was being polite.

Maybe he is. It's been such a long time since they've socialised like this that they're both out of practice.

Louise gives a little shake of her head. Pushes some pasta on to her fork and glances at Jacob. He catches her eye and smiles, his little nose wrinkling, and under the glow of spotlights above the dining table, she sees a tiny dimple appear in his chin. Louise suppresses a gasp, her gaze snapping to Mark. It's like looking at a mini-me version. Even their eyes have the same brown hue, the fleck of green. Then she looks at Richard, at his thick, wavy hair and blue eyes. More like Alfie's than his own son's. She becomes lost in the tumbling thoughts – further suspicions mounting, the evidence staring her in the face.

'Isn't that right, Louise? Lou!' Mark's voice jolts her from her thoughts, and she plasters on a smile. 'I was telling Harriet that you were also planning to go back to work. Just to try it out, see how you get on.'

Louise purses her lips at his condescending tone, but chooses not to make a fuss, instead relaying the plan Harriet already knew. After all, she was the one who encouraged Louise in the first place, providing the push needed to broach the subject with Mark.

'I'm surprised, actually, Harriet,' she says, a sudden burst of curiosity nudging her, 'that you aren't putting Jacob into a private nursery. Remind me again, why didn't you?'

'I can answer that,' Richard butts in. 'It's because of me.'

Harriet raises her eyebrows, puts her elbows on to the table. 'This'll be good,' she whispers to Louise.

'Didn't want a child of mine being brought up in an unrealistic environment.'

'Unrealistic?' Mark asks.

'Yes. Life isn't like that, is it? You don't learn if you only mix with your own kind.' His eyes flit towards Louise. 'You need to experience the entire spectrum of people from other classes. Don't you agree?'

Louise inhales sharply, her shoulders tensing. 'Um –' she fiddles with the stem of her glass – 'I'm not sure I understand what you're getting at.' She takes a slug of wine.

'Richard, for Christ's sake,' Harriet says, her hands splayed. 'Things to avoid at social gatherings one-oh-one. Who wants pudding?' And, at the delighted squeals from the boys, she pushes her chair back and starts collecting the dinner plates.

'Please, let me.' Louise doesn't wait for a response and follows suit. She snatches Richard's plate from him, smiling sweetly. 'I know my place.'

As she walks behind Harriet towards the kitchen, she hears Mark's voice, low and apologetic. She doesn't catch his words, but she knows he'll be telling Richard something along the lines of 'excuse Lou, she had a challenging upbringing and has always felt unworthy. She's been overly sensitive since having Alfie . . .'

'Men, eh?' Harriet bumps her elbow against Louise's, and it's like the first time they met again. 'So insensitive. Richard couldn't read a room if his life depended on it. I'm sorry if he made you feel uncomfortable.'

Louise takes a deep breath, exhaling slowly through her pursed lips, creating a steady release of air. Smiles. 'No worries. I'll try not to take it personally.'

'Good. Ignore him. Sometimes he's a bit of a dick. We often clash over the best way to bring up our son.'

Louise doesn't disagree. As Harriet dishes out trifle,

sprinkling a hefty amount of chocolate drops on top of the whipped cream for the kids, Louise has a sudden thought. 'Is that why Richard agreed to the pool party, too? Because he wants Jacob to mix with the local riff-raff so he *learns* from them? I'm not sure his strategy is sound, Harriet.'

Louise starts at Harriet's eruption of laughter. Harriet claps a hand over her mouth, suppressing a further outburst. Tears of amusement well up in her eyes and her hand drops.

'Oh, dearest Louise. That's funny. When I found you, I'd no clue I'd like you so much.' Harriet takes a bowl in one hand, balances another in the crook of her arm, picks up a third, then leans in close. 'And don't be fooled. I only let Richard *think* he's the one making the decisions.' She struts away, calling back for Louise to bring the other two bowls.

When Louise sits down, she's taken aback by the shift in Mark's body language. He's taken his tie off and with an arm slung over the back of the chair, legs sprawling, he's in his relaxed mode. It's how he is after having a few whiskeys. Clearly, Richard has put him at ease, and suspicion prickles over Louise's skin. What did they talk about while she was in the kitchen?

Harriet sits with her elbows on the table, watching as everyone but her eats the pudding. Louise cringes when Mark says, 'Surely you don't need to worry about calorie-counting,' and Harriet waves her hand, brushing off the compliment. Louise's grip tightens round her spoon, the whipped cream clogging her throat as she swallows a mouthful, washing it down with a gulp of wine.

'You don't have a dairy allergy, do you?' Louise asks,

recalling the phone conversation when Harriet asked her about allergies.

'No. No dairy intolerance.'

'Just an intolerance for fat people,' Richard says with a snort of laughter. Then, his expression becomes more serious. 'And a fear she'll end up like her father.'

Sighing, Harriet shares how her dad had dementia, seizures and hallucinations resulting in his death. 'They classed it as dementia and he was already hospitalised, so there was no postmortem. Had there been, I'm certain they'd have found the real reason.' She says she did her own research into his symptoms, her findings convincing her it'd been a genetic brain disorder where the body was unable to metabolise fats.

'It's ridiculously rare, but she's obsessed she's inherited it. I pay a small fortune to put her mind at ease every month.'

'Yes, and I'm so grateful, Richard. As you should be that we have a healthy son because of my *obsession*.'

Richard snaps his mouth closed, having been firmly put in his place by his wife, and Harriet continues to explain about wanting regular check-ups.

'I ensure I have monthly MRIs as a precaution,' she says with a shrug, then turns sharply to Richard. 'Something *you* should be doing, Richard.'

Mark starts talking about the importance of physical and mental health, with Harriet nodding along and agreeing. Why is this beginning to feel like a real-time personal snub? Louise is right back to being excluded, the way she was before when watching the fun mums from afar, feeling as though she'd never fit in. Only now it's far worse as her own husband is in on it; she can't even get a word in. Louise wants to direct the conversation back to find out more about Harriet's health concerns, but there's a commotion as the kids start whingeing and the opportunity passes.

The boys begin to clamber down from the table to head back to the playroom – but, exerting some control, Louise pipes up that they need to ask for permission before leaving the table – it's manners. But Mark doesn't back her up, dismissing her command by telling her not to be so strict – they're just toddlers. Louise's mouth sets in a tight line.

'Fine.' She sits back in the chair, her spine rigid. Eyes are on her. She needs to be careful not to appear like a sulky teenager. Once the boys have left, she quickly changes the subject, asking Harriet which days Jacob will be in nursery. Harriet controls her voice, but Louise sees the emotion in her eyes. She's torn. As most mothers are, she suspects, about leaving their children and returning to the workplace. There's something more, though. An emptiness Louise hadn't caught before.

'I'm not going back until after Jacob's birthday.'

'You don't *need* to go back at all, Harriet,' Richard says.

A conversation about the merits of women in employment ensues, but Louise's focus drifts. Mark's doing the annoying thing where he's virtue-signalling. Not sure why he's bothering going up against Richard. They have money, she and Mark don't. It's as simple as that. Their viewpoints are bound to differ.

Louise hears Richard use the phrase 'a woman should

bring up her own child' and is immediately back in the room. These men both know the challenges Harriet and Louise have been through. Why are they talking this way?

'So, what you're saying is, even those who've suffered with post-natal depression should stay at home, cooped up all day—'

'Louise, love,' Mark says, pressing his hand over hers. 'You've missed the intervening conversation. You don't know the context.' Louise's face flushes with heat.

'Okay, okay.' She puts her hands up. 'Well, if you'll excuse me for a moment, I've overeaten, I think I need some air.' They don't bat an eye, their conversation continuing as before. Louise's legs wobble a little when she gets up. 'Maybe a trip to the bathroom first,' she mutters, and heads out through the kitchen.

Louise brushes up against the large American-style fridge as she passes and a Post-it note from the magnetic family organiser sticks to her shoulder. She snatches it angrily from her top as she walks towards the corridor, but doesn't read it until she's sitting on the loo. It's a list of playgroup names – the first three are crossed out, and Rainbows, the one they're at now, is circled with one name beneath remaining untouched. Harriet mentioned she'd tried the playgroup next to the library, but it seems she'd tried them all, up until the one where they met. Why hadn't she tried the final one? Is it because she'd found what she was looking for at Rainbows?

Louise turns the Post-it over and her heart lurches at the two words: *He's here.*

Louise's breathing shallows. The evidence she's found so far loops in her mind: the way they look, the bond, Alfie being mistaken for Harriet's child at playgroup. And God, now she thinks about it, Harriet's reaction to that was really over the top – and the photos Louise found of Alfie on Harriet's phone. The DNA result ... And what had she said in the kitchen earlier? *When I found you, I'd no clue I'd like you so much.*

Louise had believed their first meeting was down to luck. But maybe it wasn't a coincidence at all. Had Harriet tracked her down? With a jolt, Louise thinks of Drew, the way he watches her. The café. Could he and Harriet know each other? Has he been keeping an eye on her *for* Harriet? She's dizzy, nauseous. What does Harriet know? And what the hell is she planning?

She steadies herself, makes her way back to the others. 'It's getting late,' she tells Mark. 'I think it's time to leave. Why don't you go and get Alfie?'

A splash of concern passes between Harriet and Mark. *What was that?*

After a round of thank yous and goodbyes, Harriet says she'll get Jacob ready for bed while Richard sees them out. Jacob runs to the door, calling bye-bye and waving.

'I thought you were going to bed,' Louise says. He propels himself forward, his body crashing against her thighs, and as she ducks down to his level, he throws his arms around her and buries his face in her shoulder. 'Well, thank you. What a lovely hug.' Louise smiles, and a wave of emotion crashes and breaks inside her as she holds him. The warmth of his body soothes her, and when he steps back his eyes lock with hers. Her breath hitches. There's such trust in them. Like a child who knows they're safe in the knowledge their mother will do anything for them.

When Louise stands again, Harriet's right there, watching. Her expression ice-cold.

Chapter 35

They take the exact route home from Harriet's that Drew took Louise and Alfie. Louise remembers thinking he was abducting them, or something equally dramatic, and a knot presses against her ribs. Is she just prone to melodrama? Considering her recent behaviour, the evidence certainly suggests she might be. Anyone else would think she's lost it. She looks at Mark, at his side profile. Would he think she was nuts if she told him what's been going on? Turning to the backseat, Louise gazes at Alfie, his eyelids fluttering closed. She opens her mouth to say something, encourage him to stay awake. But, actually, it serves her better if he sleeps. She needs to talk to Mark without him listening.

'You were quick to take Richard's side at the dinner table in front of everyone.'

'I'm sorry, Lou. I shouldn't have called you out like that,' Mark says without hesitation. Louise is taken aback at the speed of this apology. 'It was just an awkward situation, and you seemed to want to fuel the fire.'

'I felt really embarrassed.'

'Is that why you wanted us leave so abruptly?'

Louise sucks in a breath. Should she share her suspicions now? 'The evening had run its course, I think. And to be honest, something felt ... *off*.' She bites down on her lip, then continues. 'Probably just me; I'm exhausted.'

'Obviously I don't know them like you do, but I didn't get that. They seem nice.'

'Yeah.' Louise waits a beat. 'Did you spot how Jacob's chin has a little dimple when he smiles? And the way he gives that little shrug?'

'He's a cutie, all right. Like our boy is.'

'Yes, of course. Jacob's hair, though. It's fine, isn't it? Like yours and mine.'

A dark shadow descends on Mark's face. 'Lou. What are you getting at?' His voice brims with uncertainty.

'You must've noticed them, too, right? The similarities. Like his eye colour. It's not the same as Harriet and Richard's, is it?'

Mark tilts his head, his eyebrow arching. 'I don't know, Lou. I can't say I looked that closely.'

She sighs, sensing that she's going to have to detail her suspicions or at least explain her concerns about Harriet. Telling him how she's tested their son's DNA without his knowledge would not be a good idea.

'I think something went very wrong while we were in the special-care baby unit after having Alfie.'

'What? What do you mean?'

'I've found things – *concerning* things, Mark. And I'm worried about Harriet's intentions.'

'You're not making sense. I thought she was your new best friend, and now—'

'I think our babies were swapped,' she blurts out. 'And I think Harriet suspects the same, but somehow she knew about it before me and tracked us down. I've no idea what she's planning to do about it, and frankly I don't know what to do about it either. I—'

'Jesus, Lou! Really?' Mark cuts her off, slamming his hands on the steering wheel. He mutters a few incoherent words before taking a deep breath. She gives him a few seconds to compose himself, although this news will take longer to sink in, she's sure.

'Lou,' he says, shaking his head, 'can you actually hear what you're saying?'

'Oh, here we go.'

With as much composure as she can muster, Louise rattles through her 'evidence', though without the DNA test result, even she can hear how flimsy it is. Mark remains calm, hears her out. Maybe she's getting through to him after all?

'Louise, love,' he says when she's finished, more gently this time. 'All of this – it's just a coincidence, *barely* even that. This is just ... *mad*. You must be able to see that? Remember what Natalie said, about the depression clouding your judgement? Making it hard to separate fantasy from reality?' Heat soars through her, frustration building as he explains it all away, finally saying what she'd feared the moment she voiced her suspicion.

'I think it would be good if you made an appointment with her, or maybe the doctor. I can make the call tomorrow.'

'No, Mark. I don't need a fucking counsellor. I need my husband to listen to me.'

'Oh, I am listening, Louise. I really am.' His calm demeanour fades, his voice notching up a tone.

'Then why are you telling me to see my therapist?'

'You just told me you think our babies were *swapped*, Louise! Why do you think? You've been obsessed with Harriet since you met her and, what, now you think Jacob's your kid? Do you want to *swap* him with Alfie, our actual son?'

'That's not ... Don't be absurd, Mark. I want to *protect* Alfie. I told you, I think Harriet knows – I think she always has!'

'Maybe it's best you don't see Harriet and Jacob for a while.'

'What? No.' Louise decides to try a different tack. 'You've seen how much better Alfie is since playing with Jacob. And Harriet's become a friend—'

The loud scoff from Mark stops her dead. 'Friends, Louise? Is that what Harriet is? Because – if I'm getting this right from what you're saying – you believe she's a threat. So why would you even *want* to see her again?'

Louise knows she's blown it. She's come across the exact opposite to how she intended and, deep down, she knows he's right. The most sensible thing would be to cut ties with Harriet, get back to her life and learn how to move forward with Alfie. But if she does that she'll never find out the truth. Pain shoots through her chest. It'll mean not seeing Jacob any more, too. The thought brings tears to her eyes.

'Okay, look, I'm sorry. You're right. Of course you're right. I've had too much to drink and I just ... It must be the depression talking. But please, please don't ruin Alfie's birthday because of me.'

'What do you mean?'

'The pool party. I told you. Harriet's organising it as a joint birthday for the boys. You know, because they were born on the *same day*.' Louise screws up her eyes. 'Alfie hasn't stopped talking about it. Please don't let him suffer because of me.'

Mark rolls his shoulders, his jaw relaxing slightly. But his grip on the steering wheel remains tight.

'I promise to make an appointment with Natalie.' She leans closer to him, trying to read his expression. His focus is on the road. 'Besides, after the party, I won't see Harriet and Jacob much anyway. The kids will be at the nursery and Harriet's going back to work ...'

'True. How many others will be at this pool party?'

'Oh, quite a few. Mostly the mums from playgroup. I'm not going to cause a scene, Mark!'

Louise draws in a breath, holding it as the pause stretches.

'Fine,' he says with a huff. 'But only if you give me your word you'll stop this nonsense.'

She exhales softly, the air whispering through her lips, and nods. What's another lie among so many?

Because Alfie slept for all of five minutes in the car, he's wide awake now – refreshed and ready to play again. Mark's sitting on the floor beside him, building a tower of bricks as tall as Alfie. Louise watches them like she's a stranger on the outside, peering into a world that isn't hers. Her lack of emotion, dulled senses, remind her of when she was on the anti-depressants. She knows she needed them, and everyone is sure they helped her, but she prefers experiencing an array of feelings and reactions. Even if they're extreme. She'd tapered off the medication exactly as her doctor instructed. Well, give or take.

Had she done so too soon?

They said it was time. It was safe, because they were happy about the progress she'd made.

Because you lied.

Closing her mind to the voice, Louise backs away from Mark and Alfie and slips into the lounge. She goes to the bookcase and picks up the white-framed photograph of the three of them. Everyone – with the exception of Sue – says Alfie looks like Mark, but she doesn't see it. And there's no resemblance to her. Only their hair colour is the same.

Because Alfie isn't yours.

She replaces the photo, and, while Mark is occupied playing with Alfie, seizes the chance to nip upstairs. She grabs her laptop and sits cross-legged on the bed, biting her thumbnail as she awaits the start-up process. Drums her fingers while glancing furtively towards the door. 'Jesus, this thing is ancient.' Finally, the Windows sound plays, and her homepage appears. It's another age before the internet connects and, with a shaky hand over the keyboard, she goes into the DNA account she made. Her heart stutters. Thoughts whizz through her mind, guilt swelling in her belly once more. If she really did find out her baby was swapped, what did she want to happen? Is Harriet going through the same thing? Is it possible she's only trying to gather evidence, too?

She could confront Harriet – ask her outright why she orchestrated their first meeting, why she's been keeping tabs on her— 'Oh, my God.' Louise freezes, the sudden realisation hitting her. Was Harriet the one who took Alfie from outside the butcher's? Louise mentally flits through her memory bank. *The lollipop.* After she came to, Alfie had the lollipop. She'd assumed the butcher gave it to him, but when they went to Harriet's the first time Alfie had immediately asked her for a lollipop. Had he linked the two, recognising her as the woman who gave it to him? Surely Harriet didn't intend to *kidnap* him? Louise runs her hands roughly through her hair. She's allowing her imagination to run wild. But she's sure suddenly that *someone* took him – for all her problems, she's never hallucinated. And buggies don't just disappear into thin air. With what she knows now, Harriet is the obvious suspect. Maybe she got cold feet at the last moment, quickly wheeling the buggy into the shop and disappearing.

What if Harriet is more dangerous than she thinks? If Louise confronts her and Harriet denies it, it wouldn't be difficult for Harriet to make Louise look mad, to paint her as an unfit mother. Mark already thinks she's lost it – he said as much earlier tonight. If she gains hard evidence, though, it will be different. She doesn't want to lose Alfie, but what if Harriet's planning on taking him from her anyway?

She has to at least try to control the narrative. She needs another DNA test.

She knows now that Mark will be livid if he finds out. He'll probably run straight to her mother and together they'll have her sectioned or something. Louise opens the bank app on her phone – grimaces at the digits, the overdraft nearing its limit. Christ. She hasn't looked at their joint account since she paid for the first DNA test; she's surprised she got away with the purchase given the state of it. But another minimal post and packing cost shouldn't be flagged. Louise adds a maternal DNA test to her basket. But this time she'll swab her and *Jacob*. The only opportunity she'll get to do it is at the pool party.

Almost there.

She hesitates as Mark's voice drifts up to her, sounding louder as he moves closer. Footsteps tread on the stairs. There's no time for hesitation.

Click.

Louise slams the laptop lid down and tucks it underneath the duvet just as the bedroom door handle depresses. At least she's ordered it. She can work out how to get the money for another lab test later. Maybe this time she'll tell Mark she needs something for Alfie's birthday. He wouldn't look too closely at the bank statement then.

'Lou?' Mark's face appears round the door.

She pretends to be transfixed by her fingers as they make circular motions, tracing the pattern on the duvet cover.

'You're not sulking, are you?'

Louise looks up, shakes her head. 'No.'

'Hmm,' he says, his eyes narrowing with scepticism. 'You're not convincing me. I've only got your best interests at heart, you know. You'll feel better once you've had some space from them.'

It takes Louise a moment to realise he means Harriet and Jacob, her head full of DNA tests and deceptions. She must make an effort to appear normal.

'I know. Thank you, you know, for not going ballistic.' She shrugs in an effort to appear embarrassed by her earlier outburst, as if it were just a moment of madness. Picking your battles is something Natalie has suggested in the past – mostly regarding Alfie, but it works with Mark, too. For now, the fact he agreed to let them still go to the joint birthday pool party will have to do.

'Okay, then. Well, come downstairs. Spend time with your family.'

Louise flinches. 'Be with you in two mins,' she says, a faint blush creeping into her cheeks. He leaves, and her posture sags. She's doing the right thing, isn't she? Burying her head in the sand is detrimental to her mental health – hasn't she been told that multiple times? She's doing something about her suspicions – acting by finding the evidence that will either confirm or refute her theory. Whatever the result, she promises herself, she'll move forward. Whether that means finally putting to rest her feelings of disconnect with Alfie, accepting that they are nothing more than a psychological barrier, or ... *God*, the alternative makes her lungs freeze. If Alfie is indeed Harriet's child, won't she have to start the ball rolling by going to the authorities? What will that mean for Alfie?

Louise presses a hand over her heart. They all deserve to learn the truth. She'll decide what to do about that truth when it comes.

Chapter 36

It feels as though a week has passed, not just two days. Louise spent them moping around the house, not really present. The dispatch email for the new test had popped up last night, and last time it arrived the day after, so it should come today. It's seven a.m. and she's barely slept. All night, different scenarios ran through her head and none of them ended in a satisfactory way. How could they? Her eyes are puffy; every muscle hurts from holding herself so rigidly. But adrenaline floods her system and her skin tingles with anticipation with the knowledge she's going to push forward. Because, if she doesn't, Harriet might. Louise needs to be first.

She stands at the kitchen window, a lukewarm coffee in her hands. She's half listening to Alfie naming his toys as he lines them up on the table, while keeping an eye on the path for the postie. She hasn't taken a sip for ten minutes, afraid she'll miss the telltale blur of red. Movement spotted in her peripheral vision makes her nerves jump and she dives forward, spilling milky-brown liquid on her T-shirt.

'Damn.' She looks down at the trickle of brown on the pale yellow and sighs. The mess isn't even worth it because it turns out to be Drew walking past. It's early for him to be out and about. And his sister's car seems to have gone. Or he's parked it elsewhere. She wonders what's happened on that front.

The clatter of the metal letterbox rings out, startling Louise from her thoughts. The splat of letters hitting the mat propels Alfie into action, too, and he's out of the room, heading for the front door like an excited puppy before she has time to register what's happening. In a rush to beat him to the door, she leaps over him and almost knocks him over and he cries out in frustration. This isn't how it usually works; she always lets him get the post because he enjoys it. No doubt he's wondering why Mummy is suddenly in competition with him. She's behaving like she's in a scene from *The Hunger Games*. But, as she scoops up the mail, her energy ebbs. There's no package.

'Not seen you that eager to get the post before. Expecting something exciting?' Mark's hurrying down the stairs, tying the knot of his tie as he goes.

'Nope, just playing,' she says, passing the junk post and leaflets to Alfie and bending to give him a hug. Alfie takes the proffered peace offering, but his entire body stiffens when Louise puts her arm around him. It's a deserved rebuttal, but Louise takes it a step further in her head.

He doesn't want me.

Hot tears prick the back of her eyes, and she squeezes past Mark on the stairs, taking two steps at a time, and locks herself in the bathroom. She closes the toilet lid, sits down on it and holds her head in her hands. What is she doing? Mark's words from the other evening echo inside her skull: *You've been obsessed with Harriet since you met her.* Maybe he's right. Maybe she just wants Harriet's perfect, polished life.

'You coming down to eat breakfast?' Mark hollers up the stairs. Louise yells back, but before joining them in the kitchen, she goes to her bedside table drawer, unearths her diary and journal. She's not mad, or obsessive – she's basing it all on the evidence.

It's circumstantial. If it comes to it, she'll need hard evidence to take to the police.

'Louise! I have to go.'

'Yes, all right,' she calls. 'Bloody hell.' She takes a deep breath and closes the drawer. Whatever she does now, she knows she has to keep it on the down-low. Be even more secretive than she's been already.

'I'll be late tonight,' Mark says, giving her a hasty peck on the cheek, his eyes averted.

'How come?' Usually, she'd just nod and agree, say 'sure'. But today, his declaration feels off.

'Brad *insisted* on a meeting after work. Doesn't want to pay us for having it in his time, as per. Bloody cheek. Anyway, see you around seven? Go ahead and put Alfie to bed. Don't wait for me.'

Louise's mouth twists to one side. She's about to question him further, but her mobile rings and she leaves him to go in search of it.

'In the kitchen,' Mark calls over his shoulder as he disappears out the front door.

Louise makes a dash for the kitchen, finding her phone on the dish drainer. She doesn't remember leaving it there. Has Mark been looking through it? She picks it up, groans at the name displayed. Her head lolls back, and she closes her eyes.

'Phone call,' Alfie says. 'Phone call for Mummy.' He pretends to pick up an imaginary phone, and Louise gives a half-smile.

'Yes, it's Granny.' Louise holds the mobile at arm's length, like it's at risk of exploding.

Alfie chants, 'Gran-nee, Gran-nee,' until Louise gives in and answers.

'Hey, Mum. How are you?'

'Oh, you wouldn't believe what a week I've had …'

Louise's brain shuts down. Not even a 'Hello, Louise', before she set off on her rant this time. Charming. She puts the phone on loudspeaker, but turns down the volume, and props it up on the dish drainer while she tidies up the breakfast things, her mother's drone blurring into the background.

It's not until the word 'police' that Louise's attention is caught.

'Sorry, missed that, Mum. Say again?'

'Oh, love – don't you ever listen? I said, poor Janet – the whole dog incident. Police looked at the Ring whatsit footage and they think the white van did knock poor Truffles over. Not a nice man, by all accounts …'

'So, who *is* he?'

'I told you, dear. Someone living along Janet's street. Been in all sorts of trouble, it seems. GBH, ABH, all the acronyms . . .'

'Is he married?'

'Well, I don't know. Why is that relevant?'

'Just wondering. Could you find out? Maybe check with Janet – see if she can find out their names.'

'Detective now, are we? I suppose it must get rather boring being at home all the time.'

'Actually, I'm going back to work soon.' The words are out of her mouth before she's considered the backlash.

'Oh, *darling*. Do you think that's wise? Mark said you're acting very oddly again. Perhaps you need more recovery time.'

Louise's heart stutters. Mark didn't waste any time grassing on her, did he? What else did he disclose? The alarm on her phone rings. 'Got to go, Mum. Alfie will be late for playgroup. Bye now.'

'Remember to call your therapi—'

Louise swipes the mobile from the drainer, stabbing at the red button, her brow furrowed. Between Sue and Mark, her family really knows how to push her to her limits. Instead of allowing her mum's words to set her up for a bad day, Louise does some measured, mindful breathing, followed by some reassuring self-talk: 'Do not let her take your control. *I* am in control.' She closes her eyes. 'Not much longer until she'll be off on another cruise and out of your hair.' When she opens them, Alfie is in front of her, looking up, his lips pouty. 'Oh, hello, little man. Sorry, Mummy was miles away, then. You ready?'

'What's in your hair?' He cocks his head on one side, his eyes curiously interrogating her head, and Louise laughs.

'Oh, just some tangles. I can get rid of those easy enough.'

Seeming to be satisfied with her answer, Alfie walks off and goes to the shoe rack, pulls his blue trainers from it, then sits on the bottom stair, waiting for Louise to put them on him.

'Progress,' she says, bending down and popping them on without a battle. 'Are you looking forward to playgroup?'

He shrugs. 'I guess,' he says. Louise raises her eyebrows, smiles.

'That's good.' She hasn't heard him use the phrase before. He's picking up so much lately. His vocabulary is really coming on. Seeing as he's in a calm mood, Louise doesn't mention it's one of the last stay-and-play sessions. She and Mark have read some stories about nursery to help prepare him for the transition. But, in all honesty, Louise doesn't think it'll bother him if she's not there. He rarely comes up to her or wants her to help him or play with him – he's pretty independent in that way. Apart from Jacob, though, he hasn't warmed to any of the other children. And it's Jacob's last session with them today.

Louise blinks away tears. She's not sure who will miss Jacob more – Alfie, or her.

Chapter 37

EMAIL

FROM AngelFace
SUBJECT Next step

So pleased we had that chat! Have you thought any more about what I said? You know I'm coming from a place of kindness, don't you? I've been where you are. It's lonely. Our men don't fully understand – how can they? WE'RE the ones who grew another human inside of us. WE'RE the ones who pushed them out of our bodies. WE'RE the ones to suffer when things go wrong.

It's down to US to protect our babies, no matter what. I don't know about you, but I'd do ANYTHING for my boy.

Chapter 38

Louise spots Harriet striding towards the playgroup, practically dragging Jacob, who's trailing at least two steps behind. Before Louise can say anything, they go past her, with barely a smile directed her way. And Harriet continues on, right past the playgroup entrance. Louise's heart misses a beat. She's going to the other door – to the nursery side. Louise frowns, then notes Harriet's smart skirt and tailored jacket – and how her face is set into a stern, stressed expression. Not how she usually rocks up here.

'Oh!' Louise says involuntarily, then snaps her mouth closed again. At dinner the other night, Harriet said she wasn't going back to work until *after* the boys' birthday party. But, clearly, she is. Why the change of plan? Louise hurries after her. 'Harriet! Hey – wait up. I wanted to thank you for a—'

'Morning. Can't stop to chat.' Harriet disappears inside with Jacob, leaving Louise standing, blinking as though she's just seen something unbelievable. She turns to Alfie, who looks equally confused. She hadn't planned on making a thing of it today, but now circumstances have forced her hand.

'You'll be going there, too, soon. But today, we get to play together. Okay?' She turns, leading Alfie into the hall, a heaviness dragging her down. Mark has got his way. With Harriet at work and Jacob in nursery from today, she won't be seeing much of either of them. The fun mums are a member down. Should Louise try to step into Harriet's shoes? Heat rises to her face. Like that's even possible.

The sinking feeling that Harriet will take back her offer of the shared birthday party doesn't leave her all session. She'll text Harriet later, confirming times, or something. See what she says.

Leaving playgroup before the other mums, Louise pushes the buggy at high speed, desperate to get home and check what's happening with the parcel. According to her app, it should've been delivered. Maybe it came late, or via a different courier. She's on the home straight, her legs aching from rushing, and almost at her path when Drew steps out in front of her, putting his hand out like he's stopping traffic.

'Acronyms,' he says. Then pauses. Louise comes to a halt, panting, and cocks an eyebrow, waiting for the question she assumes is following. Drew looks down at a scruffy-looking notebook in his hands. 'You ever heard of E-D-D?'

Louise transfers all her weight on to one leg, tucks a loose strand of hair behind her ears and lets her breath return before responding. 'Got anything else to go on? I mean, in what context?'

'Oh, yeah. Er ... it's the letters E-D-D, capitalised, followed by a date, by the look of it.'

'Can I see?' Louise says, stepping forward.

Drew snaps the notebook against his chest. 'It's not mine.'

Louise's suspicion piques. What's he hiding? 'I can't think of anything. How come you thought *I'd* know?'

He shrugs. 'I've seen something like it before. Next to a woman's name, that's all.'

Louise apologises and begins walking down her path. Then stops. 'Oh! Hang on,' she says, backing up. Drew pops round the side of his house, a hopeful expression on his face. 'E-D-D – I do remember seeing that, actually. On my maternity notes. Not sure if it's the same, but in that context it stands for estimated date of delivery. The obstetrician noted it after the initial ultrasound.'

'Ah. I see.' Drew's chin drops to his chest. 'Thanks, Louise.'

'Why did you want to know?' Her pulse picks up, the thought he's asking a question about pregnancy suddenly concerning. Drew's turned away, though. He puts a hand up, mutters something under his breath. Sounded like *so that's what she was hiding*, and then he disappears from her view. It's not until she's inside and releases Alfie that she puts two and two together. She could be way off, of course, but Drew seemed dejected when she told him what EDD stands for and now she wonders if his girlfriend was pregnant when she left him and, until just now, he'd no clue. Maybe Louise has got it all wrong – looking for connections to Harriet where there aren't any. Poor Drew. She feels bad for him, but Louise has her own issues to deal with. Like the fact there's still no parcel.

She refills Alfie's beaker with water, then settles him in the conservatory. Had it been delivered to a neighbour? Drew would've said just then if he'd taken it in. She highly doubts that anyone else in the street would've accepted it and, anyway, the first test kit arrived no problem and easily fitted through the letterbox. This would be the exact same size.

It had better come in tomorrow's post. She has to know as soon as possible. This uncertainty is killing her. The birthday party is the ideal, and possibly only, opportunity she'll have to conduct the cheek swab on Jacob. Without the test, how will she gain the evidence that Jacob is her biological son?

Her only option would be to confront Harriet.

Chapter 39

'Our office hours are Monday to Friday between the hours of—'

'Goddamn it!' Louise hangs up. It's the fourth time calling the support line – two previous times she'd been held in a queue and was then disconnected, and her last attempt saw her through to an actual person, but Mark's key hit the lock, and she had to cut the call short. She should've tried a different company, but now it's too late. Her concern right now is that they're adamant the parcel was delivered, which begs the question – to whom? Frustration tipping, she turns to go back inside. She's already paced up and down beside the conservatory, trying to stay out of sight of Mark or Alfie – if she's outside any longer, she'll attract suspicion. Plus, there's no more time. Today is the big day.

They'd been up early to celebrate Alfie's birthday with him – just the three of them – before this afternoon's pool party. Mark isn't going, saying he'd rather spend his time with his son in a calmer atmosphere. She'd attempted to change his mind, then concluded she was better off there without him watching her every move. Instead, she'd asked if he would drop them off. So, while they are at Harriet's for a couple of hours, he's going to organise a birthday tea with Sue's help.

She's about to creep inside when movement along the fence catches her eye. It's near the top end of the garden, on Drew's side. He's probably seen her out in her slippers, acting like *she's* up to no good, and is curious. Or he's simply spying on her as she alleged to Mark. She flicks her gaze left and right then takes two big strides towards the fence and turns so her back is against it. Confident that Drew can't see her from this position, she takes a few slow sidesteps, then stops and listens. The movement on his side continues – it's a scratchy sound, or maybe scraping. Louise's shoulders sag. All this, and he's probably potting some plants or something mundane. She suppresses a laugh with her hand, shakes her head at her own drama. As if she doesn't have enough of her own to occupy her.

'What did you do?'

The voice, slow and raspy, pins Louise to the spot. Is Drew speaking to her?

'You stupid, stupid bitch.'

The noise of her heart thumping jams her ears and she can't make out anything else. She wants to ask what he's talking about, demand answers about why he's loitering by the fence again. Her mouth hangs open, her knees buckle and all at once she knows she has to get inside the house. With Mark and Alfie. Without trying to keep quiet, Louise pushes herself away from the fence, causing the panel to wobble, and retraces her steps, not looking back until she's in the house, behind the closed door, her breaths laboured.

She needs to check if he's still there, but there's nothing to see from this angle. Running through the house, kicking her shoes off as she goes, Louise darts up the stairs and into the back bedroom. She edges towards the window and peeks out from behind the curtains. He's probably gone, especially after she made such a racket and alerted him to her presence. Although maybe he knew she was there, and the accusation *was* aimed at her. In which case . . .

She arches her neck, chin high to create a better vantage point.

Drew stands looking directly up at her.

Louise jerks backwards. 'Shit, shit, shit,' she whispers, screwing her eyes up tightly. She counts to ten, then shifts forward an inch. And another.

Drew's gone.

'Spying—'

'Fuck's sake, Mark.' Louise spins round, her hand slamming against her chest. 'Don't sneak up behind me like that.' The power's left her voice – it comes out like a hiss of air.

'Seriously, Lou. What are you doing?'

'I thought I saw . . . I – I don't know.' It's not worth trying to explain. 'Nothing. I came in to get the swim bag, got sidetracked.'

Mark mumbles something before leaving, and Louise gets back into gear. She can't allow her neighbour's odd behaviour to derail her today. The large holdall is wedged on top of the wardrobe, and it takes several attempts to pull it down. Once she brushes off the layer of dust, Louise packs it with swimming things for her and Alfie, then tucks a small waterproof wet bag into the side pocket. In it, she has some ziplock bags so that she can pop a toothbrush inside for use later on, when she can sort out another DNA testing kit.

Mark's talking in a hushed tone to Alfie when Louise comes in, then they both giggle. Alfie pretend-whispers in Mark's ear, and they laugh again. She thinks back to a few weeks ago, before Harriet and Jacob came into their lives, how hopeless she felt, how desperately lonely she was and how she was at her wits' end with Alfie's behaviour. So much has changed in a short space of time. On the whole, his temper tantrums have lessened, and his social skills have improved. She has to admit, her own mood still swings wildly from one day to the next, but that's because of what she now believes. That Alfie is not their son. Looking at Mark and him now, though, there's nothing to suggest this. And without actual proof Mark will never believe her. Does she want to believe it herself? She loves Alfie. But if Jacob is her son, she wants the opportunity to get to know him, too.

The bigger question right now, though, is whether *Harriet* can be trusted. Things have been tense between them, so why is she still carrying on the pretence of being friends? Why throw the party for Alfie, too? Is it simply because she's kind, or does she have another agenda? Louise thinks of the lollipop, and her unease grows.

What would Harriet want? From the stories about

children in other countries being mixed up at birth and then swapped back when it's come to light, there are few truly happy endings. Will this story end any differently? If money talks, which in her experience it does, then going up against Harriet in an official capacity could prove costly. If Harriet wanted to swap back, Louise is sure she could make it happen. What had Richard said – Harriet always gets what she wants? Dread slides down Louise's spine. Is there a world where Harriet could take *both* boys from her?

Mark barely utters a word to her in the car on the way over to Harriet's, choosing to chat with Alfie instead. He doesn't throw her a single glance. Any other time, she would make a thing of it – push it, force him to speak to her. But today, with her mind on what she needs to accomplish, she's happy to let it go. She'd rather not speak anyway; her tummy is too full of fluttering wings and her lungs feel stiff, as though her ribs have turned rigid, preventing effective respiration.

The car stops and Louise gathers her thoughts, her bag and Alfie, says goodbye and heads up the driveway. Apart from one 'The Party's Here' sign with some blue balloons attached to it, the place is strangely devoid of decoration. Louise expected to see something spectacular on the front lawn, the huge water fountain spouting colourful water, transformed into something befitting Las Vegas.

'Really, Louise?' Mark calls. She turns back, shooting him a questioning look.

'What?'

'Jacob's present?' he says, shaking his head. She tugs Alfie back to the car and retrieves the gift with a smile. 'No more dramatics, or anything. Okay?' Mark says. 'Please don't make me regret agreeing to this.' Louise bites the inside of her cheek, gives a curt nod and carries on towards Harriet's house. Her shoulders relax as she hears the engine of the car grow distant.

'Oh.' Louise stops at the front door, reads the sign there. 'We have to go around the side entrance,' she says to Alfie, who's become agitated and is itching to be released from her grip to join Jacob. They follow the sound of excited squeals, and with each step Louise's heart pounds harder. What should she expect when she walks through? Given the lack of pomp and grandeur out the front, perhaps it's all very low-key. And, as much as that would be preferable in most circumstances, today of all days Louise could do with some chaos – a way of hiding her true intentions, wrapping her deceit up in a big bloody bow to ensure it remains undetected.

With her breath held, Louise opens the side gate. Releases it at the sight of a large gathering of mums, dads and kids. Balloons of all kinds hang from every available location: the large conifers, the fencing, the chalk-white pergola. There's a gazebo on the patio with a balloon arch and underneath it is a trestle table piled high with presents. Louise goes to add her gift for Jacob to it, then notices they are separated by signs – one for Jacob, one for Alfie. She hadn't expected this. The invitation Harriet gave out was for Jacob's birthday, it was only afterwards Harriet had suggested they call it a joint party. She must've rung around the parents and told them to bring gifts for Alfie, too.

'Here's the other birthday boy!' Harriet swoops up behind them and bends down to Alfie's level to wish him a happy birthday. She's dressed in a Boho-style dress, and looks like she's just stepped off the beach. And she's carrying a tub of lollipops. The same brand Alfie had been given by someone at the butcher. Alfie's face lights up as she offers him one.

Louise pushes her hand out to cover the tub. 'Are they sugar-free?'

'No added sugar,' Harriet says coolly.

Louise lifts her hand. It's not the sugar she's bothered about. She looks Harriet in the eye, searching for a sign she knows Louise is on to her. Her facial expression appears serene, but did Louise detect a fleeting look of panic? Like she's just realised she's slipped up?

'Weather is perfect,' Harriet says, standing up. 'But didn't want to bank on it, so we've got the marquee if required.' Louise tears her gaze away from her face and looks around but can't see it. 'Oh, it's in the other part of the garden,' Harriet says, when she sees Louise's confusion.

'How big *is* your garden?'

'Too big,' Harriet says, giving a light laugh. 'The upkeep is a nightmare.'

One of the fun mums flounces up. 'No wonder you didn't leave, Harriet.'

She spins round. 'Oh, it's not the be-all and end-all, Steph.

I'd prefer a house on the coast. That fresh sea air, stunning clifftop scenery.'

'Well, we have some properties coming up in Lynmouth you might be interested in, then.'

'Now we're talking,' Harriet says, her arm round Steph's shoulders as she begins to move away. 'One of my favourite spots. I just adore spending quiet moments by those cliffs ... so relaxing.'

Louise watches as they go and mingle with some of the other guests, unsure how to proceed. It's like being back at playgroup, where she's on the periphery again.

'Punch?' Richard is beside her, a tray of glasses balanced upon one hand. 'Non-alcoholic, of course.'

'Go on, then,' she says, grateful for him giving her something to hold on to, something to do with her nervous hands. 'This is amazing, Richard.' She's about to announce her thanks to him and Harriet for including Alfie, but stops herself, the memory of his admission the other night springing into her mind. She's the riff-raff, the lower class, in his eyes.

'You having a dip, too?' He nods towards the covered pool. 'I'll be undressing her in a moment.'

'Yes. Can't very well let Alfie go in alone, can I?'

'No. Of course. Mark didn't come with you, did he.' It's a small dig, but it hits Louise hard. Her gaze falls on Richard's striped swim shorts and she swiftly brings the conversation back.

'I assume you're going in with Jacob.'

'Yep! Harriet isn't much of a swimmer. More of a socialite.

I mean, look at her. She's in her element.' They both watch her for a moment, interweaving with the guests, smiling as she glides effortlessly between them.

'She's certainly putting on a good show,' Louise says. She turns to face Richard. 'She *is* okay, isn't she? I'm a bit concerned about . . .' Louise lowers her voice. 'About how erratic she's been recently. You mentioned her struggles after having Jacob. Maybe his birthday has brought some things back to her?'

'She's absolutely fine, Louise. Perhaps you should be concerned about things closer to home.' And before Louise can explore what he means by this he takes his tray of punch and continues to distribute it to the others. Was he implying that she was missing something in her own life? She swallows the lump in her throat with the aid of some punch. He was referring to *her* behaviour. Was that about her nosing in his office? Why didn't he just come out and say it, if so? Why are so many things hinted at, but left unsaid?

After the kids have played in the ball pit and on the soft-play items scattered around the garden, Richard announces the pool is ready, and there's a hive of activity as everyone gets undressed and begins climbing down the steps into the pool, the kids sitting on the edge with their water wings and the adults lifting them in. Louise and Alfie stay close to the metal steps, with him clinging to her, his confidence in the water low. She talks him through it, encouraging him to loosen his grip on her, but he begins to panic, which raises Louise's own anxiety level.

'Here. Swap a moment.' It's Richard, right next to her, with Jacob in his arms. After some twisting and shuffling, they manage it. Jacob reaches for an inflatable and laughs as Louise bobs him up and down a few times before lifting him as high as she can before plopping him on top of the bright green dragon. She side-eyes Richard and Alfie. Richard's chest is above the water level, with only Alfie's legs submerged. He's talking softly but firmly to him, which seems to be doing the trick. Already Alfie is calmer, and he's looking less terrified than when he was clamped to her a moment ago.

He can sense I'm not his parent.

They don't stay in the water for long. The weather is good today, and the pool heated, but it's not the height of summer and they soon get chilly – the collective chorus of chattering teeth and display of shivering bodies attests to that. Louise gets out first with Jacob, then goes to take Alfie from Richard. As he hands him back, she catches sight of what she'd originally assumed was a tattoo on his arm. But it isn't. Along his upper arms and on one side of his torso are a number of small light-brown patches. Flat, like birthmarks, but there are too many for it to be that. Looks more like a skin condition. She tries not to let her gaze linger.

'Thanks, Richard. You were great with him. I'll dry the boys if you like.'

'Perfect. I'll get the cover back on while Harriet sorts the c-a-k-e.' He spells it out, although she's sure the kids aren't listening.

'Enjoy that?' Louise asks Alfie as she wraps a towel around him.

'Can I play now?' he says, wriggling to get away. Louise tells him he has to get dressed first, but then he can. She turns to help Jacob, who's standing patiently. His towel slips and her breath catches in her throat as she sees the birthmark, the one she'd spotted in the photo. It's bigger and even more defined now; it looks just like Mark's. A sadness consumes her, then, in an instant, it's replaced with a deep knowing.

This is her son. Jacob is hers.

Everything points to it. She doesn't need a DNA test to convince her of it.

But she will need it in order to convince everyone else.

Alfie goes back to playing on the soft-play toys while Louise finishes drying Jacob, who natters away to her as though he's already had a fill of sugar. Her face hurts from smiling. Alfie breaks the moment, shouting to Jacob to hurry up, and, keen to join in the fun, he scampers away. Louise has to make her move soon, before the opportunity to get into the bathroom and find Jacob's toothbrush passes her by. After drying and dressing herself, Louise checks if anyone is looking, then takes out the ziplock bags and pops them into her trouser pocket. Richard's almost finished covering the pool, and soon Harriet will emerge with the birthday cake. Maybe she shouldn't do anything now. Hesitating is wasting even more time, she knows that, but a sudden surge of nerves – or maybe it's simply second thoughts, a fear of getting caught out – keeps her rooted to the spot. If she messes up – what then?

Just as she makes the decision not to act, Jacob slips and falls, face-planting on the ground. Louise rushes to him. 'Oh, darling. Up you get,' she says, helping him to his feet. Blood oozes from his nose. 'We need to mop you up, I think,' she says brightly, so as not to panic him. He's not crying, but his lips pout in readiness. Louise quickly casts her gaze around. No one else seems to have noticed, and Harriet's not in sight. 'Mummy's busy, so I'll take you in and we'll sort you out.' She turns to Alfie. 'Can you stay and play nicely with the others, please?'

And, swiftly lifting Jacob on to one hip, Louise takes him inside, managing to bypass the other mums and dads, and, more importantly, Richard and Harriet. The closest bathroom is the main downstairs one. She'll have to use that one as it would appear too suspicious to be seen taking Jacob upstairs, where she assumes his bedroom and bathroom are. If she's lucky, after she cleans him up, she could get Jacob to show her by saying he needs a fresh top to wear.

Closing them both inside the bathroom, Louise lifts him on to the closed toilet seat.

'Here we go, sweetheart.' She presses a wad of tissue to Jacob's nose. The blood soaks through the top layers quickly. 'Can you hold your nose like this?' She shows him and he does as she asks without question. She wishes she had another DNA swab so she could do a quick cheek swipe while she was here. This is the only time she's likely to get Jacob alone. She's about to throw the first lot of tissue away, then it hits her. Could she use Jacob's *blood* and send that for testing instead? The online testing company requires a swab or a toothbrush, but perhaps there are private methods for testing DNA, and surely a sample of blood would be ideal.

It's an opportunity she shouldn't waste, may as well take the tissue, anyway. Louise grabs a ziplock bag from her pocket and pops it in. Once the bleeding has stopped and Jacob's cleaned up, he runs off back to the others without waiting for Louise. She hovers for a moment, her mind working overtime, then peeks out from behind the door. No one is about. She might not be able to chance going upstairs, but she *could* make it to the en-suite bathroom to check for toothbrushes. Better to have as many options as possible for testing in case she can't find a place that'll take Jacob's blood. Louise sneaks into Richard and Harriet's bedroom and goes straight to their en suite. There on the back of the sink sit two electric toothbrushes. If she were to take both, that would alert them to something being up, and they'd check any cameras and see her going in. She can't have them suspicious enough that they'd look into it that carefully. Taking out another ziplock bag, Louise chooses the toothbrush she thinks is Harriet's, pulls the head off, and places it inside.

With an internal whoop of triumph, Louise turns to leave. She bumps right into someone. She stifles a scream by putting her hand to her mouth, in the process dropping the bags. Eyes wide, breath caught in her lungs, Louise stares up. It's Richard. But Richard's gaze is on the floor.

'What on earth are you doing, Louise?'

Flustered, all she can think is to deny all knowledge. 'Oh, that was on the floor when I came in.'

'And you were in our bathroom because?'

'Oh, well . . . funny, really,' she says, laughing a little too hysterically. 'You said to look after the boys—'

'Stop. Stop lying,' Richard says, bending down to pick up the samples Louise dropped. He inhales sharply. 'Is this *blood*?'

Louise pushes her mouth down at the corners, gives a slow shrug.

'No one else has been in here.' He unzips the bag with Harriet's toothbrush inside, his head shaking side to side in complete bewilderment. 'You're a strange woman, Louise. This *obsession* with my wife . . . It's gone beyond a joke.'

'Oh, God, Richard. I'm sorry. It wasn't meant to be like this. I'm not obsessed with Harriet. In fact, I'd say it was the other way around, actually.'

'Whatever are you going on about?'

'Harriet targeted me and Alfie, I've got proof of that – and I'm sure she knows something about our sons being swapped—'

'Oh, my God!' Harriet bursts in. 'What the *hell* are you saying?' Her expression oozes disgust. But there's something else hiding behind the façade, and Louise frowns. Harriet doesn't seem *surprised*. It's almost like she's acting . . .

Richard places an arm around his wife, a sign of solidarity, as he glares at Louise.

'I'm not sure what's wrong with you, Louise,' he says. For

a split second, Louise thinks he seems genuinely concerned more than angry. Then his jaw tightens, his tone becoming judgemental, like he'd been at dinner the other evening. 'I should've listened to your concerns sooner, Harriet.'

Louise snaps her attention to Harriet. What concerns has she been discussing? The walls seem to close in, a sense of claustrophobia clawing at her.

'I do think you should see a doctor,' Harriet says, her usually delicate features twisting as she takes a step closer. 'I thought I was helping you, but, given your actions, it's apparent that it's professional support you need. You need help, Louise – you owe it to Alfie, if not yourself.'

'Why are you doing this?' Louise's throat constricts, the realisation of what's happening hitting her. Her eyes flit between Harriet and Richard, desperately searching for a way out of this. But she's trapped. Harriet is playing her – that's obvious. What isn't clear is what exactly her end game is.

'So as not to ruin Jacob and Alfie's birthday,' Harriet says, her words slow and deliberate as if she's talking to a child, 'you can stay while they blow out the candles. Then you're leaving. Got it?'

'But . . .' She has no defence to give. Her plan has failed. Can she still convince Richard to listen?

'Please, Richard. I found her Post-it note – it proves she was following me, tracking me and Alfie down. She *knows*.'

'A *Post-it note*?' Richard is incredulous. 'You're basing this ridiculous, disgusting theory on a *Post-it note*? I don't want to make this situation any worse than you've made it already, so I'll do you a favour and not tell Mark the shit you've just pulled, if you promise to stay away from now on. Deal?'

Louise's eyes burn with tears. What choice does she have?

Chapter 40

Sue is in the kitchen when Louise returns home with Alfie.

'What are you doing back? Mark said he was picking you up at four!' She's got a plate of sandwiches in her hand, cut up into star shapes. 'We aren't ready.'

'Well, I'm so sorry for ruining your afternoon by coming home early, Mother. Just assumed you'd want as much time with your grandson as possible.'

Mark's flustered face appears around the door. 'Oh. You walked back?'

'It was all a bit much,' Louise says, trying to keep her voice level when all she really wants to do is sob. His expression darkens.

'Do we need to talk about it?' He's speaking to her like she's a naughty teenager, not a grown adult. She draws in a steady breath, and not trusting that her voice won't break, shakes her head. Sue gathers Alfie into her arms, sings 'Happy Birthday' and covers him in kisses. Louise recalls an early memory of one of her birthdays, how Sue showered affection on her then. When had it stopped?

Why? Did Louise do something to stop her mother loving her?

Will Alfie think she never loved him, if she continues down this road?

The thought crushes her. Louise longs to leave the room, escape to her own thoughts without being observed. Because they are watching her, and judging – she can feel it. It's thick and uncomfortable, like an extra layer of skin she's desperate to shed. They've probably been talking about her behind her back, too. Has Mark told her mother what she said about Alfie and Jacob being swapped? That thought's bad enough, and they don't know the half of it. Can she really trust Harriet and Richard not to mention anything to Mark? The way they reacted, the things they said...

Louise's mouth dries. *You owe it to Alfie, if not yourself*, that's what Harriet had said. It'd be easy enough for her to make Louise out to be an unfit mother – maybe that's what she wanted all along. And Louise has unwittingly provided her with all the ammunition.

As they're clearing up, Sue corners Louise in the kitchen.

'You remember you asked about the horrible man up the road from Janet?'

Louise's eyes widen; with all the other drama, it'd slipped her mind. 'Yes. Did you find out if he was married?'

'Divorced, apparently.' Sue lifts the lid of the bin, slides leftover sandwiches from the plate into it. 'But Janet said he'd been shacked up with another girl until a few years ago...' Louise's heart is in her mouth. 'She did a runner, it seems. No wonder, is it – who would want to be with someone like that?'

'Did you get names?'

Sue slumps. 'Goodness, I can't remember now. Got wrapped up in the story. I'm sure they'll come to me.' She stands with a finger to her bottom lip, her eyes to the ceiling.

'When you say *girl* . . .'

'Well, not sure how old. Just a fair bit younger than him by all accounts.'

Louise, glad of a distraction, soaks up this information, and can't help but speculate what it would mean if the white-van man is the same one who was threatening Drew. Were they with the same woman? Before she can probe Sue further, Alfie comes into the kitchen and Sue's attention goes to him. In the pause, Louise's mind flashes back to the moment Richard and Harriet caught her in their bathroom. Bile fills her mouth. Without the sample of Jacob's blood or Harriet's toothbrush, she won't be able to offer Mark actual evidence of the swap. Nothing to prove her innocence if Harriet and Richard tell him what she's been up to – or, worse, go to the police.

'Come play with me and Daddy.' Alfie pulls at Sue's sleeve. 'And you, Mummy,' he says.

Louise smiles at him. 'You go ahead. I'll follow in a minute.' Maybe it's time to finally give this up. Let Harriet make the first move.

You'll be a sitting duck.

She can't do nothing. She's already in too deep.

There's one thing she hasn't tried. Visiting Sommerby

maternity unit – the place both Alfie and Jacob were born. See what she can find out about that day. If she can't get DNA proof, the next best thing is to do her own detective work.

With a new plan in mind, Louise's muscles relax a little. She checks her phone. No new messages or missed calls. But then, if Richard were to spill his guts, he'd call Mark directly. Apparently they exchanged numbers the other night after they chatted about business. She joins her mother, Mark and Alfie in the conservatory, and the three of them play with Alfie and his new toys, like the perfect family.

Alfie crashes at seven thirty, taking no time to settle once Sue left. Louise watches him on the monitor and her thoughts wander to Jacob. Has he fallen asleep as quickly after the day's activities? Did he enjoy his birthday party? She rubs her eyes; the lids feel swollen with exhaustion. Mentally, the day has taken it out of her. And as she sits down in the lounge and Mark gets up, she knows it's not over yet.

Mark's face is serious as he takes her hands in his and crouches down in front of her. The weight of what's on his mind seems to physically cause his head to droop. Shit. Has Richard called him while she's been upstairs with Alfie?

'It's been a really long day, Mark.' She tries to pull her hands from his, but he grips them tighter.

'Yes, I imagine it has,' he says, keeping his gaze on the floor like he can't bear to look her in the eye. She feels the urge to talk, to rattle on about the pool party, how Alfie had an amazing time – anything to prevent him from getting a word in, in case those words are related to what she blurted out to Richard earlier. But fear prevents speech. 'Are you all good now?' He finally lifts his head and looks into her eyes. Tears spring to them, her lip quivering.

She nods. 'Course.'

'I mean it, love. You don't need them in your life. Look at your son.' He points to the monitor. 'You've made such huge leaps. That's on you. It's not simply because Harriet appeared.'

'Thank you,' she says.

'It's for the best you don't see them any more.' Something flickers in his eyes and Louise senses there's more to this exchange. 'Promise?'

Her throat locks up, the response he's asking for, trapped. A barely perceptible nod of her head is all she can manage.

Chapter 41

WhatsApp

I need to act . . . before it's too late . . . Are you in?

I'm leaving something for you taped underneath the bench. Be there at 8 a.m. this Tuesday to get it.

Chapter 42

The maternity unit is situated at the far side of the main hospital. Louise stands staring up at the row upon row of windows in the redbrick building with a sense of numbness. It's the first time she's been back here since the day they took Alfie home. Her memory of that day isn't clear – in fact, she skimmed through her baby diary again before leaving the house today to refresh it. It looks familiar, while also appearing alien to her. Much the same as her own baby – or the baby she'd believed to be hers – had felt to her when she held him. Took him home.

Getting inside the unit itself isn't difficult because the clinics are held in the same block. However, gaining admission to the post-natal ward is an altogether more challenging task. And the special-care baby unit is accessed via the ward. Louise watches from the stairwell for ten minutes, noting the coming and going, how people get admitted and for how long. It looks different even though it's only been three years since being here herself. She wished she had Alfie with her now. She wouldn't look so suspicious. But, then again, children aren't allowed in unless they belong to one of the mums on the unit, so she wouldn't have stood a chance at gaining entry with him.

Honesty is the best policy.

Louise strides up to the intercom and presses the buzzer.

'Hello, can I help?' a voice asks. She can't see through the double doors very well; the glass is obscured.

'Hi. My name's Louise Webb. I was in the special-care baby unit – I was just wondering if I could have a word with the staff on duty today?'

She hears some muffled speaking. Then the voice comes back, loudly, 'What's it in relation to, please?'

Her chest tightens. Is she going to have to do this without even seeing the person she's talking to? 'Well, it's going to seem like an odd request, but ... well, to be honest, I've been suffering with post-natal depression and my therapist suggested visiting the unit where I had Alfie, and kind of following the journey again to help me come to terms with the bonding issues I had initially. So I was hoping that ... maybe you'd allow that? I won't take up too much of their time, of course.'

The silence after she stops speaking stretches impossibly thin. Are they ignoring her?

There's a long drawn-out buzz, and the door clicks and swings open.

She's in.

Faced with the array of faces behind the nurses' station, Louise panics – her breathing suddenly jagged. She fights with the desire to turn and run. One woman, dressed in blue scrubs, hurries out from behind the desk and lays a hand on Louise's shoulder, soothes her. After a few moments to get herself together, she thanks the nurse for her kindness and continues her planned story. She tries to get a list of doctors, nursing staff, or anyone who was working the day Alfie was born – asks about the power outage, the flood that caused it. As Louise's motive for her visit becomes clearer – that she's questioning whether something untoward happened – the staff close down, saying she'll have to put any further requests in writing to the head of the department.

'I understand. I appreciate you allowing me in. Can I just leave my details, anyway? In case someone remembers something. Please?' She writes her name and mobile number down and hands it to them. As the unit door closes behind her, she imagines they've probably binned her information already and, with a disappointed sigh and a heavy feeling in her stomach, she heads for the lifts. While in one way, the trip has been a waste of time, in another way, it's given her even more reason to press on. Because who shuts down like that when asked a few simple questions?

Only those who know something went terribly wrong.

Louise falters at the exit to the maternity unit, half tempted to try her luck in gaining entry to the labour ward. They would have details of Alfie's birth, and they took Alfie to SCBU from there. They'd feared he'd inhaled meconium, and two of the staff transferred her baby to the lower level in an incubator. Could the mix-up have taken place during that time?

Seems unlikely. To have two babies taken to SCBU at the exact same time and accidentally swapped is a stretch. Louise's mind jolts back to the present as her body comes to an abrupt halt. Her breath expels in a huff, and she almost falls backwards from the force at which she's whacked into someone coming from the opposite direction.

'So sorry,' the man says, before he goes to carry on.

'Drew!' Louise grabs his arm, and he spins round to face her.

'Louise. Hi. I was in such a rush, didn't realise it was you.'

'What are you doing here?' Her eyes slide to the maternity unit sign and Drew's gaze follows.

'For goodness' sake. How?' He stands back, surveying the sign. 'Bloody place. I've taken the wrong turn.' He mumbles something about having an appointment and being late because of the 'rabbit warren'.

Louise's heart races, thinking about Saturday in the garden, how he was saying: *What did you do? You stupid, stupid bitch*, and she believed he was speaking to her. Now he's acting all normal towards her? How strange. He must clock her confusion because he takes a step back, squints.

'All okay with you, Louise?' His eyes lower to her abdomen.

'Oh. God. No. Not here for me.' She touches her hand to her stomach and laughs. 'No more for a while! I was just here visiting a friend.'

After an awkward pause, Drew says he has to go, and disappears into the maternity unit. Presumably to walk through the corridor that links to the main part of the hospital.

Did he follow her here?

Chapter 43

The bus home takes her around the scenic route, adding at least twenty minutes to the journey. Usually, the sight of the sea would soothe her, but it does nothing today – her mind grappling with the mashed-up thoughts swimming inside her aching head. She presses her fingertips to her temples, rubbing in a circular motion. The tension remains. Her gaze wanders to the clifftops in the distance. The sign for Lynmouth flashes past. Isn't that where Harriet said she goes to relax? Louise glimpses a property for sale, huge, modern – a perfect fit for Harriet – and raises her eyebrows. Bet that's the house Steph said she had on her list that she'd show Harriet. Oh, to have money.

Money can't buy true happiness, though. That much, she knows.

'I'm back.' Louise hangs her bag up on the hook in the hallway, looks around for her mother and Alfie. It's uncharacteristically quiet. She told Sue not to take him out, that she wouldn't be that long. She checks her mobile as she walks to the conservatory. No missed calls. But she is about an hour later than she'd said. Everything is tidy – no toys strewn about, no sign of Alfie. Panic shoots through her. What's her mother done? She calls out. But it's Mark who replies. Shit. Mark's home. Now she'll have to try to explain where she's been. He hurries down the stairs, his jaw set. Louise opens her mouth, ready to tell a lie, but he puts his hand up.

'I don't want to hear it, Louise.'

He walks towards the kitchen, so Louise follows, grasping for a possible reason for his reaction. The obvious one soars to the top of her mind, but Richard said he wouldn't tell if she stayed away from them.

'What's wrong? Where's Sue?' she says, hoping to get at least one answer from him.

He huffs, picks up a plastic container filled with food, and stands beside the table, his head shaking, nostrils flaring.

'Mark! Speak to me. What's going on?'

'You're unbelievable. How can you stand here and pretend not to know?' He drops the container down then pounds a fist into the table. Louise flinches, stuttering a feeble excuse in the vain attempt to placate him, but he's too far past that. 'You promised not to continue along that ridiculous path,' he says. His face flames, saliva forms at the corners of his mouth like a rabid dog. 'But no. Not only did you go against me and *our* son, but you were also hellbent on ruining another family, too.' Louise's heart beats out of her chest, thoughts rushing through her mind like a whirlwind whipping up debris and flinging it around. She stays quiet so as not to incriminate herself; there's still an outside hope that he's enraged for a different reason. 'Telling Richard that Harriet *targeted* you and Alfie? That our sons were swapped? What were you *thinking*?'

So Richard did call him. What a fucking liar.

'Seriously, Lou – I had to beg Harriet not to involve the police!'

'Sorry, what?' Louise squeezes her eyes closed. '*Harriet* called you?'

'Yes. She was distraught, Louise. The things you said to her and Richard. Poor woman was beside herself because she felt so guilty coming to me behind your back.'

'Hang on – poor woman? The woman you said wasn't my real friend, the one you demanded I no longer have contact with?'

'Well, none of this is on her, is it? *She's* not the one making wild accusations about our baby, our *son*, being swapped at birth!'

Louise staggers back. Hearing it in his words, it sounds insane. Of course Mark's upset. 'Maybe you should've let her call the police. We'd get to the bottom of it then, wouldn't we?'

'You seriously think Jacob is our son, not Alfie? Can you hear yourself?'

'There's evidence, Mark. I tried to talk to you about it. You shut me down.'

'Oh, yes. The "evidence". Louise, there are plenty of children who have similar characteristics to other children and parents. You don't think every child with fine blond hair and brown eyes is ours, do you?'

'Of course not.' Heat soars through her, frustration building. 'There's more to it. I haven't told you the half of it ...'

'So I gather.' He rubs his hands over his face. 'I looked at your laptop, Louise. You've lied, manipulated – taken me for a fool.' He pulls a padded envelope from his back pocket and waves it at her. It's the missing DNA kit. He had intercepted it. 'You've gone too far.'

He strides into the lounge and comes back out carrying a suitcase.

'What are you doing?'

He disappears again, returning with Alfie's dinosaur suitcase, plus a bag of his toys. Alfie is trailing behind him, silent, his eyes wide as saucers. 'I'm taking Alfie to see my parents for a while. Give you time to sort yourself out.'

'No, you're not.' She launches towards Mark, pushing him back. '*You're* the one taking this too far, Mark.'

He glares at her, huffs, then shakes his head. 'Please, Lou. Listen to yourself, eh?'

'So, you think leaving me all alone is the best way to handle this? You said—'

'No! *You* said you'd call your therapist. I can't help you if you don't want to help yourself.'

'I did call. Well ... I was about to. If you'd given me half a chance—'

'You've had more than that. Now, do everyone a favour and don't make this worse for Alfie; he's upset enough. I'll check in, but right now I don't think it's safe for you to be around him.'

Louise watches in stunned silence as Mark walks out of the door with Alfie, up the path and disappears towards the car.

She stands at the kitchen window for a few moments, her mind numb. It isn't until she's about to turn away that she spots Drew. He hadn't been very long at the hospital then. His expression fills with a sadness she knows she should be feeling herself, and she wonders if he's thinking about the scene he's just witnessed. For a fleeting moment, their gaze meets, and Louise puts up a hand.

He doesn't return the gesture.

Chapter 44

Louise paces the conservatory, the silence too much for her. She never envisaged herself alone here, though sometimes she longed for it. But the days since Mark and Alfie left have been torture. In all the time seeking answers, she hadn't fully contemplated what it would do to them. A sense of dread now consumes her. If she continues on this path, she might lose her family either way. If she's wrong, Mark will leave her for good, and take Alfie. And, if she's right, the lives of two families will be forever altered. If Harriet really does want to cut all ties, maybe she's decided to leave it. But Louise doesn't trust her.

She stands at the conservatory window, scanning the fence line. No Drew. Seems to be keeping a low profile since he saw Mark and Alfie leave with their suitcases. Wonder what he thinks. Perhaps it wasn't news to him. He's known all along because he's acting as Harriet's spy. Her nails dig into her palms. No. She's not deluded. Not imagining all of this. They just want her to believe that, so she stops digging. She might not know Harriet's motivation, her plan – but the way Harriet has behaved isn't exactly sane either.

Louise searches the forum she'd come across previously and joins it – it's similar to the ones she'd been encouraged to use when Alfie was a newborn and she was struggling to cope with the transition into motherhood. Only this one is filled with desperate people like herself who believe they took the wrong baby home. Tears streak down her face as she reads about others' desperation. How no one believes them. Message after message details their fight to gain support. Even those with inconclusive DNA tests – and one woman with a negative result – have failed to be reunited with their biological baby. Some are saying they're getting hold of journalists, as that's the only way of sharing their experiences and gaining awareness of the issue. One thing that strikes Louise as she reads the comments is how she is in a unique position.

Because she knows who her biological son is.

Gathering herself, Louise gets up. She needs to see Jacob.

Chapter 45

EMAIL
FROM AngelFace
SUBJECT Our deal

My other half is beginning to suspect something's up. All the time I'm spending 'researching' is causing him to ask questions, because as far as he's aware, we don't have the money to get our son the treatment. To be honest, I'm not sure I want him to be part of our future. When our deal is done, I'm thinking of going it alone. Our arrangement should be just between the two of us anyway. Less risk that way. Neither of us should end up in prison simply for wanting better lives for our children!

Chapter 46

The car isn't in the driveway. Louise's mind blanks – she can't remember if this is one of Harriet's working days. If it is, Jacob will be at the nursery. Why didn't she think about that before setting off? She's here now, though. It's worth checking, just in case. Knowing the Ring doorbell will alert them of her presence, Louise is careful to edge her way to the side entrance, keeping her back against the far fence. With her breath held, she lifts the gate latch. If they've locked it from the other side, she's screwed.

It opens. Her breath escapes her dry lips in a long stream of air.

When they were at the pool party, Louise hadn't clocked any CCTV cameras, but that's not to say there's not security of some kind, so she must remain vigilant. Harriet had said the garden was massive, but Louise had not had the opportunity to venture far at the party – other important tasks had been on her mind. If she stays along the perimeter of the fence, she could check out the rest of the area now. Find places she could conceal herself if she hears anyone coming. Places she could use in the future: good spots to watch Jacob. It'll only be from a distance; she's not doing any harm. It's not like she's going to steal him.

There are two huge bushes, and several trees, and the borders are filled with flowering plants – all of which could offer camouflage. The pool cover is on – and remembering what Harriet said about it being that way all the time, Louise debates whether she could duck down and creep up to the end of the pool, where the large manual roller is situated, to give her a closer view. It's risky if there are cameras, but from the distance she is currently she won't see much. It's a chance she's willing to take.

Crouching, then moving as though she's on an army training exercise, she swiftly makes her way to the pool. The roller for its cover is situated high enough above ground level that she can get into a position behind it and be confident she won't be observed from inside the house. And there she waits, her eyes flitting between the glass corridor and patio doors, hoping for movement. After around ten minutes of immobility, her muscles cramp, and she slowly stretches her limbs to alleviate the stiffness.

The sky begins to dull, the clouds taking on a dark hue; she's lost track of time – is it late afternoon already? Louise tries to pull her mobile from her pocket, but a flurry of activity stops her. Adrenaline spikes though her veins as her patience is rewarded and she finally glimpses Jacob. She smiles, a warmth radiating through her chilled body. He's traipsing behind Harriet, whose hand is pressed against the side of her head – her other arm flailing. Louise squints.

Harriet's on her phone and she doesn't seem happy; her face is screwed up, her mouth twisted. If Louise were closer, she's sure she'd hear heated words. Who's on the end of the line? Suddenly, Harriet's face is at the patio door, peering out, and Louise shrinks back behind the pool. Was she too slow?

Oh, God. Please don't have seen me.

She closes her eyes. Stops breathing at the noise of the patio door sliding open. She's been rumbled. What will she say: 'Oh, hi, Harriet. I thought I'd lost an earring at the pool party, decided I'd come looking for it without even asking you . . .' That won't go down well. She exhales slowly as her pulse thuds hard against her neck. With the door open, Louise makes out some of the one-sided conversation.

'I can't believe this is happening. How could you let it?'

A tingling sensation creeps over her skin. Why does Louise get an awful feeling Harriet is talking to Mark? She wishes she could see Harriet's expression. She strains to hear what's being said over the whooshing in her ears and catches something about a test, then, just as the door starts to close, she hears: 'He was never meant to survive.'

Louise's blood runs cold.

Her legs, heavy with tiredness and achy due to being crouched uncomfortably in Harriet's garden, move slowly, the walk home taking almost twice the usual time. Inside the house, she collapses on to the sofa, arms splaying, eyes closing. She dips in and out of microsleep, each brief lapse ending with a flash of memory – a series of snapshots of

Mark leaving with Alfie, and Louise lost and sad, unable to bring the fractured pieces of her life back together again.

Waking with a jolt for the third time, Louise sits up. Wipes away the tears she's shed in her sleep. She turns on the TV, anything to replace the deathly silence in the house. Then she checks her mobile for messages. Not one.

'Unbelievable,' she says. Not even one from her mother. If there was a time for Sue to show her love, or any ounce of support, it would be now. But no. It's easier for her to spout crap like how Louise was so wanted and so loved as a child because of the lost twin, because they're simply empty words.

Now the house is empty, and she is empty. This can't be all there is. She deserves her family. She scrolls through her contacts, taps on Mark's name, her heart hammering while she waits for him to answer. The ringtone continues. Is he screening his calls? The voicemail will click in any second and, with the heat flushing her face, she prepares to leave a narky message. But then he answers.

'Hi, Louise.'

His voice sounds far away, like he's at the end of a long tunnel. She waits for him to ask how she is, gives up when the seconds silently tick by. Louise picks at a loose thread on the arm of the sofa as she tells him she's missing them both, that the house is too empty and quiet without them in it. Mark mutters, 'Yeah, I'm sure it is.' She ups the level of remorse; she has to show him she's serious about changing. 'I'm really sorry for disappointing you. For letting Alfie down. I know I've messed up.'

She hears a heavy sigh and a sharp heat pulses through her veins. She can barely keep her frustration contained, but knows she must. 'And, by the way, did you tell my mother?'

'Tell Sue what? That your behaviour's gone too far, and I've brought Alfie to my parents' place?'

Louise brushes over the acidic comment; she has to show him she can handle it if she's to convince him she's deserving of them coming home.

'Yes. Because I've had no contact from her since you left.'

'Sorry. I guess she's tired of being lied to, Lou. We all are.'

'That's unfair.'

'Is it? You know, Harriet sent me some interesting Ring doorbell footage today. You, sneaking around – not to mention she saw you snooping inside their house last month. What were you playing at?'

'I . . . well, I was just—'

'No more. I'm so tired, Lou. You're lucky, because Harriet said she doesn't want to escalate this. But only if I make sure you get the help you need.'

Louise folds forward as if she's been punched. Harriet has wasted no time getting Mark onside, painting a picture of Louise as the unhinged, obsessed mother. But then, maybe she is.

'I am getting help,' Louise says quickly. 'I saw Natalie today and have another appointment booked for Thursday.' She screws her eyes up, shocked at how easily this lie comes out of her mouth. It seems to have the desired effect, though, bringing a lighter, more upbeat tone to Mark's voice. He tells her he's pleased she's made some progress. There's always a 'but', though, and she senses it coming even before he utters the word.

'But I need you to be in an altogether better place before I consider coming back with Alfie. A couple of sessions with Natalie is a good start. You need to build on that. And no more loitering around Harriet's house. Christ, they'll have you arrested for stalking next.'

'I promise, Mark,' Louise says, her jaw clenched tight.

'Take this time alone to work it out – make sure you listen to the expert. Natalie knows what she's talking about. Then we'll see where we're at.'

'I'll do what it takes to get my family back,' she says, then hangs up.

Chapter 47

Louise tosses and turns, her mind overactive and unwilling to give in to the night. What if Mark and Alfie don't come back? What if she ends up with no one? Nausea builds and she sits up, letting the bile slip back down. This level of sleep deprivation is reminiscent of the first weeks having a new, tiny human to take care of, adapt to – it's what started her spiral into depression. And now it's as though she's right back there in the depths of despair. Only this time there's no Alfie. No Mark. No one to bring her back from the brink.

After getting up and knocking back a double dose of sleep aid medicine, she finally succumbs to sleep, but even then her mind fills with nightmarish visions and she wakes up drenched in sweat with a deep sense of loss tugging at her from every angle, like she's being ripped apart by a pack of ravenous wolves. A lasting image from the dream is Harriet, walking away from her with Alfie in her arms, laughing.

Could that happen? She's been so focused on figuring out

the truth, she hasn't properly engaged with how she'd feel if the boys really were swapped back. Leaping from bed, Louise grabs her laptop and starts searching for real-life stories of swapped babies being returned to their biological parents. Of the cases she finds worldwide, two couples chose to keep the babies they'd brought up, and not their biological offspring. And one woman fought for years to get her own child back.

Even if she can prove without doubt that Jacob is her and Mark's son, and that Alfie is Harriet and Richard's – what if only one set of parents wants to swap them back? What would *she* want? Louise claws at her throat, fighting to regulate her breathing. She can't deny the bond she feels with Jacob – she wants the child that's rightfully hers, the one she birthed. But Alfie is her son, too, the boy she raised. It's an impossible question.

Louise gets to her knees, fumbles inside the bedside cabinet, pulling the journal, baby diary and a number of random items from it, flinging them to the carpet to reach the paper bag. She hasn't used it for ages. Now it's all she has.

After she's blown into it and rebreathed the exhaled air a dozen or so times, she regains a steady rate of respiration, and her panic subsides.

The room is too quiet. Louise leans over the bed and smacks the button on the alarm clock – music blares out and she sinks back into the pillows, allowing it to assault her ears. It's not until the banging breaks through to her conscious mind that she focuses on the time on the clock.

03:33. She raises her eyebrows at the repeated numbers, a niggling thought on the edge of her mind that they must mean something, then jerks upright. It's gone three in the morning. The banging is from next door.

Leaning across Mark's empty side of the bed, Louise turns the sound down.

'Sorry!' she shouts at the wall. Then she presses herself up against the flower-print wallpaper, her ear against the barrier separating her bedroom from her neighbour's, listening. It's not loud, but she can hear Drew talking. He's likely cursing her for waking him. She knocks gently, calls, 'I'm sorry, Drew,' again. Waits.

'No worries,' he shouts back. 'Just letting you know I'm here.'

And then, without warning, she cries.

Chapter 48

Louise has visited Harriet's house three days in a row now. She enters the back garden the same way each time but switches up her positioning. She's not sure why but feels it's an important precaution to prevent being seen. While she's never spotted a camera out the back, she wouldn't put it past Harriet to conceal the nanny cam in a bush. She's noted down the times Harriet is working and knows that Jacob will be at nursery then. Richard picked him up yesterday, and Louise followed, making sure to keep a safe distance behind them. Today, Jacob has been at home with Harriet all morning. As is the norm, he's spent most of his time in the playroom, alone, while she's been on her laptop, sitting at the island in the kitchen. She's taken several phone calls – one of which had her pacing the floor like an expectant mum, her fingers idly twiddling the key charm on her necklace. She never seems to wear a different necklace.

Harriet appears distracted, her face pale. Something is visibly bothering her. Richard pops in and they have a brief but animated conversation. What was that about? Then Louise hears the roar of a car engine, the screeching of tyres as he drives off. Harriet appears at the patio door, slides it open and screams. Louise jumps, almost yelping in shock. Then she hears crying.

Jacob.

Harriet's soothing voice drifts out the open door. She's suggesting they go to the park. Louise readies herself to follow but waits for a few minutes after they've left before coming out from her hiding place. She's about to take her usual route along the line of the fence towards the side gate, when she lets out an involuntary gasp.

The patio door is still open. In her haste, Harriet's forgotten about it.

Louise falters between the desire to leave unseen via the gate, or grasping the opportunity to sneak inside the house, where the likelihood of being caught on camera is high. While she enjoys watching Jacob, being near him, and would dearly love to watch him play at the park, this is a chance she can't waste.

It's happened for a reason.

With a surge of confidence, Louise pulls the hood of her jacket up and snakes along the exterior of the house, then stealthily slips inside. As they've not seen each other since Louise was caught red-handed taking a sample of blood and a toothbrush from their house, she assumes Harriet will have let her guard down. The last thing she'll be expecting is Louise undertaking a mad covert operation, so maybe, along with her inattention at leaving the back door open,

Harriet has also been careless and left something important out on view.

Louise tiptoes through the kitchen, careful not to disturb anything. Harriet's laptop is right there, the screen display visible; she hasn't even locked it. Louise surveys the area, looking for the nanny cam or any other recording device. Frowns. There's nothing. It's too easy. What if they've set up hidden cameras? No time to worry about that possibility now – she's in already, may as well go for the full crime of trespass.

Ignoring the warning prickling sensation running over her skin, Louise approaches the laptop. Its homepage shows an array of apps, and at first glance, they all appear to relate to kitchen design and other work-related files. Her eyes scan over them, and she's drawn to the calendar app – it could prove beneficial for her future reference. The week and months show up and Louise takes a photo on her mobile of the upcoming work meetings and schedule. There's a hospital appointment booked in for next week. This looks to be the regular monthly one Harriet has – an MRI scan. She clicks back through the calendar to the week they first met at playgroup. There's a tick, but nothing written on that day about her or Alfie, nothing the previous week either. But then, going back further still, an entry leaps out: Louise Webb/Rainbow. Harriet marked it down three weeks *prior* to them meeting. This is it, the proof, in black and white. Louise's pulse is racing – she feels both vindicated and horrified. Because this means she was right: Harriet sought them out; she already knew who Louise was. She must have known about Alfie and Jacob.

Pulling her attention away from the laptop, Louise glances around the kitchen. It's not as neat as when she visited before. Possibly a side effect of being back at work. Why doesn't Harriet employ a cleaner? She'd once have assumed it was because Richard wouldn't agree to it, but as Harriet put her right on that score during the meal – how she only let Richard believe it was him making the decisions – it must be Harriet who doesn't want one. Because of what a cleaner might find? Louise taps a finger against her bottom lip, does a three-sixty turn. Harriet was careless enough to leave the door and her laptop open, so there's a chance she left the cabinet in the study open, too.

Popping her head round the corner first to check for new cameras, Louise makes a quick dash through the glass corridor towards the other end of the house. Then, checking all is clear, moves to Richard's office. With a silent prayer that she'll find the cabinet drawers open, Louise enters the room. It's even more sparse than the first time she snuck in. Or, maybe she's remembering wrongly – but it feels . . . hollow, almost. The antique cabinet is in the same position as before. Closing her eyes, her tongue between her teeth, Louise tugs on each of the handles. Frustration thrums in her chest. The drawers remain stubbornly shut. Short of forcing them open, there's nothing she can do. If she were to prise them open with a knife, or break the entire cabinet, it would be clear she was responsible, and any hope of convincing Mark, or anyone in authority, would be lost entirely. She must play it carefully.

Is it easy to pick the lock on an old piece of furniture?

Louise scrambles around Richard's desk for a paperclip, kicking the box that's beneath it and sending the lid flying. She's already searched its contents, so it's a waste of her time doing so again. She'll replace the top in a second. Unfolding the metal paperclip she finds, she inserts it into the lock, giving it a twist first one way, then another. Nothing. She slams the flat of her palm against it, groaning in frustration. She's no idea how to pick a lock. There's likely an instructional YouTube video, though. After searching them for a few minutes, Louise gives up. It's no good, she just doesn't have the required tools to do it. Tracing her fingertip over the lock, something clicks in her mind and it's now she puts two and two together. Harriet wears a necklace with a key on it. Never seems to take it off. And – now that Louise considers it – it has the same pattern on it as the ornate legs. What's the betting it's to unlock this cabinet?

And for Harriet to have it on her person means it *must* be important. She's protecting something inside – and it's this, Louise reckons, that holds the proof of the baby swap.

Chapter 49

EMAIL
FROM AngelFace
SUBJECT Re. your text

Everything is falling into place. Don't worry. I've thought of everything. I've got you. I'm your guardian angel, don't forget!

Chapter 50

With her mood dipping from the weight of another failure, Louise turns to leave the study. Stops dead. The box lid she kicked is still under the desk. She runs her hand over her forehead. A slip like this would have alerted Harriet and Richard to something untoward, and they'd have reason to check the monitor. She's not sure the footage is recorded, but she doesn't want to find out the hard way. Nipping back, Louise bends down, picks it up. It's heavier than it looks. Turning it over, she sees something stuck inside the lid.

Steadying it on the desk, she tucks a fingernail underneath and teases it away from one edge, then runs her nail under each of the other sides. A dark brown card envelope pops out. Swallowing down the foreboding lump in her throat, she opens it. Immediately her posture droops. It's just a birth certificate. Why hide it? On closer inspection, Louise realises it's not Jacob's, and with mounting confusion reads the details.

Name and Surname: Benjamin Richard Faulkner

Sex: Male
Date of Birth: 24/05/2021
Place of Birth: Hastings, East Sussex

Louise's legs tingle with pins and needles and she shifts positions. This child would be four years old now. Where is he? Did they give him up for adoption? It's only a small gap between the two pregnancies. The certificate is one of those 'short' ones, so there's no parental details on it. Is it possible Richard had a child with someone else and this is Jacob's half-brother? Louise pulls her phone from her pocket. The battery icon flashes and she taps the screen, taking a photo of the certificate just before her mobile dies completely. A car door bangs outside, jolting her into action. She quickly replaces the envelope in the lid of the box and exits the house the way she came in.

At least she has something new to look into.

Instead of going straight home, Louise takes a detour to the library to use a computer. She approaches the friendly-looking librarian at the desk; she might know the quickest way to gain information about adoptions.

'Oh no, dear,' is her very quick response. 'I'm afraid you won't find that information easily. They're separate documents to births and deaths.'

'Okay, thanks. Can I look up birth records, then?'

'Yes, there are sites that give free access, though the searchable years are often limited.' She shows Louise through to the computer room and gives her a code to access the internet.

Coming up against brick wall after brick wall with the so-called free access, Louise is about to give up for the day when the librarian asks if she's tried the births and deaths notifications in the newspaper archive.

'No, I haven't. Can I do that here?'

Five minutes later, rubbing her strained eyes after all the scrolling, Louise finds something.

'Oh, God. No.'

She'd been wrong. Benjamin wasn't a half-brother, and he hadn't been adopted.

Louise's heart breaks.

Harriet's baby had died.

Chapter 51

Now she's able to lie in, Louise doesn't want to. She's been awake since 5 a.m., after barely sleeping, thinking about Harriet and the baby she lost. She's endured something no parent should ever have to experience. Louise wishes she'd known – maybe she'd have understood her better. She thinks of the lack of family photographs, Harriet's coolness with Jacob. What if this was never about Alfie?

But, no. The fact remains that Harriet tracked her and Alfie down. There's still something going on. This is just an added, terribly sad complication.

'He was never meant to survive.' She remembers the words she overheard Harriet say the other day. Was she talking about her first baby? She recalls Harriet or Richard mentioning a genetic condition, about Harriet not wanting to end up like her father. Is it possible her first baby died from the same condition? The realisation hits her like a brick: if Alfie is Harriet's son, what if he gets sick, too?

The morning has only just begun, but she's already on

her third cup of coffee. She needs fresh air. Somewhere to *think*. Away from her usual spots.

After mindlessly walking, she ends up at the park. Sits on a bench, under the tree furthest away from the play area. She hears excited squeals, children's laughter and dogs barking, but with her eyes closed she manages to shut out the noise. It's the ice-cream van that penetrates and brings her out of her thoughts. The tinkling, slightly out-of-tune music transports her back to her 90s childhood. There was nothing like running out to the van with a pound coin pressed into her palm to make everything brighter, better. Life was so simple then. The nostalgia of the moment brings a smile to Louise's face, and she opens her eyes to fully appreciate it. The van has come to a standstill somewhere on the other side of the park, but her attention doesn't reach it.

Because there's Jacob. Her breath snags on the inhale. He's got a *Cars* sweatshirt on – Lightning McQueen, his favourite character. He's skipping between the slide and see-saw, oblivious to all around him. In his own carefree world. An invisible cord tugs Louise, drawing her heart towards him. She closes her eyes, lowering her head to break the spell, and then she moves from the bench, as though that will detach her from its force.

Walk away.

But she *misses* Jacob. And she misses Alfie. She just wants to see them both.

The prickling in the back of her nose brings tears to her eyes, and a gust of cool air helps release them. She presses the heels of her hands to her cheeks as she heads blindly on.

'Lou-Lou!'

Louise turns to the sound of the little voice. 'Well, hello, Jacob.' She sniffs, quickly wipes away the remaining tears, and smiles. He puts his hand in hers – it's warm and soft and her palm tingles with tiny electrical pulses. Losing herself in the pleasure of the moment, she closes her eyes, but a thought bursts into her mind, and they snap open.

'Can I have ice cream? Pur-leeease!' he says. Louise looks around. No one's watching.

'Of course, darling.' And they're walking, arms swinging, her heart thudding wildly in her chest as she checks over her shoulder, back at the play area. 'Where's Har— Mummy?'

Jacob shrugs. 'My favourite is chocolate,' he says, pulling her hand. He laughs as he drags her towards the ice-cream van. It's in sight of the park, she's not taking him far. Harriet's nowhere to be seen, though.

'Okay, okay.' She smiles and allows herself to be led. 'I'll send Mummy a text ...' But she doesn't get her mobile. Swept along by Jacob's cheerful chatter, Louise's mind settles into a place she can't remember having been for a long time. If ever. A calmness engulfs her; a sense of everything being in its rightful place. After she's bought the ice cream, they could go somewhere else. Just the two of them.

How easy it would be.

When they reach their turn at the van, Jacob jumps up and down excitedly beside her as Louise hands over the money in return for the chocolate ice-cream cornet. She ducks down and places it in Jacob's outstretched hands, and as she bobs back up her eyes catch the frantic look in Harriet's.

'What the *fuck*, Louise?'

Louise gasps. 'No need to swear like that.' She places her hands over Jacob's ears, protecting him from the further cursing she assumes will spill from Harriet's mouth. Given the alarming colour her face has turned, the way her lips form a tight line and her fists clench as she launches herself towards her, there's every chance Louise is about to be hit.

'Take your hands off *my* son.' She says this loud enough that everyone within earshot turns their way, their attention fully on the three of them. Suddenly caught like an animal in a trap, Louise lets go of Jacob, backs away from him and lowers her head in submission.

'Sorry. I was going to text ... He asked for ...' She indicates the ice-cream van. 'We were on our way back.'

Harriet glowers, shaking her head. 'You've gone too far this time.'

'But, Harriet ...' She doesn't have a leg to stand on. What's she going to do – blame a three-year-old?

'You purposely lured him away, didn't you? Are you trying to punish me for something, Louise? What on earth did I do that was so wrong, apart from be your friend when no one else was interested? Maybe this is why.'

'I promise, Harriet. We were –' her words jerk out from her mouth, staccato as she gulps in air – 'on our way. Back.' She's going to have a panic attack.

'Yeah, right. You say that now you've been caught. I've

seen you, you know. Sneaking around outside our house like some *stalker*. To think I felt sorry for you.'

Louise wants this crushing humiliation to end. Harriet's enjoying this – Louise can tell. She tries to hold on to the sympathy she feels for Harriet, for the awful thing she went through. But one look at Harriet's furious puce face, the nasty words pouring out from her, and Louise's resentment comes roaring back. *She knows*.

'Stay away from my family, do you hear? Because I swear, if I see you anywhere near Jacob again, I'll call the police.'

'Do you want me to call 'em, now, love?' a voice asks. Others join in and, knowing it could escalate quickly, Louise mumbles further apologies and strides off. The voices don't grow distant, though, and she swears she hears someone yell, 'Don't let her get away!' She picks up speed, fear pounding through her veins, not daring to look behind. Her breaths become shallow, as if a tight band restricts her chest. Hurried footsteps keep pace with hers. She has visions of everyone from the park and surrounding area giving chase, one behind the other, and new people joining in when they realise what's going on, just like the scene from the children's book *The Big Pancake* she loved as a child, where the mother, hungry children and passers-by give chase. If she remembers rightly, it's the clever pig who pretends to offer his help who gobbles it up in the end.

Trust no one.

Reaching the perimeter of the park, she has two choices – go right and head straight for home and risk the police being there waiting for her, or go left and wander around town for a while, wait it out in the hope no one carries out the threat of calling the cops.

'Need a lift?'

She hadn't noticed the car, let alone the person sitting in the driver's seat, the window rolled down.

'Drew!' Any ounce of concern she might've had about him evaporates in this instance. She's still not chanced looking behind her, afraid of what she'll see. So, with Drew her only ally, and the quickest way out of the terrible situation into which she's got herself, she rushes round to the passenger side and jumps in.

Chapter 52

Louise's breaths heave, and she presses a hand against her chest, attempting to contain the sobs threatening to escape. Did Drew witness what happened? He must have done, but he doesn't ask questions. Whether because he knows she isn't capable of answering, or because he doesn't want to know, she's not sure. But she is grateful.

They sit in silence – and Louise welcomes it. As the distance between her and the park grows, and she doesn't hear any sirens, she sinks back a little, and the rhythmic dinging of an alarm breaks through her consciousness.

'Is that me?' she says, reaching for the seatbelt. The alarm ceases when she clicks it into place.

'No worries. Didn't think the extra restriction would help.'

Louise considers him for a moment, her frown deepening. She still can't work him out. He's always been kind to her, she realises, especially of late. And if he is in cahoots with Harriet, then, well, he's done her a solid by rescuing her today. She wishes she could ask him about her, but she doesn't want to open up that can of worms. Not after what just happened.

'You're staring,' he says, and Louise immediately snaps her head away. He laughs. 'If you've something on your mind, do go ahead.'

'No. Nothing.' She doesn't sound convincing. Should she come straight out and ask him?

'I'm sorry you're having such a hard time, Louise.' His voice is soft, kind. Filled with compassion.

'Not your fault.' Louise looks out of the window, doesn't want him to see the tears in her eyes.

'I saw Mark leave with Alfie and a suitcase. Assumed it wasn't a holiday.'

Her muscles tense at the mention of their names, but she doesn't respond.

'Is everything okay with you? After seeing you at the hospital the other day . . .' she asks instead.

'Oh, yeah, fine, nothing to worry about. Just standard "man of a certain age" stuff!'

He's quick to brush off the question. Noticeably uncomfortable when the roles are reversed. She's about to say as much, when he shifts his attention from the road to her.

'Seems we're both learning about things we'd rather not know.'

Louise's mouth drops open as his watery blue eyes penetrate hers. He blinks rapidly, breaking the connection, and she senses he has more he wants to share. Maybe she needs to open up first.

'I miss them, Mark and Alfie. So much. I – er, don't know

how much you saw back there, but today was a bit of a wake-up call for me.'

And it was, in more ways than one. The fact that it not only crossed her mind to take Jacob, but that she nearly acted on it, fills her with horror. If she were asked in this very moment what it is she actually wants, she would say it's to have Alfie and Mark back home. It's not simply DNA that makes a child yours – it's all the little things, it's love and memories, sharing the moments of joy and laughter, watching them grow into an adult. But it isn't only the happy times – it's being there for them when they're sick or sad, scared or lonely. She'd lost sight of all this. If she's willing to put this whole thing to bed, maybe she can put it all right.

'Not to push my thoughts or suggestions on to you,' Drew says, 'but I've had some counselling. It's not for everyone, I know, but might you find that helpful? Having someone independent to talk things through . . .'

'I've done that. Was seeing a counsellor for a while, actually. In fact, I'm supposed to be seeing her now. Agreed I would when things started getting tough again.'

'But you haven't?'

'No. I – I lied to Mark. Told him I'd made an appointment.' The confession sends heat to her face; she touches her cheeks with her palms.

'Wouldn't take much to rectify that one little lie,' he says, nodding towards her mobile.

Drew's right. May as well make a start on some of the easier things to remedy. It'll be one thing ticked off her long list of things she needs to do to make it up to Mark.

She takes her phone, scrolls through her contacts until she sees Natalie's name. Takes a breath, then taps call. Her heart plummets when voicemail kicks in, but she stays on the line, leaving a message saying she wants to book an appointment as soon as possible.

Drew smiles. 'Small steps,' he says. 'You can't eat an elephant in one bite.'

'Thanks. You're pretty good at this stuff. And lately you've been in just the right place at the right time for me.'

Despite herself, she thinks again of him watching her, of the times she saw him near Harriet. Screw it, she's just going to ask him.

'Funny question,' she ventures, trying to sound casual. 'Do you know that woman, in the playground? Harriet? I'm sure I saw you in the same place as her once or twice.'

Drew doesn't look at her – simply presses his mouth down at the edges while shaking his head. 'Can't say I do. It's a small town.'

She's not convinced, but she's not in a position to push him on it. If she's going to put this to bed, she doesn't need to. And, she realises, she finds him a comforting presence now. Unless he's an extremely good liar, he can't mean her any harm.

'Look, if I can get my shit together, get my family home again – please can we agree to keep ... *all this* – what happened at the park today – between us, do you think?'

He nods. 'Course. Besides, I've got my own stuff to deal with.'

* * *

The second Louise gets inside the house, she calls Mark. After a slightly awkward greeting, she gets straight down to begging him for forgiveness.

'I've called Natalie. I wasn't ready to accept it before, not really – but I am now. I know I need help with all of this.'

'You lied before, then.' Mark's voice breaks.

'I was scared, desperate to say what you wanted to hear. It's different this time, I swear.'

'I hoped the space would make you realise …'

'And you were right, Mark. I'm so sorry it took you both leaving to make me see more clearly. I promise, wholeheartedly –' she places her hand on her chest, feels the emotion flowing through her – 'that I'm willing to do whatever it takes to keep our family together.'

Only Mark's nasal inhale and exhale breaks the silence. Time slows to a crawl, each second dragging out. Louise bites the inside of her cheek, holding back the urge to fill the void. Finally, she breaks.

'Please, Mark. I can't do this without you. I love you.'

'Okay, Lou,' he says. 'If you can prove to me that you can be trusted, we'll come back.'

'Thank you.' Louise ends the call, curls up on the sofa and sleeps.

PART THREE

Chapter 53

The light breeze tickles Louise's face as she lifts it towards the sun. Her son's hand is warm in hers, and she walks with him slowly, relishing the moment. Practising mindfulness has given her a new way to cope with everyday life. Natalie is impressed with how she is moving forward. How she's open about what's happened and has embraced honesty, her desire to overcome the irrational belief that Alfie isn't her biological son. Over the past few sessions, Natalie's explained the theories and research she thinks are linked to how Louise felt, how she twisted the evidence to suit her narrative. The newly prescribed medication helps keep her level. Her suspicions, and everything that happened between her and Harriet's family, are no longer at the forefront of her mind – and the more she talks it through with Natalie, the stronger her belief becomes that she got it all wrong about Harriet's motivations, about the baby swap. Mark's pleased she's progressed, and they're in the best place she can remember being for a long time. But she keeps her mother at arm's length – at Natalie's suggestion, she chooses to spend time with those who bring her joy. Not those who are toxic and bring her down.

Today marks a new beginning. Not only is she dropping Alfie to nursery, the first time since he's been back home, but she's attending an interview for a PA role at a local marketing firm. It's a step down from her previous role, but the hours suit, and it means she'll get to spend time with Alfie, too.

Louise doesn't see any sign of Harriet or Jacob when she takes Alfie to nursery. Knowing Harriet, she's likely taken him to another place now, rather than chance another incident like the one at the park. She wants to ask the fun mums if they've seen her, but judging by the withering look Steph gave when Louise said good morning she assumes Harriet's told them something and asking them anything is futile. It doesn't matter anyway. She doesn't want to know about them. She's good. Alfie's good.

She doesn't need them.

Once Alfie runs happily into nursery, Louise heads to the interview, walking at a slow pace to avoid getting sweaty. She's dressed in a smart dark-blue pencil skirt with a white blouse and a tailored jacket. Getting to the building fifteen minutes earlier than her appointment, she signs in with the receptionist, then nips to the loo to check her appearance. She pulls her jacket off, inspecting under her armpits. Sniffs, spritzes some perfume for good measure before replacing her jacket. She pulls at the sleeves, straightens her skirt for the fourth time, then reapplies her lipstick while mentally repeating the mantras:

You are worthy.
They'll be lucky to have you work for them.

Louise's cheeks burn when she stumbles on the first question, then falters on the second. She's ballsing this up. *Stay calm. Stop panicking.* She must take her time, stop her racing heart from making her rush her answers. Think of the end goal. A place on the workforce again, back to feeling she's contributing – not only to finances, but to life. A sense of belonging, of importance. She takes a long, slow breath before answering their next question and nails it.

The interview lasts almost an hour, and by the end of it she's fully in her stride, as if she's never been out of employment. Walking out with her head held high, confidence radiates from her. For the first time in a while, she's beginning to enjoy life.

Her mobile vibrates in her bag. She'd forgotten she'd muted it while she was being interviewed. It'll be Mark, wanting to know how it went. She should buy some champagne on the way home. Even if she doesn't get this job, she's confident she'll get another. And, besides, she and Mark can still call it a celebration – they're a family again. Snaking in and out of people along the bustling pavement, she hits the accept button, a smile ready, unable to contain her delight about how well it went.

But the voice on the end of the line isn't Mark's. She takes the phone from her ear, checks the number displayed. Unknown.

'Oh, sorry, thought you were someone else,' she says,

waiting for the inevitable 'have you been in an accident' line so that she can hang up.

'Is that Louise ... er ... Louise Webb?' The woman is quiet, tentative. Unless it's her first-ever sales call, it's not the reason she's contacting her.

'Speaking.'

'My name's Clara. I work at Sommerby Hospital ...'

Louise stops walking, her legs unstable. Not the woman's first sales call, but possibly her first giving bad news. While she's been in the interview, something bad's happened to Mark or Alfie.

No. Surely the police would contact her in the first instance. She breathes again, but she can't shake the dread filling her nervous system.

'How can I help?' The wobble in her voice is audible.

'You came into the maternity unit last month. Left your details in case anyone remembered something about the time you and your son were on the special-care baby unit?'

'I did.' She swallows hard, her heart galloping as though she's been running.

'Well – I think there's something I should tell you ...'

Chapter 54

Clara won't say more on the phone. With her world verging on exploding again, Louise debates ignoring this woman. As much as one part of her yells '*walk away* – this is just another waste of time, another chance of losing what you've got', the other part can't bring herself to say no. She'll regret not hearing her out. Louise agrees to meet her in fifteen minutes at a coffee shop on the edge of town, making a pact with herself that if this is a dead end and what Clara tells her is nothing more than she knows already – she won't continue.

It's as though she's self-sabotaging. Something her mother would say is a trait she got from her father. Because isn't everything currently moving in the right direction? She's put the past behind her – to a degree, at least, certainly enough to be able to focus on Mark and Alfie, on their life together. She's doing well. Feeling good. Why risk rocking the boat?

This is a test.

Is she failing it by simply turning up at the café?

On the flip side, should she ignore a blatant sign from the universe? The questions slosh about in her skull and, before she knows it, she's there, looking in the window of Joe's Café. A woman, late fifties, sits fidgeting with a ring on her finger, her mouth pressed in a tight, worried line, her eyes flitting around nervously. Louise pushes her shoulders down, the ache from rigid muscles spreading between her blades.

In and out. Listen to what she's got to say, then go home.

She opens the door and strides up to Clara.

There're a few moments of silence as Louise sits down. Up close, Clara looks older. Louise takes in the spidery lines and crepey skin, and tries to recall her face from the maternity unit or SCBU.

'You don't remember me, do you,' she says.

'It's not just you. I've huge gaps in my memory.'

Clara gives a knowing nod. 'I won't bother with a long backstory; I don't wish to waste your time. I'm very sorry for keeping this to myself for so long.'

A throb begins in Louise's neck. 'Go on,' she says, her eyes focused on Clara's.

'It's been bothering me, really, since the day of the flood.'

Louise's stomach plummets as if she's fallen from a great height. Clara's referring to the flood written about in her baby diary, the one she didn't recall. She puts her hands on the table, steadying herself as the ground feels like it's shifting beneath her feet. 'Keep going.'

'The power went off for a moment. Not long, as the generator kicked in, of course. But it managed to cause some confusion, all the alarms going off and whatnot.' Clara's face goes in and out of focus as Louise listens. Waits for the punchline. 'We don't usually have very sick babies on the special-care baby unit, but on this occasion we had a couple of high-dependency little ones awaiting transfer to the neonatal unit – and it got a bit chaotic. Myself and the other senior nurse were busy attending to them, and that meant the healthcare assistants and agency nurses were left to support the other babies and begin moving the mums to different rooms, those furthest away from the water leak, until it was fully assessed.'

Fragments of memories creep in from the perimeter of her mind, hearing Clara describe the aftermath of the power outage caused by the flood. She *does* remember having to leave the bay in the ward she was on, along with a few other mums. The sense of panic when she was ushered down the corridor without Alfie. It went against every instinct to leave him behind.

'Is it normal to move mums without their babies?' A situation such as that could certainly give rise to babies being accidentally swapped.

'It depends, really. If the babies are in incubators, then yes. If the babies were in the standard cots beside the beds, then they'd go together. But, as no one was going outside of the building because the flood wasn't major and the power was reinstated quickly, it didn't get flagged as a problem to move them separately.'

Clara takes a sip of her drink, the cup clinking against the saucer as she places it back with a shaky hand. When she continues, telling Louise how she had to rush into the next treatment room for a monitor, her voice trembles and her words stutter.

'What happened, Clara?'

'See, this is the part I've struggled with. I've questioned my recollection of it, replayed the scene over and over in my mind and tried to view it without prejudice.' Clara puts a hand on her chest as she inhales, her eyes closed. 'I thought I saw one of the agency nurses, Emma, switching two of the babies. As I swung the door open, she was taking a baby and placing him in an empty cot.'

Louise's eyes narrow. 'Why did that make you think she'd switched them? I don't understand.'

'Because she'd had two babies in a single cot moments before I entered, and the look on her face when she realised I'd seen was one of pure panic. She uttered something about thinking she'd transport both babies together for speed, but realised it was a bad idea, and so was putting the baby back. Her explanation appeared plausible in the circumstances.'

Louise draws in a ragged breath. The babies being accidentally swapped was one thing, but deliberately? Why the hell would someone – a *nurse* – do that? Louise saves her questions, Clara continuing the story. 'But, later, it came to light someone had purposely caused the leak. I had my suspicions about Emma – had been taken in by her stories before – but ultimately felt sorry for her when she told me her son had a rare condition. She showed me photos on her phone; he looked so sick. I even gave her money. She was going to start a funding page; she might have actually done it. I can't remember now.'

'What happened to her?'

'That's the thing. After the day I caught her in what I thought was her swapping the babies, she called in sick. It was a couple months later that we were told she'd left. Gone to America to seek treatment for her terminally ill boy.'

'The timing is weird, that's for sure.'

'My thoughts, too. But you know, at the time ... The fallout of me saying something when I wasn't sure – it didn't bear thinking about. I feel terrible now, because had I mentioned it, told *someone*, a simple test would've sorted it there and then. I'm so sorry. I just couldn't be sure enough. Everything looked as it should. The babies both had identity bands. I assumed I was mistaken—'

'Alfie didn't, actually. Have two bands, I mean. But probably lost it in a Baby-gro ...'

'That's the usual issue,' Clara says, offering a small smile. 'Anyway, I ended up putting it, and her, to the back of my mind, if I'm honest. And life went on. Until I overheard you talking in the maternity unit the other week. I didn't put two and two together for a bit, then, all of a sudden, it hit me. Your Alfie was one of those babies. I'm certain of it.'

Louise's blood runs cold. She'd guessed where this was going, but having someone else – a professional – put a voice to her fear is almost unbearable.

'And the other baby?'

'I'm really not sure I should say ... I—'

'Clara,' Louise says, pressing her hand over hers. 'I don't think you came to tell me half a story, did you?'

'No.' She gives a huge sigh. 'The other baby was called Jacob.'

It's like a guillotine falling, slicing off the last part of her doubts. 'Jacob *Faulkner*,' Louise states.

'Yes.' Clara's eyes widen. 'How did you know?'

'Because he's a little boy I met through playgroup. From the first time I saw him, I sensed something – a closeness. A bond. I couldn't explain it.'

Clara's hand goes to her chest. 'I'm so very sorry.' Her skin is pallid, waxy with shock and regret. 'You must be going through hell.'

'I'd just concluded I was wrong about everything. Decided it was me, that I was suffering from ... Well, it doesn't matter now.'

'What will you do?'

What *will* Louise do? She doesn't know – she has never known. She thinks of the weeks since Alfie and Mark returned. How free she's felt.

'Maybe I should just leave it. My life is beginning to get back to some kind of normal, you know? If I start this again ... I took a DNA test, you see. It was inconclusive, which I took to mean I definitely wasn't Alfie's mum, and my husband found out. He took Alfie and left for a while. I can't go through that again.'

'I understand. There's a lot at stake. But you deserve to know the truth; there are questions that need answering.'

'I don't think Harriet, Jacob's mum, would agree. She's already threatened me with the police.'

'Oh, I'm sorry, that must've been distressing. I wonder, though ...' Clara says, sitting back. 'Things stick in your memory for a variety of reasons. And quite apart from what

I thought I saw, the thing that stood out with Harriet was how she didn't *look* at her baby.'

Louise's brow creases. Although this seems odd, she can relate because she felt the same. 'Can't that be normal, though? I mean, having been through the pain of birthing, the exhaustion, all that – it's understandable you feel disconnected from the little human who caused it. Isn't it?'

'Yes, it is. But with Harriet it just seemed ... different. Purposeful. Until after that day – then she just changed, as quickly as a light switching on.' Clara lets out a sharp sigh. 'It's easy, I guess, to assign meaning after the fact. The years might've altered my own recollections. I definitely remember that her behaviour did strike me as being strange, though. But one of the reasons I let it go when I thought I saw Emma swap them was because I couldn't think of a reason *why*. What would be the point? All I could think later, when I considered a motive, was that it was for financial reasons. Emma would do whatever it took to get her son that treatment.'

'So you think she was *paid* to swap them?'

'It's possible, although I don't know why a parent would *knowingly* swap their baby for another. Doesn't make the slightest sense to me ...'

But, all of a sudden, it *does* to Louise. A deep ache in her body tells her that what happened three years ago in SCBU, Harriet not only knew about it, but she was also the one responsible for it.

Chapter 55

WhatsApp

Time is running out for my son – soon he'll be too sick to travel to the US. It's devastating watching him suffer and having to leave him each day to go to work. You're the only one who understands me – the lengths I'm prepared to go to. Our Plan A must work, I honestly don't think there'll be time for the Plan B.

> Putting my trust in you. You say you will pull off Plan A – I have to believe that. I know you've a lot to lose. The less I know, I think the better, but remember – the target **must not** be sick.

I'm doing all I can before D-day.

> OK, great. Tell me only what I need to know.

I've got eyes on the prize, as it were! So, as soon as the time comes, I'll message you as we agreed. You'll have to do all you can to make sure you're in there at the same time.

God, I hope it all aligns.

This will work. It has to.

Chapter 56

The noise of the world around her fades to a low hum as Louise walks home, each step feeling as heavy as her thoughts. Before she'd left the café, Clara asked again what she wanted to do now that this new information had come to light, but Louise's mind had refused to think straight. 'I don't know. I need time to think about it,' was all she could offer. Clara, adamant she should help put things right, said to contact her once she'd absorbed the details, and if there was anything she could do to help gather evidence, to let her know.

Her first instinct is to tell Mark and together go to the police, but even with Clara's account, it's still hearsay. And she doubts Mark would even let her get that far – certainly not if he finds out about the playground incident. She was sure Harriet would've told him, since she'd told him everything else, but for some reason she's stayed silent – perhaps because Louise has finally stopped bothering them. As a result, she can't confront Harriet either; she knows too much and has already proven to be an expert liar.

Back to square one.

Mark and Alfie greet her at the front door.

'Well, hello, you two.' She summons her earlier enthusiasm and high spirits back to her voice. Hopes the fact that the stuffing has just been knocked out of her isn't immediately detectable. She smiles down at Alfie, a sadness once again filling her heart. 'Oh, you've had chocolate, have you?' She laughs, hoping it conceals the onset of tears, and reaches down, wiping her thumb gently over his mouth to remove the rim of brown.

'First day at nursery is a big deal, isn't it, mate?' Mark says, stepping into the hall so Louise can get inside the house.

'Did you have fun?' she asks. But he slips away, toddling off towards the conservatory.

'He's tired,' Mark says. 'Right, shall we have a takeaway? To celebrate?'

Her face twists in confusion before it clicks. 'Oh! The interview.' She doesn't feel the slightest bit hungry, but nods anyway. 'Though, a bit premature to celebrate . . .'

'There's a message for you on the answerphone,' he says, his face lighting up. She hasn't seen him this happy for a long while, and the guilt of where she's been since the interview, the direction her thoughts have gone again, crushes her. Mark follows her to the landline. She forces a smile as she plays it back. She got the job.

'I'm so proud of you,' Mark says, wrapping his arms round her waist. 'You've been through a lot, but here you are, smashing it!'

'Yeah.' Louise struggles to summon the enthusiasm to match his. 'Sorry. It's really great. I'm drained is all. That's the most mental energy I've had to sustain for years,' she says, laughing.

'Your mother even said she'd do the nursery pick-ups if you need her. When you start.'

'What do you mean? I haven't even told her ... Oh,' Louise says, her lip curling. 'You already listened and immediately told my mother.'

'I was dead excited for you, didn't want to waste a moment trying to ensure it happens for you. No point getting the job then worrying about childcare. I wanted it to be in the bag.'

'That's thoughtful, but it would've been nice to enjoy my own success first, *before* involving my mother.' Her words land badly, the atmosphere changing as quickly as a flip of a coin.

'Not that long ago you were moaning she doesn't take an interest in you or Alfie. Now, finally, she's stepping up to the plate and that's wrong.'

'It's not that.'

'Sometimes, Louise, I don't think you *want* to be happy.'

'I do. Trust me, I do.' Her voice dips, mental exhaustion disabling her ability to continue talking.

'Fine. Well, I'll make sure I get off work early and do the pick-ups the first couple of times. But I really think you should let your mum help out at some point.'

Louise nods. She'll fight this particular battle another time.

'I'm going for a shower.'

Pain radiates up her back into her neck. She stands under the jets of hot water, pressing her fingers into the knot, kneading gently as she replays Clara's story in her mind.

She knows, deep down, that she has to act. But how? At least she has Clara onside now – only a phone call away. But there's no point doing anything rash. If she's to do *anything*, it has to be smart. Only concrete evidence will do. She rests her head against the shower screen, waiting for an idea to materialise. Nothing comes.

Five minutes later, Louise sits on the bed, wrapped in a towel, and her eyes fall to her bedside table. She begins rummaging inside the drawer, but doesn't find the journal or the baby diary. Her mind blanks. She can't remember moving them, but, then again, she was putting it all behind her, forging ahead on her new path, so she must've boxed them up. Filing her concerns away with them.

Until Clara's call, she had been doing a good job.

Mark's cooked an evening meal. He's making a huge effort since returning home, consistently back from work earlier, helping out around the house more. After they've eaten, the three of them play until Alfie's gaping yawns and drooping eyes indicate he's ready for sleep. Mark jumps up, about to take Alfie by the hand. Louise intercepts him.

'You've done your share today,' she tells Mark. 'I'll take Alfie to bed.' And she grasps his hand in hers and leads him upstairs.

He's asleep before she even finishes the first story. The

book lies open on her lap as she leans back against the wall. How easy it's become lately. So far from the exhausting battles she had with him only a few short months ago. Natalie was probably right about him picking up on her emotions. There's been less stress oozing from her recently – she's been in a better headspace, learning to live with her shortcomings. But, today, everything has been thrown up in the air again. She watches Alfie's chest rise and fall in steady respirations, his lips slightly parted, the gentle puffs of air vibrating through them. It's so close to being perfect. But how can she bring up this little boy if she knows he was never really hers?

It's not fair to him, and it's not fair to Jacob. They didn't choose to be swapped. That decision was made by selfish people driven by greed and ... and what, though? *Is* there something wrong with Alfie? Surely, if there had been some kind of genetic disorder, it would've been picked up by now? She feels a rush of anger. How *dare* Harriet and Emma conspire to ruin her life. Why her? Why her baby? The rage grows in Louise's stomach, twisting and pulling, pushing upwards. She bolts for the bathroom, hot vomit expelling from her like lava.

Chapter 57

Louise watches from the top of the path as Mark and Alfie disappear from view. Mark is taking Alfie to feed the ducks, to give her some time to go through paperwork before she begins her new job.

'Hey, Louise.' A hand waves in front of her face. 'Everything all right?'

'Oh, hi. Yes, I'm fine.' She snaps back to the moment, sees the concern on Drew's face and quickly explains Mark and Alfie are off to the park for a bit. Relief softens his jawline. It's touching that he cares. Since Mark and Alfie returned home, she hasn't seen much of Drew, guessing he was keeping his distance while she got on with rebuilding her life.

'I could take your "I'm fine" answer at face value,' he says, narrowing his eyes, 'but ...'

She looks him in the eye and decides it's now or never.

'No. Everything is not all right.' Louise looks up at him. 'I asked you before, whether you knew Harriet, and you denied it ...'

His head drops.

'I thought you were moving on from all of that,' he says sadly.

'You *do* know her, don't you!'

'Look, do you want to come in for a coffee?' he asks, hooking a thumb towards his house. 'There are some things I need to tell you.'

Louise's stomach contracts. She's just started to like Drew, but maybe she was right about him all along. She follows him down the path to his house, waiting behind him as he opens the door.

'Erm ... excuse the state of the place. Don't get many visitors.' He waves a hand around, then fills the kettle.

She doesn't give a shit about the state of the place. She wants answers.

'Why did that guy, the one in the white van, want to hurt you so much?' The question is out of her mouth before she's considered it. Drew sighs heavily.

'It's all part of a bigger story,' he says, reaching into a cupboard and taking out two mugs. She takes a step back, peering into the lounge through the open door. It's dark in there, only a sliver of sun breaking through the slit where the curtains don't meet fully in the middle. She glimpses the clutter – what look to be old newspapers, magazines piled high, a ton of unopened post; it reminds her of the programme she watched about hoarders. Is that what Drew is? But if that were the case, what the hell is he filling his bins with every week? He's certainly not throwing anything away from the look of it. The kitchen is clutter-free, though.

She refocuses on him. 'And this *bigger story* – does it involve Harriet? Does it involve me?'

He gives a long blink, inhales and exhales slowly. 'It does,' he says simply. 'But probably not in the way you think.'

Her pulse skips. 'I need to know, Drew. Do you have any links to her? Were you keeping tabs on me for her?'

'I wasn't, and I'm still not, conspiring with Harriet.'

'So what, then? What's the connection?'

'It's . . . it's hard to explain. Why don't you start by telling me what's happened?'

And for some reason, despite everything, she feels she can trust him. She tells him the whole sad story, starting with that first, hopeful playdate with Harriet and ending on the bombshell that just fell into her lap.

As Louise talks, she finds herself almost hoping Drew will laugh, tell her Clara must've been mistaken and it's all some terrible coincidence. Talk her out of following it up. But, instead, something shifts, his face becoming more serious, the colour draining from it.

'I'm so sorry, Louise.' He bows his head. 'I should've come clean about everything before. I hope you will appreciate why I didn't.'

A dizzying lurch catches her off-guard, the sensation that she's falling stealing her breath.

'What do you mean?' There's a tremble in her voice.

'I haven't been entirely honest with you about my ex-girlfriend.'

Louise stiffens. What's his ex got to do with this?

'What did you do to her?'

'Do to her? God, Louise – it's not what I did to *her*.'

Shit. Apparently she doesn't trust him as much as she'd thought. 'Sorry. What did your girlfriend do?'

'I wasn't sure how much you knew. When I bumped into you at the maternity unit, it wasn't by accident.'

So he *had* been following her. 'You weren't there for an appointment.'

'No. I was doing some digging of my own.'

Louise locks her gaze with Drew's as something clicks in her mind. 'I forgot your girlfriend's name. Remind me.'

Drew pushes his hands down his thighs, blows out his cheeks.

'It's Emma.'

Chapter 58

Louise's mouth falls open. 'Emma, as in the nurse, the one Clara saw switching the babies?'

Drew nods sadly.

'What the fuck, Drew?' Her breath is coming in short, sharp gasps.

'Louise, please, you're okay. I'll tell you everything – I promise. Just go sit down in there and I'll get you a glass of water.'

He gestures to the lounge and runs towards the sink. Louise is still standing in the middle of the room when he comes in with a glass. She takes a grateful gulp then goes to put it down, but there's no clear surface.

'Oh. Shall I?' She bends forward, about to shift some things to make space.

'No!'

She jumps. 'Uh ... sorry.' Louise puts her free hand up.

'Everything's in order.' Drew takes her glass from her and sets it on a small nest of tables, then goes to the window, sweeping the curtains back. Louise squints as the light floods in. When her eyes adjust, she sees a two-seater sofa, asks if she should sit there. Drew nods, then passes her the glass. Takes his mug of tea and kneels down opposite her, on the other side of the table.

'Emma left me,' he says, his eyes avoiding Louise's. 'Vanished in the middle of the night without explanation – not so much as a Dear John note.' He goes on to explain how in her hurry she'd left some of her things behind. He tried to contact her, but she never responded. 'I always wondered what being ghosted meant.' He gives a brittle laugh before continuing. Because he couldn't understand why she'd gone, he'd looked through the items for clues. He already knew she had an obsessive interest in Louise, though he couldn't work out why.

'Now that you've told me what she did, her obsession makes more sense. I can't help thinking Emma was more deeply involved. Your story has certainly shed some light on what I've found. I've been collecting bits and pieces over the past three years since she left,' he says, giving a melancholy shake of his head. He picks up a notebook Louise recognises as the one he was holding when he stopped her to ask about the acronym E-D-D. He flicks through the pages, then stops, placing his finger in it to keep his place. 'A lot of it hadn't appeared relevant. But when you told me what E-D-D stood for, well, it all started adding up. And, like a huge fucked-up puzzle, a few of the missing pieces slotted in.'

Louise places her glass on top of a pile of magazines, takes the notebook from him. On the page, there is a list of names. All females. *Louise W* is fourth down. Alongside the estimated delivery date for Alfie's birth. There's no good reason she can think of why Emma would have written this information down.

'I realised Emma must have been up to something,' Drew says. 'I just didn't know it would turn out to be this bad. It now seems clear she upped and left after she'd swapped babies and got her money.'

Louise's heart aches – for herself and for Drew. 'She had everyone fooled,' she says as a way of offering some degree of comfort.

He smiles, shrugs. 'I admit I was sucked in by her. She had a way of spinning the truth, and I suppose I wanted to believe she was a good person. "The One", you know?' Drew says, running his hands through his hair. 'I don't want you to think I had anything to do with it, Louise. Honestly, I knew nothing about what she was doing. I suspected she had issues, and genuinely wanted to help her. Just before she left, she became more volatile. Would go out of her way to start arguments. But when I called her out on her behaviour, she turned on me.'

The picture starts to build, and Louise listens in stunned silence as Drew tells her how he begged Emma to seek help because he was worried about her obsessive behaviour. He'd no idea the lengths she'd go to.

'Until I found the diary, the most I'd worried about was her pissing you off if you caught her watching you. Now I think she used her knowledge of you and your pregnancy to work out if you were a good candidate for the baby swap.'

Louise picks the notebook back up, looks at the list of

women registered at Sommerby maternity. There are other details, lots of crossings-out – mainly of the names of those who had already given birth prior to Harriet.

'Only two were left.' Louise puts a hand to her tummy, remembering the first flutters of movement, then the later kicks, the long moments where she felt her growing baby wriggle and move beneath her skin.

'I wonder if she targeted me, too,' Drew says.

Louise frowns. 'What do you mean?'

'Well, we got together pretty quickly. She knew where I lived, made a thing of staying here most nights, and she was the one who suggested moving in. I think now it was purely to be close to you.'

Louise casts her gaze across the other items strewn on the table and floor, including baby items. Drew follows her gaze. 'It's a lot, isn't it? I began finding baby "memorabilia": knitted booties, a blanket, soft toys – I even dug up a small chest she'd buried by the garden fence. It was filled with photos of babies and children – ones where she'd written dates and notes like "first birthday", "first hospital visit" – she'd hidden items all over the place.'

'Enough to make it seem she had a child,' Louise says. She realises this must've been what Drew had been doing when she overheard him on the day of Alfie and Jacob's birthday.

'Yep. Must've collected things to help make her story plausible. You mentioned Clara had seen photos of her alleged son – hadn't even questioned their authenticity. I'm guessing Harriet didn't either.' He exhales sharply. 'It's taken a long time to suss out the web of deceit she weaved. I half expect other victims to come knocking; I doubt it's the first time she's done something like this.'

'Is the white-van guy one of them?'

'Sort of. He was one of her ex-boyfriends – well, not entirely "ex", as it turns out. He obviously didn't know what she was up to, blamed me for her disappearance.'

Although Drew's story fills in many gaps, Louise's mind still whirs with unanswered questions.

'Why, though? Why make those things up?' Louise says, her head ready to explode. 'To pretend she had a son who needed life-saving surgery in the US, that's some high-level shit.'

'I was aware she had some . . . *odd* . . . tendencies and I'd often catch her out in a lie. When I was trying to get her to seek professional help, I looked some stuff up. There's something called Machiavellianism – a personality trait that manifests as manipulation, lying and a willingness to do whatever it takes, regardless of the moral consequences, to achieve one's goals and gain power. In this case, I assume her goal was money. She was always jealous of others who, in her opinion, were doing better than her. Knowing that she latched on to Harriet makes absolute sense.'

Louise's head swims; it's all so much to take in.

'Look, Louise. I feel sick about this. I should have said something earlier, but it just seemed, well, mad. I hoped I was wrong. But, if you need me to, I'll tell Mark, Harriet's husband, whoever. I'll back you up.'

Would it be enough? With Clara's testimony, too? It's possible, but, while Louise can't say it, she knows Mark has never been that keen on Drew. And Clara is a stranger, with nothing to prove her suspicions, just like Louise.

'I can't ... I can't risk it. Mark might take Alfie away for good.'

'Can you think of anything that might implicate Harriet? Something she's told you? Something you've seen while at her house?'

'Well, I did snoop around her study a couple times.' Any guilt Louise felt about these invasions has long since vanished. 'I found a birth certificate for a boy and, after some digging, realised it was for Harriet's first baby who died not long afterwards. I think this had something to do with the reason Harriet wanted to swap babies.'

'That's devastating,' Drew says, inhaling sharply. 'A trauma like that could make her vulnerable. Though by itself it isn't incriminatory.'

'She has a locked cabinet; I've always thought she must be hiding something inside it.'

'Okay, that's a start. Any idea where the key could be?'

'Harriet wears a necklace with a key on it; she never takes it off. I'm pretty sure that's it.'

'So how do we get hold of it if Harriet wears the necklace all the time?'

Louise circles her shoulders, squeezing her eyes closed to think. Snaps them open. 'Clara!'

'What about her?'

'She said to contact her if I wanted help gathering evidence. She's really keen to help, Drew.'

He frowns. 'Still not getting how Clara can—'

'I'm surprised you don't already know,' Louise says, her eyebrows arching. 'It's safe to say that the times I saw you around Harriet was because you were keeping tabs on her, right?'

'Only in so far as her name appeared in Emma's notebook. I wasn't following her every move.'

'Well, anyway – she has regular MRI scans at the hospital. And for that she'd need to remove her necklace.'

'Genius,' Drew says, nodding. 'If Clara can obtain the key and pass it to you, we can access the cabinet. But how do we get into the house?'

'How do you feel about a bit of light breaking and entering?' Louise says. Drew doesn't so much as raise a brow as she tells him her plan.

'So we wait until one of them is out and I distract the other so you can sneak in through the back door, get what you need, then sneak back out again?' Drew repeats. 'Right. And you're sure the back door will be unlocked?'

'They always leave it unlocked when they're in – I remember thinking it was a bit of a hazard. What if Jacob got out?'

'Sure.' He rubs his thumb and finger over his chin. 'Run it past Clara and let me know what she says.'

She almost laughs at the absurdity of it all. She just needs to steal the key, break into the house and find out what's inside that cabinet. Who does she think she is, *Ocean's Eleven*? But, with Drew and Clara onside, maybe they can pull it off. It's a long shot – but it's the only one she's got.

* * *

As soon as Louise goes back inside her house, she calls Clara to run their idea by her.

Just one more attempt to get the proof she feels sure lies in the antique cabinet. Louise tells her about the MRIs and Clara confirms she has seen Harriet at the radiology department before.

'I took a photo of Harriet's calendar, actually ... Hang on.' Louise frantically scrolls through her phone – did she delete it when she made her promise to Mark?

'Yes, got it,' she says, then puts the phone back to her ear. 'It's at ten forty-five on Thursday the fifteenth. Or at least it was. No telling if she's altered it.'

'It's fine. I can check if she still has it booked.'

'Won't it be difficult, given you work in the maternity unit?'

'I've worked in the hospital for twenty-odd years – everyone knows me. It's not unusual for me to be in other areas of the hospital. Once I confirm the date and time, I'll make sure I'm around.' Clara sounds confident she can get the key from Harriet's necklace and pass it to Louise. 'I can probably only give you around an hour, tops, though. Will it be possible to get in and out of her home in that time?'

It does seem optimistic. Will it be long enough for her to do what she needs and return the key to Clara before Harriet notices it's missing?

'I'll make sure it is.'

Chapter 59

The day is here now, and Louise's head is heavy, her eyelids red and swollen. Mark left for work early, dropping Alfie to breakfast club at nursery before heading for a meeting with Brad about flexi hours. He's doing all he can to ensure she's supported in going back to work. She gazes at herself in the bathroom mirror. Tries to tell her reflection that she's doing this for all the right reasons. That she's not the one who started the chain of events currently in motion. Something was done *to* her. *To* her baby. Others' actions are why she's having to lie to her husband. Having to go behind his back – again.

Snatching a lipstick from her make-up bag, Louise draws the dark burnt-orange stick across her mouth, the colour bleeding above her top lip from the shakiness of her hand. Why is she even bothering with lippy? She rips a square of toilet paper from the roll and rubs it off.

Only a few more hours and it'll be done. Over. This part, at least.

She needs Richard to be home while Harriet's at the MRI

so the back door is unlocked – she can't break in; it would be the nail in the coffin for her if she were caught – but she can't guarantee he'll be there. She's lost track now and isn't sure if Jacob goes to nursery on a Thursday – and there's a possibility Harriet's moved him to a different one since the park incident, though Louise has been careful not to raise concern by asking. Would Richard stay at home with him if it's not a nursery day? Probably, now she thinks of it; Jacob is usually confined to the playroom.

These are all the unknowns she's already verbalised to Drew. And he gave a calm and simple solution: they could drive over early, prior to Harriet's scan time, and check it out. Louise ties her hair up in a ponytail, grabs her hoody and leaves the house before she can change her mind.

Drew is waiting in the car a little way up the road. By the time she reaches it and climbs in, her breaths are short and ragged.

'Morning,' he says. 'Been on a run?'

'Very funny.' She wipes the condensation her breath has caused from the passenger window.

'Louise,' he says. 'Take a moment to calm down. Can't have you passing out.'

He puts the radio on, turns it up and starts singing along to the song. She doesn't even recognise it, but his out-of-tune vocals give her something else to concentrate on. Soon, she's laughing.

'Hope you're not laughing at me, Louise! I'll have you know I did solos in my school choir . . .'

Despite Drew's attempts to keep the drive light-hearted,

an invisible weight presses down on her as they near Harriet's. She wraps her arms tightly round her stomach, as if holding herself together – but it doesn't calm the churning inside.

He parks further up the road, and they sit and watch and wait. Louise checks her mobile every thirty seconds, each time verbalising how close it is to when she thinks Harriet should leave. Finally, Harriet leaves in Richard's car, and Louise allows hope to sprout. He mustn't be going to the office today, then. Drew says if Richard is not in when they get back he'll help her break in.

He sets off, following Harriet at safe distance.

Harriet walks towards the hospital outpatient entrance. The radiography department is accessed from there. All good so far. Louise nervously checks her texts – looking out for one from Clara.

'Fingers crossed Clara's been able to slip away from the maternity unit. What if she's caught up?'

'Relax, Louise. She'll keep her end of the bargain.'

'But—'

Drew puts his hand up, tells her to stop panicking. To breathe.

Her phone pings.

'Okay, Harriet's there. God, I feel sick.' Louise grips her stomach. She turns to look at Drew. 'But I've got this. I'm going in,' she says.

'Good luck. Keep calm. If you start acting weird and suspicious, it's game over.'

Louise sucks in a breath, pulls her shoulders back, gets out of the car.

Inside, the corridors stretch on, and at the end of one, there's a choice of several others. Trying to still her nerves, Louise stops near the hospital shop and leans against the wall. Closes her eyes for a moment to visualise the layout. Becoming flustered now and taking a wrong turn could cost her. If she misses her opportunity today, she'll have to wait another month.

Her phone vibrates. With trembling fingers, she taps on *Messages*. Doesn't even need to open it, the single word from Clara is visible.

Problem.

Louise's pulse stammers, then picks up speed. Had she been realistic in assuming this plan would go without a hitch? She waits, air expelling forcibly from her nostrils.

'Come on, come on. Tell me,' she says, under her breath. She checks the time. It's two minutes past Harriet's appointment. Only having the ability to text Clara means she's at the nurse's mercy. Her only course of action is to sit tight until she receives further information.

Another vibration.

Can't access locker.

Shit. It's over, then. How will she get the key if Clara can't reach the necklace? She was so sure it would be easy, based on Clara's confidence. She sends a message back asking why, and, while she awaits the response, walks towards the lifts. Just as she reaches level 3, she gets a text from Drew saying he's had to move the car to a different spot. She gives an exasperated sigh. Things aren't aligning. Maybe it's a sign to stop, go back, retire this mad plan. She presses the heel of her palm into her forehead, rotates it, massaging the tension headache that's brewing.

You've come this far.

Her phone vibrates again. Not holding out much hope for anything positive, Louise glances at it. Straightens.

See you at the lifts, level 3.

The lift pings and the doors open. The only other person riding the lift with her gets out, and Clara, her head turned away from Louise, gets in. Hits the button for the level and waits, her back turned, for the lift to begin moving. Then she backs up until she's next to Louise, and slips the key into her pocket.

'You've got fifty-five minutes,' she whispers. 'See you outside the lifts on level 3. Don't be a second late.'

Louise gives a slight nod of the head, then gets out, not looking back at Clara. As soon as she's out of the building, she calls Drew.

'Where are you?'

'Coming back around. You should see me ... about ... now.' The car appears and Louise runs up to it, jumping in and slipping her belt on.

'Go!' she says. Drew drives off, his face set in a serious expression. 'We have to be back here at 11:54.'

His head snaps towards her. 'That's not even an hour. Will we make it?'

'You tell me. You're the one driving.'

He whistles. 'I'll give it a go. But you might not have a lot of time in there.'

'I'm literally grabbing what's in the cabinet, locking it up again and leaving.'

'But won't you need to check that what's there is worth taking?'

'It is.' Louise's fingers are so tightly curled into fists, her nails bite into the flesh of her palms. 'It has to be,' she adds. She's not going through all of this for nothing.

While he drives, Drew goes over his plan to distract Richard. Louise has to hand it to him, he's thought it through.

'How come you're so good at all this?' she asks, her eyes narrowing.

'Oh, you know – as an ex-con, it comes easy.' He side-eyes her.

'Very funny,' she says. In spite of the seriousness of the situation, she laughs. The tension releases her hands, and her fingers relax. 'Almost had me.' She stares at the indents her nails have left. 'Thanks again. You know I really appreciate your help.'

'Yeah, well – let's not be premature, eh?'

'No matter the outcome, though – I misjudged you and I'm sorry.'

He takes his eyes off the road to look at her, gives the sad smile she's seen before.

'Me, too.'

The heartfelt moment comes to an abrupt halt as Harriet's house comes into view.

'Oh, God – here we go, then.'

Chapter 60

Drew puts on a baseball cap and gets out first. Louise waits a few seconds, then follows, keeping a little way behind him. They know there's a doorbell camera, that if Richard is still here, he'll be able to see Drew's approach once he reaches a certain point. Harriet mentioned she'd seen Louise at their property skulking about, but Louise doesn't know if that's because the camera has greater range than she realised, or because there are cameras showing the rear of the property. Either way, this next part of the plan is risky. Drew has to keep Richard distracted long enough for her to get in and out of the study. Then she has to pray the back door has been left unlocked. If not, plan B will come into play. And she really hopes to avoid that. Using any kind of force will mean they'll no longer be under the radar and, once police get involved, this shit will blow up. She only needs enough time to get the cabinet open and grab its contents.

Louise stops on the pavement just out of view of the house and drops to one knee to do her shoelace. She's close enough to hear Drew's voice if Richard answers the front door. Her eyes flit about, checking if any of the neighbours are watching. Luckily the houses are widely spaced – there's no direct view into Harriet's. Why hasn't she heard Drew speak yet? What's he doing? She's been pretending to tie her lace for too long. She'd never make a private investigator using such basic ploys – and, given Harriet had spotted her previous attempts to sneak around their garden unnoticed, guesses she's not that skilled at covert operations, either.

Maybe her heartbeat is too loud to hear conversation.

Then she hears him.

This is it.

Louise pauses once she gets round the back of the house, her lungs heavy, as if they're filled with wet sand. There's no pounding of footsteps, no raised voices, so she must've gone undetected so far. She takes a two-second breather before heading to the patio.

Be open. Please be open.

A quick look through the glass shows no sign of Jacob. If he's here, he'll be in the playroom. She grips the handle, pulls to the left.

It slides open.

Thank you!

Should she close it? Or leave it open for a quicker getaway? If Jacob's here, though, he could get out if she leaves it.

Just get on with it! the voice in her head screams.

There's no time for indecision. She closes it, then sneaks through the kitchen. As she nears the playroom, Jacob's *vroom-vroom* noises stop her in her tracks. He's right there.

It would be easy to take him. He'd go with her willingly – she knows that.

But then what?

With a dragging feeling in her gut, she glides past the playroom and heads to the study. She must get the evidence first. How long has she been? Feels like only seconds, but, checking her mobile, she sees it's already been five minutes since she left the car. Richard and Drew's voices are close. The front door is in view of the corridor she needs to go down. Edging out from behind the corner, Louise checks if it's safe to cross the hall. Richard has his back to her, his hands on his hips. They're talking about the fountain. Drew is pretending to be interested in buying it from him despite it not being for sale. She has to hurry this up. There's no way he can keep Richard talking for too much longer about a bloody water feature.

She takes two big strides and reaches the other side without issue. Now for the study.

Louise goes inside. She is relieved to see it's the same as before and the antique cabinet is in the same position. She takes the key from her pocket, holds it in a shaky hand. Ducks down and pushes it into the lock. It turns easily and, with a small tug, the top drawer scrapes open.

Her eyes scan the contents. There are several folders, nothing that immediately stands out. The second drawer contains photos and a metal box. Louise takes the canvas bag that she'd folded and tucked in her trouser waistband. She'd assumed she'd take all the contents, but now, looking at it, should she check what's there first? At least if she only takes a fraction of it, at first glance it might seem as though nothing's missing. If she grabs the lot, it'll be obvious someone has been in here, and she'll have far less time to figure out her next move.

Time check.

Seven minutes since leaving the car. She's got another eight minutes before they need to be on the road, heading back to the hospital.

Time to at least flick through this stuff.

Careful not to make a noise, she removes the cardboard folders from the first drawer. Opens the one on the top. Inside is a pile of paper – what appear to be printouts of correspondence, messages occurring over a forum she recognises called Mumstogether. Her mouth dries. There's no time to read through all of it, but she skim-reads parts of a couple of pages, getting the gist that ExhaustedNewMum0593 is struggling with her new baby. What Louise gleans from her posts is that she was desperate for support – for someone to tell her they understand how she feels. Clearly, if these printouts are anything to go by, she didn't get what she hoped for. Skipping ahead a little, Louise finds someone did jump in, backing her up. The name AngelFace pops up quite a bit, each time coming to the defence of ExhaustedNewMum. Flicking through to the later printouts, she notes that the forum messages between them hint at meeting in person. Louise chooses a different folder. Inside are private messages dated a couple of years later, but still using the same usernames from the original forum – maintaining some form of anonymity? In these, ExhaustedNewMum shares her fear of losing another baby. Louise knows for sure now that this is Harriet. But who is AngelFace?

Hastily searching the other folders, Louise finds copies of emails. She closes her eyes for a second, silently pleading to find actual evidence in here; so far all she's got is meaningless forum chat and, while it's adding context and building a picture of Harriet's state of mind, it isn't proof of anything untoward. She flicks through them, one catching her attention:

> My other half is beginning to suspect something's up. All the time I'm spending 'researching' is causing him to ask questions, because as far as he's aware, we don't have the money to get our son the treatment. To be honest, I'm not sure I want him to be part of our future. When our deal is done, I'm thinking of going it alone. Our arrangement should be just between the two of us anyway. Less risk that way. Neither of us should end up in prison simply for wanting better lives for our children!

This has to be the nurse, Emma. Jesus, Clara was right.

A burst of laughter jolts Louise from her thoughts. Drew's giving her a warning. She needs to hurry this along.

She's running out of time.

Another folder – this one has mobile-phone screenshots of messages that must be from Harriet's phone, although not a number she recognises. Emma and her carried on with their plans and Harriet's kept every bit of correspondence, dating back four years. Why would she store evidence that incriminates her? Although, so far, it doesn't seem there's

THE OTHER CHILD

anything suggesting the plan went ahead – or, crucially, which baby was targeted for the swap.

Louise stuffs the contents of a few folders into one file and slips it into her bag, closing the drawer and opening the other. She removes a single-ring binder and thumbs through the pages – yet more correspondence – skipping to the last email dated a week after Jacob and Alfie's births. It looks to be the last communication between Harriet and Emma – a copy of an email stating that Emma received a huge sum of money from ExhaustedNewMum to switch the babies.

Proof that it happened. Without painstakingly reading everything right now, she can't be sure if any of it helps in identifying her or Alfie. But it's surely enough to get an investigation underway. She tears the last pages from the binder and adds them to the bag, readying herself to leave. There's no more time. But as she's closing the drawer, the metal box catches her eye again. There's no lock. Her fingers shake as she opens it. There's an umbilical cord clamp inside. She smiles, the memory of Alfie's coming to her. She hadn't been compelled to keep it, though. Her smile fades when she sees a baby's hospital bracelet. Just one. She picks it up, her vision blurring – her subconscious already knows, but it takes a moment for the reality of what she's seeing to sink in, blinking rapidly in case her brain is playing tricks on her. There's no mistake.

Baby boy WEBB

It's Alfie's. The one she thought she'd lost.

It's the last piece of the puzzle, and holding this tiny piece of proof in her hand pushes her over the edge. Her entire body shakes and she collapses on to all fours, inhaling deeply, attempting to regulate her breathing before she's heard.

This whole time she's been right. If it hadn't been for Clara's call, she might never have found out for sure. Mark and Natalie had convinced her it was all in her head.

Louise relocks the cabinet, takes the canvas bag filled with the evidence and ducks back out of the study, her legs barely holding her weight. She hangs back when she hears Drew's voice, now asking Richard about what water purification system they have in place. Checks her mobile for the time – only twenty minutes to get back to the hospital and return the key to Clara to slip onto the necklace before Harriet realises it's missing. As agreed, Louise calls Drew to give him an excuse to leave immediately.

Within minutes, they're back inside the car, Drew hurtling down the road so fast her head spins. She rattles off what she found, her words rushed, urgent.

'Harriet did pay Emma to swap Jacob and Alfie. I've got the proof.' Saying it out loud, the truth of it laid bare, hot tears stream down her face. She wipes them with the back of her hand and continues. 'There are loads of messages between Harriet and AngelFace – that's Emma. I need to look at them more thoroughly, but it could be enough.' Drew's silence is filled with a brewing anger. 'I'm still not clear why Emma made up the backstory. According to Clara and the correspondence I found, she needed the money to take her sick child to the US for some kind of specialised treatment, so that fits what you found. But it's a very detailed lie. Why go to those lengths?'

Drew's jaw tightens, and he shakes his head. 'She really was conning people. I guess a part of me hoped there was an innocent explanation for everything I found. God's sake.'

'It's not your fault, Drew.'

'I should've realised sooner. In hindsight, it was obvious she had a history of manipulation. But I guess I was smitten with her. She was a nurse, compassionate, caring. Or so I thought.' Drew slams his hand against the steering wheel. 'As soon as you mentioned the screenshots and emails, said the name "AngelFace", I remembered it from the diary. Emma had infiltrated the Mumstogether site, using it as a way of homing in on victims and manipulating them – giving them sob stories and faking a sick child who needed care only available in the USA to defraud them. It was all for money and a sense of power. She just got lucky when she landed on Harriet - who was not only rich, but also in need of something Emma realised she could offer,' Drew says. 'I'm so, so sorry, Louise.'

They fall silent until Drew swings the car into the hospital. He turns to her.

'You need to run like hell to get that key back to Clara.'

Having delivered the key to Clara with less than five minutes to spare, Louise takes a few minutes to recover her breath – it's going to take a lot longer for her muscles to stop shaking. Drew is super quiet on the drive back home, both of them drained from their part in the day's drama. It's not until he parks up in their road that he speaks again.

'How long before she realises, do you reckon?'

'I don't think she'll have reason to suspect anything untoward today – might be ages before she even thinks to look inside the cabinet. No need to rush the next part. And I really have to find the right time and way to tell Mark first.'

'Sure. You should sleep on it,' Drew says, getting out the car. She follows suit and joins him on the pavement. He puts his hand on her arm, squeezes it. 'And I'll do the same.' Then he disappears inside his house.

He's right. Sleeping on it is the wisest move. It'll allow everything to sink in, and she can read the evidence she's gathered in more detail, and without the burden of adrenaline coursing through her veins. Assimilate it before shocking Mark with the truth.

Later, she watches from the doorway as Mark reads Alfie his favourite bedtime story, her eyes blurring with tears. He asked if she'd like to read to him, but she said she was too tired.

She wants to give him one last night to put Alfie to bed without the knowledge that Alfie isn't his son. The truth will tear him apart.

Chapter 61

Louise plasters on concealer, although nothing can hide the swollen bags that have settled under her eyes, then she sponges foundation over her sunken cheeks. Food hasn't been a priority, other things being more important. She must tell Mark everything this evening.

With a heavy heart, she walks Alfie to nursery, leaving the buggy behind so she can savour the time with him. During the hours she lay awake last night, thoughts turned to what will happen next. How, exactly, this situation will be resolved.

She's due to go into her new workplace today to meet the team. Mark has arranged to pick her car up from the garage – it's now the proud owner of a brand-new battery and, apart from a few minor tweaks, she's good to go according to the mechanic – and he's collecting Alfie in it at three p.m.

There's a sense of freedom that comes with knowing she will soon be driving again, but also a pinch of fear. She hasn't sat behind the wheel for over three years – will she even remember how to drive? Having both cars running will make their lives easier, especially now she's working – that's the reason she asked Mark to sort it.

However, the thrill of starting a new job has been overshadowed by recent developments. As much as she's tried to suppress them, thoughts about getting her biological son back have weighed heavy on her mind. Because to have him will mean losing Alfie, the little boy she's brought up and cared for every day, despite the challenges. It's Alfie she breastfed, cradled in her arms hour after hour, whose tiny hand she'd held, his fingers curling round hers. Through the recent battles, she has to admit things are now much improved. Great, even, prior to Clara's call. The thought of handing Alfie over to Harriet and Richard is almost too much to bear. But what other choice is there? It's not as though she can have both.

Her new colleagues are reassuringly down to earth and, even though her mind frequently wanders off down dark alleyways of possibilities, the time goes quickly. On her way out of the building, she dials Drew.

'Can I pop over for a quick chat?' She hears a scraping noise in the background, like he's cleaning stuff up. Hopefully, he's cataloguing Emma's stuff now they're clearer on what constitutes evidence of she and Harriet planning the swap and Harriet paying her to do it.

'Course. Have you decided what to do now?'

'We'll chat when I'm there. I'll be about twenty minutes.'

There are a few loose ends, things she's not so sure about,

and before she takes the next step she wants to run them by Drew. The fluttering sensation in her gut tells her what she's really after is reassurance – maybe someone else to tell her she must act quickly on what they've found.

She doesn't waste time on niceties when Drew opens the door, bursting through like a cop carrying out a raid.

'Come on in,' he says.

'I'm sorry, I've got this niggling feeling today. Like it's all about to blow up.'

'Okay. Tell me what's on your mind.' He's his usual calm self – using a slow, soft voice, the one he often speaks to her in. Yet, she knows full well he's had his moments of distress; she's heard his raised voice, overheard his panicky tone at times. Isn't everyone capable of being measured when the situation isn't about them?

'So, now we have all this – do you think it's enough? Because I've been thinking, and it suddenly seems to me as though it hangs on so much uncertainty,' she says, pacing. 'Like, Emma couldn't know who would actually go into labour at the same time as Harriet, or at least within the small window of time required for her to swap babies. Surely too much was down to chance.'

'And, had it not worked out the way it did, maybe the plan would've failed. Some of the other stuff Emma had noted was in relation to security. Maybe there was a plan B – where, instead of swapping, she'd steal a baby instead.'

'She did make reference to a Plan B in the correspondence I found,' Louise mumbles.

'But Emma was focused on plan A first. And she kept such a close eye on you, asked lots of questions.' Drew explains how she managed to tease information from Mark. And then Emma saw her leave in the car, and unmistakably in labour. 'When you left the house, Emma, who'd been snappy and irritable for a couple of days, seemed overly happy, said "thank God", and I remember how she beamed, saying how perfect it was.'

'Oh, my God.' Louise stops pacing, putting her hands up in the air. 'One of the printouts I took was of a message from Harriet saying she was two centimetres dilated – she'd just had a midwife confirm it.'

'There you go – she had her finger on the pulse the whole time. I remember Emma making a call, and moments later she told me she'd been called for an agency shift on maternity. She orchestrated it, Louise.' Drew holds his head in his hands. 'Just being a part of it, even though I'd zero clue what she'd been up to, kills me.' He looks up. 'I'll come with you to the police. Bring all this,' he says, waving his hand at the table. 'Together with what you've found, it's enough. Has to be. I'll do whatever you want me to do to rectify this mess.'

Louise checks the time. 'Mark will be picking Alfie up now. I'll go back home and wait for them. I'm not making this decision alone.'

She gets up, puts a hand on Drew's shoulder as she walks past. 'Thanks for all you've done.'

This has to come out now. She can't wait until this evening.

Chapter 62

It's almost three thirty. Where's Mark? She stands by the kitchen window, tapping her fingers on the sink as she leans forward, eyes peeled for the car.

'Come on, come on.' What should her opening line be? She'll have to wait for Alfie to be out of earshot. Should she sit Mark down before delivering the news? She'll have to tell him where she's obtained the evidence – maybe she'll lead with what Drew's just told her. If she makes this less about what she's done and more about what Emma did, he might be more likely to believe her. Not make a call to Natalie the second she utters 'swapped babies' again.

Why isn't he home yet?

The ringtone blares out, and her heart stutters seeing Mark's name displayed. Now what? She accepts the call and before she can even say hello, Mark's voice penetrates her eardrum.

'Why did you go behind my back again?'

Louise shakes her head, trying to expel her confusion. 'What are you talking about?'

'Got your car, as agreed. Came to pick up Alfie. As agreed. But no. You've changed the plans. When were you going to tell me you've been in contact with Harriet?'

He's fuming, but all Louise feels is bewilderment. 'Seriously, Mark. Listen to me. I have not spoken to Harriet. I don't know what you're on about. The plans are exactly as they were when we arranged them. So you have Alfie?'

'No, Lou. That's my point. Harriet has already picked him up, as agreed with *you*.'

Her heart slams against her ribs. 'No. Shit, no. I don't understand.' Her mind races. How was Harriet able to waltz in and take Alfie? 'Oh, God. She was on the safe list. I put her on it when we first discussed going back to work. We were each other's, just in case.'

'I'll come and get you first and then we'll go collect him. Where are you?'

'I'm already home. Hurry up.'

Mark won't get the urgency, he doesn't know half the story. Louise can't stay still; she strides up and down the kitchen, waiting for him. Minutes stretch and she can't bear it any longer. Dials Harriet. No answer. After her third attempt, Mark storms in, his eyebrows drawn together, face pale.

'Harriet's not answering,' she says.

'I know. I already tried a dozen times. Why would she pick Alfie up without agreeing it with you? And especially if you say you haven't seen her. Like you promised.'

'I promise I haven't arranged this with her.' She's going to have to confess all. But it's not a story that can be told quickly, and right now she needs to find out what's going on.

'I'll try Richard,' Mark says, his mobile to his ear.

'What's he saying?'

Mark puts Richard on speaker, places the phone between them on the kitchen table. With a rising dread, Louise waits for him to speak.

'I'm at home with Jacob,' Richard's taut voice declares. 'And I've no idea why Harriet would possibly pick Alfie up from nursery. I presume you've fact-checked this with your wife?'

The way he says 'your wife', Louise knows things are about to come to a head. And as she listens to him accuse her of orchestrating this drama simply to have an excuse to be in contact, to attempt to see Jacob again, her eyes dart to Mark. A realisation dawns on his face and he glares at her.

'I'm not sure I know what you're talking about, Richard.'

And, as suspected, Richard spills the beans about the day in the park – how Louise had practically abducted Jacob, and that it was only because Harriet had begged him not to that they didn't call the police.

'So, what? This is some kind of revenge? Now Harriet has taken our child?'

'Don't be so ridiculous. Harriet wouldn't do that.'

Louise reaches across to the mobile, picks it up. 'I don't think you know what she's capable of, Richard. She's obviously played you, too.' And she cuts the call.

'Louise!' Mark snatches the phone from her. 'What are you doing?'

'Don't call him back,' she says, her eyes wide. 'We don't have a lot of time for me to explain. I need to show you something.'

She collects the folder of evidence she found in Harriet's cabinet. Lays it out over the kitchen table. 'Seeing is believing.'

She tells him everything she knows – about Clara's call the other day, and how she told Louise what she witnessed; about Drew's confession that his ex, Emma, came up with a wild plan in order to gain money for her sick – and turns out, non-existent – child, pulling a susceptible Harriet into the web of lies. I think Harriet was so desperate for a healthy child that it seemed she would stop at nothing to ensure she didn't lose another.

'I am so sorry, Mark. I didn't . . . I didn't want it to be true. Not in the end. I had stopped looking. I was ready to put it behind me. But I can't ignore this – *you* can't ignore this.'

Mark slides down the kitchen unit, sits on the floor, his face blank. Lost. Tears start to stream down his face as Louise sinks to the floor next to him.

'Mark, I know this is a nightmare. Believe me. But we need to hold it together right now – we need to find Harriet and Alfie.'

He says nothing, just hangs his head.

'Give me the keys,' she says, feeling for them in his pockets. 'I'll go. You get a cup of tea, get over the shock before driving your car, but then head to Richard's – and, between you, work out where she might've gone. In the meantime, I'll start hitting the usual spots, check the parks. Okay?'

He runs a hand through his hair. Nods. 'I'm so sorry I didn't believe you.'

Louise gathers up the evidence and shoves it back in the file, popping it under her arm. 'We'll get our son back,' she says, and runs out of the house.

Chapter 63

Louise drives to the playpark where she took Jacob for an ice cream. With no luck, she continues around town. Harriet could be anywhere. *Think, think.* Is there anywhere she mentioned that's important to her? They talked about work, schools, what else? Harriet usually focused on Louise. Probably for good reason. If she's gone somewhere to clear her head, where would be a good place?

A church?

Did they have their first baby buried in the grounds of St Andrew's? It's worth a try.

There are so many headstones spread out over a wide area. Louise spots a few people tending graves, but none are Harriet. A thought comes to her: in some of the emails and messages between Harriet and Emma, there was mention of a bench – it's where Emma left things for Harriet to collect, so it must be local. When she and Alfie stopped to rest after being practically thrown out of her house that time, it'd been on a memorial bench. She remembers because the inscription was poignant, saying something like 'until we're together again'. It didn't have a name plaque, but could that bench be a memorial to Harriet's lost child?

Her hope is dashed when she slows up beside the pavement and there's no sign of her there, either.

Okay, stop. Put yourself in Harriet's shoes. Louise closes her eyes. She needs to think like Harriet. If she's taken Alfie, is it in retaliation? She wants Louise to feel the fear, the sadness of losing a child. Could Harriet even be thinking she's doing this *for* her? To make her realise just how much she loves Alfie.

No. Harriet gets what Harriet wants. She said as much herself. She swapped her biological son with another woman's, because she wanted to ensure she had a healthy baby to bring up. So why take Alfie now if she believes there's something wrong with him?

Her head hurts trying to understand Harriet's actions, the reasoning behind them. She left Jacob with Richard and took Alfie with her. She's not around town. She's taken him somewhere. To do what?

Then she remembers Harriet mentioning her favourite spot: the cliffs. Louise's foot stamps on the accelerator, the tyres screeching.

Oh, God. Why do people go to the cliffs?

It takes fifteen long minutes to reach the road leading to the coastal path of Lynmouth. All the while she prays she's wrong and that any second now she'll receive a relieved call from Mark saying it was a mistake, that he has Alfie with him. Louise steers her car off the road, taking it slowly across the rough ground. The sky is a deep grey, the horizon smudging into it. No cars are permitted here; she drove on past the closest parking area a while ago.

There's just one other vehicle up ahead.

Harriet's car.

Louise applies her handbrake and jumps out. She doesn't slam the door. Although it's likely Harriet has heard her approach, she doesn't wish to startle her, cause her to drive off again. She takes the last few yards to it on foot. With each step, her breaths shorten, pain fills her lungs and her brain feels as if it's banging against her skull. What will she find?

When she reaches it, she peers through the passenger-side window first.

There's no one inside.

A wave of relief is swiftly replaced with a stab of horror, like a blade of ice being driven into her chest, when she spots a figure standing by the cliff edge. Louise edges closer until she can see Harriet clearly. She's clutching Alfie to her as she gazes out to sea. One misstep, and they'll both fall. There's no movement from Alfie; he seems to be sleeping. He never goes to sleep this time of day – what's she done to him?

Suppressing her urge to shout out, Louise gives a gentle cough to make her presence known. There's no response.

'Hey, Harriet,' she begins gently. 'Can we talk?' She's not sure of the situation yet; at this point she's in the dark about her reason for bringing Alfie here. A heavy sensation presses down on Louise's chest. Why isn't Harriet responding? Is she in a catatonic state?

'Can you step back from the edge, Harriet? We can chat

THE OTHER CHILD

in the car.' But Harriet doesn't move. Louise asks again, louder this time, and to her relief, Harriet turns her head slightly, appearing to finally hear her.

'I knew something wasn't right,' Harriet says, her voice tight, mechanical. Alfie remains completely still in her arms. He must be getting heavy by now – what if Harriet loses her grip on him? 'The key on my chain ... that was my first sign. After my scan, when I went to put it back on, I realised it was reversed. And then I recognised Clara from the maternity side of the hospital and alarm bells rang. Of course, as soon as I reached home, I checked the cabinet drawers. Chastised myself for my paranoia when I saw the files. But couldn't quite let go of the feeling and searched each one. Then I knew the game was up.'

Louise doesn't interject, makes no attempt to deny knowing what Harriet's talking about. Would she even listen anyway? She seems to be in some kind of trance, her eyes glazed as she continues to describe how she went to get Alfie, her real son.

'I plied him with medicine,' Harriet says. 'I had to make sure he was sleepy, so he wouldn't feel any fear when I—' She looks down, and Louise's breath catches, the gravity of what Harriet's implying leaving her numb. Louise needs to keep her talking.

'If he's asleep, maybe it's better just to pop him in the car. It's getting cold.'

Harriet carries on speaking as though she didn't hear Louise. Her voice is a monotone as she shares that her first baby died at three months old.

'They told me it was sudden infant death syndrome, but I knew it wasn't.'

Harriet says they claimed there was no evidence to support her fear that there was something biologically wrong with him. Shot her down when she suggested the blame lay with her family's medical history – even Richard did everything he could to talk her out of it.

'Half of me thinks now that it might be his side, actually. Did you know he has a genetic condition – neurofibromatosis? I researched it – he's got those café-au-lait spots and that's a sign. But he won't see a specialist, no matter what I say.'

Yes, Louise had seen them at the pool party. Maybe Harriet had a point.

Either way, Harriet continues, she hadn't wanted to try again, certain another child would inherit something that would prove fatal. But it happened and Richard was overjoyed. Convinced her it would all be fine this time. Lightning doesn't strike twice.

'I couldn't break out of the cycle of doom I'd created, though. Drove myself crazy with anxiety and worry – not healthy for an unborn baby. Ironic, now I think about it.'

Harriet lowers her chin, resting it on Alfie's head. Breathes him in.

'That's when I popped back on to the forum I'd joined when I first had . . .' Harriet chokes back tears – the first emotion Louise has seen since they've been standing on the cliff. Perhaps she's coming out of the slump that brought her here. Louise shifts her weight, taking the opportunity to move a little closer. 'When I first had Benjamin,' Harriet finishes. 'Found my guardian angel again. Or, rather, she found me. Started messaging privately, emailing ... Well, you know that. And after she told me where she worked, how she was desperate for money to take her child for life-saving experimental treatment, I knew that there had to be a way to help us both. We came up with a plan where I would pay Emma to swap the babies.' Harriet shudders, as though saying it out loud has just made it real. She's tried, she says, to bury what was done, almost convincing herself it never happened.

'Emma told me that Jacob's birth mother had moved away, taking my baby with her. I accepted it to begin with; it suited me. But as Jacob grew I started to wonder how my own baby was doing. If I'm honest, I suppose I wanted confirmation I'd done the right thing?' Harriet tilts her head back, looking up at the sky. 'I remembered you from the special-care baby unit, overheard your name. God, I wish I never went down that rabbit hole now. It took a while before I found any trace of you online. Seeing a photo of you and Alfie together on your social media was the catalyst. All I thought I wanted was to find you both to check. Told myself it was only meant to be a brief glimpse that first day. Maybe I knew then I wanted more. You made it so easy. I could've taken Alfie before you knew what hit you. Such an idiotic plan. I can't believe Emma lied, after everything we shared. I tried calling her, when I realised. Over and over, on the number she gave me for emergencies. But of course she never answered – probably a fake. God knows who's been listening to my messages!' Harriet gives a wild laugh, the sound jarring.

He was never meant to survive. Was that what Louise had overheard – Harriet trying desperately to reach the woman who had ruined both their lives? Despite herself, she feels a pang of sorrow for Harriet. Maybe she can still reach her, convince them to bring Emma to justice together.

'Emma lied about more than us moving away, Harriet. There was no sick child – no trip to America. She manipulated you for her own financial gain. And, in the process, she ruined my life!'

Harriet shakes her head. Did she already know? Maybe she doesn't care about Emma's motives, because she got what she wanted out of the arrangement.

'We can find her, make her pay,' Louise says, hoping this sparks a need for revenge and a desire to live to carry it out.

'I've tried, Louise. She's a ghost. And, besides, you know I'd end up in prison, too. I thought I was being clever, ensuring my communications with Emma were anonymous; I collected it all because it was my link to reality – I couldn't quite let go of the proof that Alfie is really mine. I don't know what I was thinking. And now it's in the wrong hands ... It's over for me.' Harriet's eyes fill with tears. 'I didn't think my little boy would survive – I did such a terrible thing to you. I willingly gave my baby to another mum knowing she'd end up heartbroken at his loss. I was thinking of myself. I didn't want to go through the pain of losing another child.'

Harriet had tried to persuade Richard to move after

the birth, but he was resolute about staying there, where his family are, and obviously she couldn't tell him the real reason.

'One time you were at my place, a memory shot into my mind of you standing by the cot next to my baby's – yours was the only other baby who wasn't very sick and Emma had indicated it was the one she'd set up the switch with.' Harriet readjusts Alfie in her arms, and for a horrifying moment Louise thinks they'll fall and lurches forward.

'Don't come closer,' Harriet says.

'I'd feel better if you stepped away—'

'Shush, Louise. I'm talking.'

Louise puts her hands up. 'Okay.'

'I kept the ID bracelet Emma gave me,' she says, looking down at Alfie again, 'but hadn't looked at it since the day I brought Jacob home. Buried it along with what I'd done.' Silent tears stream down Harriet's face, and while Louise feels she, too, should be crying, hers remain unshed. There's so much to say, yet the words stick in her throat. 'I knew the first day I met you and Alfie that I should leave it there. Stop going to the same playgroup. Then I found myself asking you over. I watched you bonding with Jacob in a way I hadn't, and I was equally drawn to Alfie. God, the guilt flooded me. It all got too complicated. But I couldn't bear to cut myself off from my real son, who, despite all my fears, had clearly lived and was healthy.

'You were right, Louise. You knew all along. For what it's worth, I am sorry, for all of it. For taking your baby, for making you seem crazy. But now you have proof. Everyone will believe you now. Perhaps the police are already on their way.'

'They're not, Harriet, I promise. There's still time to rectify this.'

'Don't lie, Louise. Today, I realised I was going to lose everything. I'm so tired of it all. Of all the secrets and pretence. There's no point now.' She takes another step closer to the edge, the toes of her shoes hanging over the cliff.

Louise is at a loss as to what to do, her mind reeling. What can she possibly say to stop Harriet from jumping?

'Why don't we just swap them back? Isn't that what you've wanted all along? You don't need to take yours and Alfie's lives! It's simple, Harriet.'

'Of course it's not simple,' she shouts. 'Too many people have got involved. And Richard will never agree. Never.'

'Okay, okay. But we can still talk about it. Don't make rash decisions now. Everything is fixable.'

'He will die, though, Louise.' She looks down at Alfie, fat new tears sliding down her cheeks. The wind whips her hair across her face and she wobbles. One wrong step and they'll fall. 'He's cursed. The only way we'll be together now is if I take him with me. We can all be together then, me and my two boys.' Louise gasps as Harriet shifts her upper body and looks over the edge at the jagged rocks below. She might only have moments before all is lost.

'You say you feel guilty for what you did!' Louise shouts. 'How do you think jumping to certain death with Alfie is in any way better? You *swapped* a life before. You didn't *take* one. Give him a chance, Harriet. Don't take his choices away.'

Harriet's eyes flicker with uncertainty. Has she broken through to her? But she still teeters on the edge, and every fibre in Louise's body itches to leap forward, pull them back from the brink. Her feet, though, are planted, fear keeping her muscles rigid. If she moves now, freaks Harriet out, it could spell disaster. There's no way she could reach them in time.

'We've been through such a lot, Harriet. We've both suffered with post-natal depression. You were the first person to *see* me. You have no idea how much you helped me and Alfie.'

Harriet smiles. 'We really could've been great friends,' she says, taking a step towards her. Louise allows herself a brief moment of relaxation. It's working; Harriet is coming back from the edge.

'Maybe we still can,' Louise says and, finally able to move, she takes a few slow steps forward. 'We can at least come to an arrangement. Between us. Just you and I.'

Harriet lowers her head to look at the sleeping Alfie. Brushes her fingertips through his curly hair. 'He's such a good boy.'

'He is.' Louise nods in agreement, her words clogging in her throat as tears form. 'And so is Jacob. We're both very lucky.'

Louise holds her arms out as she approaches Harriet. The breeze is cool against the side of her face, and she closes her eyes for a second. When she opens them, Harriet is right in front of her, thrusting Alfie towards her. Louise grabs him tightly, turning to run with him, away from the danger of the cliffs. She assumes Harriet is behind her.

But when she looks over her shoulder Harriet is no longer there.

Chapter 64

Alfie doesn't wake up. Louise gives him a little shake, but there's no response, though he's warm to the touch and breathing, albeit it very slowly. She places him in the car seat, thankful Mark had fitted it ready to pick him up from nursery earlier. His head lolls forward. How much medicine did Harriet give him? She gently pushes on his forehead so he's positioned in the seat better. Kisses his cheek.

'It'll be okay, Alfie.'

Then she climbs into the driver's seat and calls Mark.

'I've got Alfie,' she says. 'But Harriet gave him something to make him sleep. I'm driving him to the hospital.'

'Where are you?'

'At the Lynmouth cliffs.'

'Oh, Christ. And Harriet? Where is Harriet?' It's Richard's voice in the background.

'I'm so sorry . . .' She can't finish the sentence; the words 'she jumped' trapping in her chest.

There's a commotion on the end of the line, and the words blur. But she gets the gist. Richard will call the emergency services and Mark will meet her at the hospital. And, with a sleeping Alfie, Louise drives the car back on to the main road, leaving the cliffs behind her.

Mark rushes to Alfie's bedside, hugs him, relief coming off him in waves. He explains that, moments before her call, Richard had found a letter from Harriet. Mostly, it repeated the information Louise had told him.

'There's other stuff, too, Lou. It's such a mess.'

'Like what?'

Alfie groans and they both look at him. 'Let's not get into it now. What's important is we have our son back.'

'We don't, though, do we? We have Harriet and Richard's son.'

An hour later, Richard's head pops around the door. 'Sorry to interrupt.' His face is tear-streaked, his eyes dark. 'Can we have a word? The police are going to want statements. Thought we should, you know, figure *it* out.'

They go to the family room – no one else is in there – and stand in a huddle.

'Where's Jacob?' Louise asks.

'With a friend. Look, this is an impossible situation. None of it has sunk in. I've lost my wife . . .' A sob escapes him and he presses a hand to his face. 'I can't lose my son, too.'

Mark says something similar, the words moulding into each other as Louise gathers they both want to keep the boys they've brought up. Aren't they going to bother asking her what she wants? She gave birth to Jacob. It's her body that grew him. It's her who's had to deal with the repercussions of Harriet's betrayal.

Blood rushes to her cheeks. 'Hello!' Both the men stop speaking and turn to look at her. 'You both seem to have forgotten one very important fact here.'

'Sorry, love.'

'You want to keep the boys you've brought up. What about what I want, as the mother who birthed Jacob? Don't my wishes count for anything?'

'Of course, of course. Yes,' Richard mumbles. 'Maybe we could come to an arrangement that suits us all?'

'So, for clarity, you're both saying we *shouldn't* swap them back?'

They shake their heads in unison. 'There's been enough heartbreak, wouldn't you say?' Richard says. 'Jacob's mother is dead.'

'Well ...' Louise starts, but Mark goes to her side, squeezes her hand.

Richard continues. 'We need to think about what's best for the boys, not simply ourselves.'

A bit late for that. Harriet's already done everything up to now with her own wishes in mind. But Louise has to admit Richard has a point.

'It's not as though there's anyone left to punish, Louise,' Richard says, his voice acidic. 'According to the letter Harriet left, and from what Mark has told me, there's not much likelihood of tracing that *Emma* woman. And, while the evidence is all there, who exactly benefits from seeing it? We know what happened. We're the only ones who know ...'

'Apart from Emma's ex-boyfriend,' Mark says.

'He won't say anything,' Louise states. 'He's devastated enough knowing he could well have prevented it.' She almost adds that Clara knows too, but leaves it. She was never sure what she'd seen that day and if Louise tells her she's not pursuing it Clara would accept that.

'So are we agreed?' Richard asks, looking at each of them as though he's in charge.

'We don't inform the authorities. We keep the boys we brought up. Yes,' Mark says.

Louise won't be railroaded this time. Won't be undermined as she's been previously. She gives it some thought. Deep down, she knows she can't give up Alfie.

'Only if we are allowed contact. I refuse to leave Jacob without a mother,' she says firmly. There're a few seconds of silence, then Richard speaks.

'As long as we set boundaries, yes. Agreed.'

Mark and Richard shake hands.

PART FOUR

Chapter 65

The playground swing swoops up in the air and squeaks with every downward motion. Louise's stomach muscles clench. He's pushing him too high.

'I think that's enough, don't you?' She elbows him out of the way, takes over.

'Christ, Louise. You worry too much. They need to experience some risk otherwise they won't learn. Mollycoddling is detrimental, don't want them growing up soft.'

Richard isn't someone Louise would choose to bring up her son. The decision they made three months ago has come back to bite her.

'Lou-Lou, push me!' Jacob cries, his legs kicking. 'Want to go high.'

'See,' Richard snorts. Then he turns his back, and starts pushing Alfie instead.

The weekly playdates are getting trickier. While it's great for the boys, Louise comes away from each one with a tension headache she can't rid herself of for several hours.

Each time she walks away from Jacob, knowingly leaving him with Richard, her heart aches.

The inquest following the cliff-edge drama returned a death-by-misadventure verdict. As agreed, Richard didn't disclose Harriet had left a letter. None of the evidence of the baby swap was divulged. And Louise didn't tell the full story about what happened on the cliffs late that afternoon.

It's almost as though none of it ever happened.

'Do you like your new nanny, Jacob?' she asks as she lifts him off the swing. There's an edge of judgement to her tone and, given the sharp snap of Richard's head as he turns to glare at her, he picked up on it.

'A bit,' Jacob says. Louise closes her eyes, tries to shut out the sad look in his eyes.

'He'll get used to her,' Richard says. 'It's only for a few hours here and there, between nursery sessions. And it's not long term.'

'You said she coming to France,' Jacob says, his mouth in a pout. Richard mumbles something, then changes the subject. But Louise pulls him aside.

'You didn't mention you were going on holiday.'

'No, well, it's all happened rather quickly.'

'What has?' She sniffs, the bridge of her nose tingling with a sudden sense of dread.

'Oh, it's for work, that's all. Not a holiday. Nothing to make a fuss over.'

'I'm not making a fuss, Richard. I'm only asking because it might affect our arrangement. How long are you going for?'

He gives an exasperated sigh as though she's asked something impossible of him. God, how did Harriet ever put up with him? Any envy she once felt about Harriet's life has long since disappeared.

'I appreciate we made an arrangement,' he says finally. 'But you must also appreciate nothing is in writing, is it? Things *change*, Louise.'

Her heart beats out of her chest.

Is he saying he's going back on their agreement? That he's taking Jacob abroad? She mustn't react, not in front of the children, but her insides burn with the effort of containing her anger.

What the hell is he playing at?

Chapter 66

It's been a week since Richard dropped the bombshell about France and now he isn't returning Louise's calls.

When she gets back from picking Alfie up from nursery, she cooks him his favourite dinner and smiles as he chats about his day. Then she gets him ready for bed, reads three books of his choice and tucks him in. He's having an early night tonight. She wants him settled before Mark returns home from work. Make it easier for him. She'll feel less guilty going out and leaving them then.

'Night, night, Alfie,' she says, closing the door slowly. 'Sleep tight,' she whispers.

She takes her time getting ready. Doesn't rush downstairs when she hears Mark's key in the lock. When she does appear, Mark's head is buried in his laptop.

'I'm off now,' she says.

Mark glances up from the screen. 'Oh, there you are. Have a good evening, love.' He gives her an appraising look. 'Make sure those new colleagues of yours don't lead you astray. You're a married woman, don't forget.'

As Louise bends to kiss him, he shields the screen from her. 'What are you up to?' she asks.

'It's a surprise.' He smiles. 'Go on, get out of here or you'll be late.'

'Love you.'

She stops, leans on the doorjamb and regards him for a few seconds. He's been on edge since the huge revelation, snappy at times with both her and Alfie. It's to be expected, of course. They've had to come to terms with the knowledge the boys were swapped. The knowledge that they chose to keep this information from the authorities. And with Harriet's death came a different set of complications. Sometimes, Louise feels their marriage is hanging together by a thread. It's also hanging together with lies. She watches as his frown deepens. But there's no time to stand and decipher. She can't be late.

As she drives the car away, she looks in the rear-view mirror, catching sight of a shadowy figure at the upstairs window of Drew's house. He's back to keeping his distance, only the odd exchange of hellos and how are yous if they catch each other outside. With Louise working and no further need for them to communicate, they've fallen back into the old routine. She did notice his bins were overflowing the other day, and the local Scout collection for magazines took some hefty bin liners from his, so she guesses he's finally sorted through the hoard of stuff he'd accumulated since Emma left him.

By all accounts, he's given up trying to get hold of her. He's run out of leads and white-van guy has finally stopped harassing him. Maybe *he* found her.

But, even if he has, it doesn't matter any more. Her gaze catches something just as she's about to turn off their road. She thinks it's Mark, waving. She inhales slowly. That's what she'll tell herself. It was her husband, waving goodbye.

It's a nice last impression.

Chapter 67

She leans over his sleeping body, inhaling the clean, soapy scent as she places her lips to his soft cheek. He stirs, ever so slightly, eyelashes fluttering. She hums his favourite nursery rhyme until he settles into a deep slumber once more. Tracing the tip of one finger over his forehead, down the side of his face, she lets out a contented sigh.

At last.

This is how it should be.

Loving your child unconditionally is the one thing you expect. It's your purpose as a mother. It should come naturally. Having to fight to find it, that special bond, isn't normal.

But it's all okay now; that's over with. Everything has worked out in the end.

'We're always going to be together, sweetheart,' she whispers.

She checks the straps of his car seat, then closes the door as quietly as she can. It wouldn't be good to wake him now – not with what lies ahead.

Sitting behind the wheel, she glances in the rear-view mirror. Smiles at the reflection of her perfect child.

'You're such a good boy. Mummy loves you.' And she presses her foot hard to the accelerator.

Richard won't find out he's missing for a while. And then what's he going to do? He's not going to call the police, because he has already lied to them and won't chance being caught out. He will, no doubt, try to find them. But she still has the evidence that proves Jacob is her son. No one can deny her that. She tries not to think about Alfie. It's temporary, she tells herself over and over. When things have settled, maybe she'll be able to come back for Alfie. The boys belong together, really. For now, it's not possible and her priority has to be her flesh and blood. For the time being, Alfie's got Mark and her mother, who seems to have finally taken an interest in being part of their lives. He'll be well looked after.

Jacob is in a deep sleep now, will be for a few hours yet. Harriet isn't the only one who can dose the kids up. Her heart flutters at the thought of giving him over the recommended amount of medicine; it went against her motherly instinct. But she had to get him from his bed to the car without alerting his nanny. Not that she would've heard a thing, too busy making out with the boy she snuck in through the patio door. She was very helpful leaving it open. And Richard was trusting her enough to take her to France with them? Louise's instinct was right again.

The trip ahead is a long one. She must put as much distance between them as possible. Her chest fills with contentment. From the moment the electricity shot through her when their hands touched, she knew there was something special about Jacob. Knew there had to be a reason why she didn't fully bond with Alfie aside from depression. It's taken too long, and she has a lot to make up for, but at last she has her son, and their journey together can finally begin.

Chapter 68

As planned, Louise stops off at a garage for food and drink. She hadn't wanted to chance raising suspicion by stockpiling supplies in the lead-up to this evening. Her boy is asleep – if she's quick, it should be fine to leave him. She locks the car and jogs to the garage shop. Taking a basket, she begins filling it with water, juice, packs of sandwiches, sausage rolls, crisps and chocolate. He'll need something sweet when he wakes up. She's got no idea when he last ate. She almost laughs when she reaches the counter. At the side of it, there's a stand containing toys from *Cars*. It's a sign. She takes Lightning McQueen and Cruz Ramirez – Jacob will be delighted. She'd not been able to take any of his toys, only packing basic items for him and a couple of toys Alfie wouldn't miss.

As she takes her phone to pay for the items, it begins ringing. She glances at it quickly before diverting it to voicemail. It was only Mark and he thinks she's on a work's night out, so he's probably not expecting her to answer. He'll leave a message. She thanks the guy behind the counter and returns to her car. She deposits the bags in the footwell and checks that Jacob is still asleep before nipping into the toilets. While hovering over the toilet seat, she scrolls through her phone and spots a text message.

> Lou – tried to catch you before you left.
> Give me a call when you can.

She breathes a sigh of relief. No mention of Jacob. He doesn't know yet. If he tried to catch her before she even left, it can't be urgent.

As she washes her hands, she looks up, her heart jolting at the distorted reflection in the bathroom mirror. A scream catches in her throat before she realises the fake glass is smeared with dirt.

Why is she so jumpy? She shrugs off the anxious feeling, shaking her hands dry and rushing back to the car.

She checks Jacob again. Puts her head to his chest, listening to his quiet breathing. With contentment returning, she climbs into the driver seat, slings the phone in the middle compartment, turns on the radio and pulls back out on to the road. There's a break in the songs, adverts beginning, and as Louise reaches across to switch the stations, she sees her phone flashing up that she's got a voicemail. She can't listen to it now; she doesn't want to take her attention from the road.

There's more flashing. She tuts. Why can't he let her be. But then she realises it's not her phone but police cars creating an ominous blue glow behind her. They're a way off yet, and there's plenty of room on the dual carriageway for them to pass her. She hopes there's not an accident up ahead. Doesn't need a delay at this point.

The wailing sirens creep closer now, and as Louise stares into the rear-view mirror the rapid, rhythmic strobing blue lights become almost hypnotic. The vehicles don't appear to be speeding up, though. Not trying to get past her.

'For God's sake,' she mutters. The noise could wake Jacob. She puts her foot down on the accelerator – maybe she can at least create some distance between them. With luck, they'll turn off at the next junction anyway.

Jacob groans and Louise takes her eyes off the road to turn round and check he's okay.

She watches her child for a moment. He stirs but doesn't open his eyes, despite the flashing. But when Louise turns back to face the front she loses focus, and in the blink of an eye she also loses control of the car. The steering wheel jerks, slips through her fingers.

She gasps, the central reservation hurtling into view a split second before the jarring crunch of metal explodes in her ears.

Then, silence.

Epilogue

VOICEMAIL

Hi, Lou. Look, I've got great news. I mean, really great! You'll be angry with me for going behind your back, and I'll take the rap for that, but at the time I didn't know what else to do. I did my own DNA test on me and Alfie. I'd forgotten about it after you presented me with all the evidence about Emma swapping the babies. And I know it looked convincing – especially after the confession from Harriet, too. But Emma must've bottled it when Clara caught her, then told Harriet she'd done it so she'd still get the money. It's the only explanation because the DNA test came back and it states categorically that *I'm* Alfie's biological father.

So then I looked at your result again, Lou. I never understood why it would be inconclusive, but I spoke to your mum. Turns out she had the missing piece all along. Remember you were a twin pregnancy? Well, there's this thing called chimerism. Your twin didn't survive in the womb, but some of their cells stayed in your body, so you ended up carrying two sets of DNA. That explains it.

We'll talk when you get home, but I just wanted you to know it's all going to work out, Lou. We get to have a happy ending.

Alfie *is* your son.

THE END

Acknowledgements

Though writing a novel often happens in solitude – and for me involves long hours sitting at a desk, developing an intimate relationship with coffee and questionable snacks – bringing it into the world is anything but a solo effort.

Deepest thanks to my wonderful, long-standing agent, Anne Williams, whose consistent support and belief have been invaluable.

It's been a privilege to work with my fantastic editor, Lucy Dauman, who – with enthusiasm, skill and patience – worked her magic on each draft. This story wouldn't be the same without such thoughtful feedback. Thank you.

Thanks to my copy-editor, Sharona Selby, whose sharp eye and revisions helped bring out the best in these pages.

My thanks also to the proofreader, Sam Stewart; editorial assistant, Ayana Playle; production controller, Victoria Lord; designer, Anna Goldfinch; marketing and publicity team, Katrina Smedley and Lily Birch. There are so many more people involved in the process, including the sales, rights and audio teams, and I'm grateful to everyone who contributed. Thank you all for your incredible talent and hard work getting our books into readers' hands.

To my family and friends: your support, love and encouragement have meant everything to me throughout this journey. I couldn't have done it without you.

And to every reader who picks up this book: thank you for inviting this story into your life. I hope it stays with you.

RAISING READERS
Books Build Bright Futures

Dear Reader,

We'd love your attention for one more page to tell you about the crisis in children's reading, and what we can all do.

Studies have shown that reading for fun is the **single biggest predictor of a child's future life chances** – more than family circumstance, parents' educational background or income. It improves academic results, mental health, wealth, communication skills, ambition and happiness.[1]

The number of children reading for fun is in rapid decline. Young people have a lot of competition for their time. In 2024, 1 in 10 children and young people in the UK aged 5 to 18 did not own a single book at home.[2]

Hachette works extensively with schools, libraries and literacy charities, but here are some ways we can all raise more readers:

- Reading to children for just 10 minutes a day makes a difference
- Don't give up if children aren't regular readers – there will be books for them!
- Visit bookshops and libraries to get recommendations
- Encourage them to listen to audiobooks
- Support school libraries
- Give books as gifts

There's a lot more information about how to encourage children to read on our website: **www.RaisingReaders.co.uk**

Thank you for reading.

---

[1] OECD, '21st-Century Readers: Developing Literacy Skills in a Digital World', 2021, https://www.oecd.org/en/publications/21st-century-readers_a83d84cb-en.html

[2] National Literacy Trust, 'Book Ownership in 2024', November 2024, https://literacytrust.org.uk/research-services/research-reports/book-ownership-in-2024